Dispatches

Alex Fletcher Book Five

a novel by

Steven Konkoly

Stribling Media
Books Games Graphics

Work by Steven Konkoly

The Black Flagged Series
Black Ops/Political /Conspiracy/Action thrillers

"Daniel Petrovich, the most lethal operative created by the Department of Defense's Black Flag Program, protects a secret buried in the deepest vaults of the Pentagon. A secret that is about to unravel his life."

The Alex Fletcher Books
Suspense/Action/Adventure/Conspiracy thrillers

"Alex Fletcher, Iraq War veteran, has read the signs for years. With his family and home prepared to endure an extended disaster, Alex thinks he's ready for anything. **He's not even close.***"*

The Zulu Virus Chronicles
Bioweapons/Conspiracy/Action thrillers

"Something sinister has arrived in America's heartland. Within 24 hours, complete strangers, from different walks of life will be forced to join together to survive the living nightmare that has been unleashed."

Hot Zone (Book 1)
Kill Box (Book 2)
Fire Storm (Book 3)

Fractured State Series
Near-future Black ops/Conspiracy/Action thrillers

"2035. A sinister conspiracy unravels. A state on the verge of secession. A man on the run with his family."

Fractured State (Book 1)
Rogue State (Book 2)

To my family for their tireless support and love.

About Dispatches

After finishing *Point of Crisis*, I thought the series was finished. I couldn't have been more mistaken. As I walked away from the series, glancing fondly over my shoulder, two main themes emerged from emails, reviews and blog comments. 1.) What's happening in the world outside of New England? 2.) I can't wait to see what happens to the Fletchers after the winter.

I tried to keep walking, but eventually I turned around and stared at these loose ends. Ideas formed, and before I knew it, a new concept emerged. One that would address both themes voiced by readers. The format for this concept changed several times, ultimately resulting in a hybrid novel. Essentially two stories in one.

Dispatches is broken into two parts. *Big Picture* and *Little Picture*. *Big Picture* takes readers across the globe, to conflicts arising in the absence of the United States' foreign presence. Of course, America is not out of the fight—she's just taking a quieter, more satisfying role in the unfolding events. *Little Picture* pulls you back to Maine, to once again walk in Alex Fletcher's shoes (and many others), as the Fletcher crew is once again faced with drastic choices that will ultimately decide their fate.

But first—Happy Reading!

A list of military/government acronyms and
definitions used throughout *The Alex Fletcher Books*
is available at the back of the book.

DISPATCHES

PART I

"Big Picture"

Winter 2019-2020

"Meet the New Soviets. Same as the Old Soviets"

Chapter 1

Colonel Egon Saar drifted to sleep in his seat, his head snapping up to greet the same digital screen he'd stared at for the past several hours. He checked his watch, already knowing the time. Zero-two hundred. Two in the damn morning and the Russians were still playing games across the river.

"Let's get this over with already," he mumbled.

His artillery battalion had been moved to Narva two weeks earlier, based on NATO satellite intelligence suggesting a buildup of Russian armor units east of the Luga River. Three days ago, Estonian agents in Kingisepp reported T-14 "Armata" tanks crossing the Luga. He hadn't slept since receiving that message. The presence of T-14s, Moscow's latest generation main battle tank, meant one thing. Invasion was imminent, spearheaded by the Moscow-based, elite 4th Independent Tank Brigade. The Estonian Defense Forces assembled in the vicinity of Narva would be little more than a speed bump on the road to Tallinn for a Russian tank brigade.

He prayed his wife had listened and taken the kids to Stockholm. If they hadn't left by now, they might never get out. The Russian invasion would undoubtedly be combined with an air and naval blockade of Tallinn,

1

cutting off any possible means of escape. Unfortunately, he had no way of knowing if they had left the country. Saar had surrendered his cell phone before deploying. It was better not knowing, because there was nothing he could do to help them.

He'd said goodbye in their apartment, a few blocks from the main gate to the sprawling Estonian Defense Force base in Tapa—fighting off tears his children couldn't fully understand. His wife knew there was little chance that he would return. She had heard enough about Russian artillery from him to know that he'd be among the first casualties. Kissing them goodbye for the last time was the hardest thing he'd ever done.

The Russians would pay a dear price for this.

He removed his headset, stood up in the cramped command vehicle, and weaved through the equipment operators, pulling his headset cable with him. A small coffee station stood on the map table, rigged directly to the armored personnel carrier's electrical system. Besides the heating system, the coffee maker represented their only luxury in the field. A gust of wind buffeted the thirteen-ton vehicle, barely audible through the armored hull. Conditions outside were miserable. Positioned in a thick forest on the bluffs northeast of Narva, his artillery battalion was exposed to the bitter northerly winds sweeping off the Gulf of Finland.

The weather didn't matter to the men and women of his artillery battalion. They were all tucked inside heated vehicles. The battalion consisted of twelve self-propelled ARCHER systems and three times that many support vehicles. Not a single soldier in his unit needed to be outside in the subfreezing temperature. The same couldn't be said about the infantry battalion guarding his position. Their perimeter extended several hundred meters in every direction, consisting of observation posts, machine-gun nests and squad-sized rapid response teams—huddled in shallow holes carved out of the frozen ground. They were miserable.

"Colonel, I've lost the ARTHUR feed," said the operator next to him.

Colonel Saar turned his attention to one of the screens behind him. ARTHUR, or Artillery Hunting Radar, represented their only chance of detecting an incoming artillery attack. Since his battalion's artillery batteries were the only viable threat to Russian tanks crossing the Narva River, he fully expected to be the focus of an intense artillery strike at the outset of hostilities.

"Get a report from them immediately," said Saar.

A few seconds later, the operator lifted the headset above his ears. "I think we're being jammed."

Saar pressed one of the buttons connected to his headset. "Vortex, this is Thunder actual. Lost contact with Watchtower."

When he released the button, a shrill, oscillating sound filled his ears, causing him to throw the headset onto the map table. They were most definitely being jammed. Somewhere high above the cloud layer on the Russian side of the border, several aircraft were flooding his battalion's radio frequency spectrum with "noise," rendering digital communication impossible. He started the stopwatch function on his sports watch.

"Contact battalion spotters via landline. I want to know what's happening in Narva."

"Colonel, spotters report heavy small-arms fire at the Narva Bridge.

"Which side?" demanded Saar.

"Ours!"

"Copy," said Saar, contemplating the situation.

The Russians had probably sent a sizable Spetsnaz force to secure the western bridgehead. There was only one course of action left, and Saar needed to act immediately to give it any chance of success.

"Transmit over landline to battery commanders. Execute Fire Plan Alfa X-ray. Expend all rounds."

The sergeant stared at him for a moment before quickly lowering his headset to pass Saar's command. "Alfa X-ray" was a northern-front battle plan devised several days earlier under the direction of his commanding officer, Brigadier General Lepp. It wouldn't prevent the Russian invasion, but it would buy Tallinn some time to petition NATO. Not that NATO was in much of a position to help. They had been completely unprepared for the sudden withdrawal of U.S. military forces from Europe.

"Battery commanders have acknowledged the order, sir."

Saar nodded before grabbing his combat helmet hanging on his seat. "I suggest everyone gears up."

He didn't need to elaborate. The combined firepower of an entire Russian artillery brigade would be leveled against them. There wouldn't be much left of his battalion after the Russians' first salvos. Before he'd finished snapping his chinstrap, the vehicle shook from a hollow crunching sound—the first of his battalion's two hundred and fifty-two high-explosive artillery rounds had been fired.

The command vehicle continued to rattle and drum as the ARCHER Artillery Systems fired shell after shell into the night sky.

ARCHER was a fully automated, self-contained system utilizing a preloaded magazine drum filled with twenty-one artillery shells. The 155 mm field gun could fire the entire magazine in less than a minute in salvo mode, nearly quadrupling the sustained firing rate of conventional artillery pieces. Fire plan Alpha X-ray's success depended on this unique capability. By his best guess, the first enemy rockets would strike Saar's battalion in less than—he glanced at his watch—forty seconds. He needed to empty the battalion's guns before the rockets struck.

Fire Plan Alpha X-ray had two components, split between the battalion's twelve ARCHER units. When initiated by the gun commander seated in each ARCHER vehicle, the system's fire control computer took over and delivered the ordnance according to the plan. The first eight rounds fired from each gun would target the two vehicle bridges spanning the Narva River, focusing most of the barrage on the solidly constructed Tallinn-St. Petersburg Highway (E20) Bridge.

Twenty of the ninety-six precision-guided shells would hit the smaller bridge south of Ivangorod. Shutting down these crossings would either force the 4th Independent Tank Brigade one hundred and eighty kilometers south to press their attack into Estonia, or stall them outside of Narva—until Russian combat engineers figured out how to get the brigade's tanks across the river. Not all of the Russian tanks would make the trip across.

The remaining one hundred and fifty-six shells would arc over Narva, targeting a six-mile stretch of the Tallinn-St. Petersburg highway. Each specialty projectile carried two self-guided sub munitions, which independently detected and attacked enemy tanks or armored personnel

struggle at the terminal, he had warned them. He'd been right about everything, except for Terminal D. Now she was fighting for enough space so her children could breathe.

At seven, Erik barely came up to her navel. Fortunately, Helina was taller and could somewhat hold her own, letting Mari focus on keeping her son off the ground. She wasn't sure how much further Erik could continue like this. The look on his face told her not very long.

"We're almost there, sweetie," she said, forcing a big smile.

He pursed his lips and nodded, tears streaming down his dirty cheeks. Mari was glad that Erik couldn't see over the crowd. An endless sea of wool hats, matted hair, backpacks and piggybacking children extended to the staircase leading to the third-floor departure gates. She dreaded the stairs. They almost didn't make it up the last staircase. Helina kissed her fair-haired brother on the temple.

"It's fine, Erik. We'll be out of here soon," she said, pushing against a dirty black backpack that hovered inches from his face.

"I miss Daddy," he whimpered.

"Daddy's fine. He'll join us in Stockholm," said Helina, her eyes meeting Mari's for a moment.

They both knew the truth. Colonel Saar would undoubtedly be among the first Estonian soldiers to fight the Russians.

"Helina, how are you doing?" she said.

"Fine, Mom, but I need to go to the bathroom," said Helina.

Mari didn't know what to say. She hadn't put any

thought into how long they might be trapped, unable to move in any direction except forward. She scanned the yellow walls of the terminal, not spotting a bathroom nearby—not that it would have mattered. A few seconds later, her son looked back at her.

"I have to go too," he said. "Really bad."

"Soon, sweetie," she said, rubbing his head through his gray hat. "Maybe it's time to have something to eat. I'll break open some candy."

His eyes lit up briefly as she dug into her coat pocket for the chocolate bar she had been parceling out to the kids for the past hour. She snapped off a large piece and handed it to Erik, breaking off another for Helina. Even at eleven years old, the allure of chocolate hadn't worn off her daughter. The kids seemed placated for the moment, while she checked her smartphone for messages. Her parents had made it to Riga by car, though she wasn't sure if that made things better or worse for them. They lived on the southern coast of Estonia, on the Bay of Riga, and Mari begged them to drive south immediately. At least Riga put them farther away from the Russian hordes. Nothing from Egan, which didn't surprise her.

The lights flickered in the terminal, followed by a sudden rumbling as military jets flew over the port. She hoped they were friendly jets, but somehow knew this was wishful thinking. The crowd pressed tighter around them, causing Erik to moan. His chocolate-stained mouth quivered as the smell of urine hit the air.

"I couldn't help it, Mommy," he said, turning his head to escape the backpack pushing into his face.

Mari wanted to scream at the young man in front of them. She'd asked him to reverse the backpack twice

9

already, but he'd just shook his head and mumbled something about it being her fault for having kids.

"It's all right, Erik. Next time make sure you pee on the man in front of you," she said, shoving the black backpack as hard as she could.

She instantly regretted her action, seeing that it caused a ripple effect in the crowd. The man spun around and raised a fist, his hand hesitating. Mari squeezed in front of her children.

"I'm very sorry," she said forcefully. "But your backpack has hit my son's face nonstop since we started. I wish you would wear it on the front of your body. Just until we get on the ferry."

"You should have thought of that before having a bunch of illegitimate kids." He snickered.

"My husband is the commanding officer of an artillery battalion stationed at the border," she stated. "Why haven't you reported to your Defence League unit? The reserves were called up weeks ago. I don't see anything wrong with you."

"What's the point of dying in a frozen foxhole on the border? Fucking stupid if you ask me," he replied, keeping his hand up as if he might hit her.

A thick hand grabbed his wrist. "Her husband is on the border, buying the rest of us time to escape. It's a time-honored tradition called sacrifice. Something your generation doesn't know the first thing about."

A stocky man with graying hair, dressed in a thick, gray and orange weatherproof jacket, held the man's wrist in place.

"Now you will reverse the backpack, or I will beat you senseless and let them walk over you. Your choice," he said.

"Fine," said the young man. "I guess this is how your generation solves things."

"That's right," he said, nodding at Mari as the guy carefully removed his backpack.

"Thank you," she said.

"No. Thank you," the older man said, squeezing between the young man and Mari. "Get behind your kids again, and I'll make sure you have smooth sailing for the rest of the trip."

She noticed that he carried no backpack or luggage.

"You're not carrying anything?" she said.

"I didn't have time. My daughter is at Stockholm University. I have to be on this ferry," he said.

"Let me know if you need water or food. We have plenty to last the trip—if we ever get on the ferry," she said.

"We'll get on. It's moving slowly because there's only one ferry at the terminal, and they're loading it carefully. All of the ferries will be here shortly. Right now they're waiting," said the man.

"Waiting for what?" she said.

He leaned back and whispered, "Waiting for NATO to sink the Russian blockade."

"What? How could you know that?" she whispered back.

"Because my son is a lieutenant at the Miinisadam Naval Base a few kilometers from here. I dropped him off before coming here. All hell is breaking loose on the water. I'm pretty sure we just heard our own jets fly over."

"God help us," she said, hugging her children.

"God—and people like your husband and my son," he said.

"Say a prayer for them, children," said Mari, buoyed by a complete stranger's kindness.

Chapter 3

Baltic Sea
Fifty-two miles north of Gotland, Sweden

Through the night-vision-enhanced visor on her flight helmet, Lieutenant Commander Robyn Faulks watched the coastline slip past her F/A-18F Super Hornet. At three hundred and ten knots, the light green strip was long gone when she glanced right. She caught a glimpse of another attack aircraft in her flight of six Hornets. In less than a minute, they'd deliver their payload and turn for the Swedish coast, disappearing just as quickly.

They'd launched from the USS *George H. Bush* nearly eight hours ago, stopping at Royal Air Force Base Mildenhall to refuel and wait for the final mission "green light." They didn't wait for long; the pilots and flight officers rushed to their aircraft less than two hours after arriving. They left with a pair of KC-135 refueling aircraft, the last strategic aircraft still stationed in Europe. The flying "gas stations" topped them off north of Denmark and returned to the protective cover of the United Kingdom's air defense zone. With the secret approval of the Swedish government, the Hornets flew a low-level profile over the sleeping country, heading toward the Baltic.

Her helmet-integrated HUD flashed a thirty-second warning, which she knew would be seen by the flight officer seated behind her. The mission profile required the strictest emissions control (EMCON) standards, prohibiting the use of radar, radio gear or internal communications circuits. Silencing the internal link was overkill, but mission planners didn't want any of the pilots "fat fingering" the wrong button and giving the Russians an excuse to escalate tensions. American forces could not be implicated in the upcoming strike. The two stealth missiles attached to her wing pylons were a testament to their quiet, yet continued commitment to NATO.

Twenty seconds. In her HUD, the green tinted missiles' status field change to "Armed." A string of secondary symbols confirmed that latest targeting data uploads had been received less than a minute ago, ensuring that the missiles would reach their targets without using radar.

Capable of autonomous targeting, the LRASM (Long Range Anti-Ship Missile) would use a combination of radar, infrared signature and electronic intercept data provided by Finnish sensors to independently detect and track their targets—ensuring the simultaneous delivery of each one-thousand-pound warhead. Only one missile was needed per ship, since the Russian's Baltic Fleet consisted of nothing heavier than a Sovremenny class destroyer. A reserve missile would loiter twenty miles away from the first Russian vessel, just in case one of the ships got lucky. Within the span of seconds, the naval blockade of the Baltic States would be lifted. *Ten seconds to launch.*

She watched the countdown timer, giving a thumbs-up to her flight officer when it hit zero. The aircraft shuddered, adjusting to the sudden reduction in weight. A brilliant yellow-green flash filled her visor, as the LRASM's booster propelled the cruise missile ahead of the Hornet. The light faded as it pulled away, the missile travelling two hundred knots faster than her aircraft. A second shaking, followed by another night-vision bloom confirmed the successful launch of their final missile. She counted a dozen successful booster ignitions from her strike force before the last LRASM's were swallowed by the night.

Her HUD displayed a Time-To-Target (TTT) of twenty-eight minutes. They'd be long gone before the Russian ships hit the bottom of the Baltic. Faulks eased her aircraft into a shallow turn, proud that the United States was not out of the fight.

"Red Dragon Redux"

Chapter 4

Lieutenant Commander Gayle Thompson stared into the darkness beyond the starboard bridge wing. The frigid air stung her face, forcing her to squint against the wind created by the ship's transit. Not even the horizon was discernible.

There's nothing out there, she thought.

She still couldn't fathom the sheer absence of shipping traffic outside of the Delaware Channel. Four months into the crisis, and the humanitarian aid from Europe had trickled to nothing—not that it had ever really started. Russian aggression across the Eastern European front started within a month of the EMP attack against the United States, effectively drawing NATO into a quagmire of idle military threats and useless political posturing across Europe. One former Soviet satellite nation after another fell to bloodless coups, or in some cases, Blitzkrieg-like attacks. The brief battle in Estonia had been particularly bloody, for both sides. In less than a week, Russian Federation borders extended to Poland, Slovakia, Hungary and Romania. NATO didn't expect the Russians to stop, not with the United States out of the picture.

Tensions at sea had returned to Cold War levels, an

era Thompson had never experienced during her eleven-year career. Few of the sailors onboard *Gravely* remembered the days when a constant, low-grade fear of the Soviets ruled the sea. NATO and Soviet seaborne units played endless games of cat and mouse, the contest occasionally turning deadly. The Russian surface navy posed little threat in 2019, the supremacy myth surrounding their missile-bristling warships was busted more than two decades earlier. The same couldn't be said about their submarine force, which was why *Gravely* had spent the past one hundred and four of the past one hundred and eight days at sea. A four-day stop to reload weapons at the Yorktown Naval Weapons Station represented the crew's only break since the "event."

Thompson had expected to take on additional crewmembers during the stop, but the Atlantic Fleet barely had enough sailors to put the minimum number of required ships to sea. The asteroid strike south of Richmond, Virginia, had killed, injured or "disappeared" more than a quarter of Naval Station Norfolk's sailors and officers. Even more surprising, she had retained command of *Gravely*. It seemed logical that Atlantic Fleet commanders would put someone more experienced in charge of one of their most important assets. Thompson had half the sea-time experience of a typical captain. Either she had proven herself worthy during the three weeks following the event, or they had run out of command-eligible officers. She guessed it was a combination of both.

The door next to her clanged open, spilling red light onto the bridge wing's crisscrossed metal decking. The officer of the deck held the door open several inches against the wind.

"Captain, CIC reports a POSSUB bearing zero-six-five/two-nine-five relative. Sonar is working on a classification. TAO requests permission to bring the ship to a new heading of one-one-zero to resolve the bearing," said the officer.

She instinctively turned her head toward the relative bearing of the possible submarine, staring once again at a black canvas of howling winds and crashing waves.

"Come right to course one-one-zero," she said, grabbing the door handle and pulling it open far enough to slip inside. "Tell the TAO I'm on my way down to CIC."

The bridge felt like a sauna compared to the bridge wing, the temperature outside barely hovering above freezing. The familiar smell of burnt coffee permeated the dark space, competing with the salty, open ocean air. She closed the watertight door and locked the handle, hearing the door hiss. The ship's positive pressure system, designed to prevent biological or chemical weapons intrusion, had recharged the pressure behind the door. The system ran continuously while they were underway.

"OOD, let's get a lookout on that relative bearing with night vision. You never know," she said, heading toward the ladder that would take her off the bridge.

"Aye, aye, Captain," said the young officer.

"Captain's off the bridge," announced a hidden petty officer to her right, startling her.

She felt the ship turn as she slid down the ladder, landing in front of the door to the captain's stateroom. Her stateroom. Located between the bridge and the Combat Information Center, it gave the commanding officer quick access to either critical station, a necessity she had never fully appreciated before assuming responsibility for the lives of *Gravely*'s crew. A few twists and turns later, she descended to the Combat Information Center entrance.

"Captain's in CIC!" yelled a sailor at a nearby console.

A petty officer at the chart table announced, "Ship is steady on course one-one-zero."

Lieutenant Mosely rushed to meet her.

"Ma'am, I have every sonar tech on the ship crammed into sonar control, trying to figure this out. There's no traffic out here, so they were able to isolate the signal," he said.

"The contact just appeared out of nowhere?" she asked.

"We've had the passive towed array below the thermocline layer for several hours, looking for any long-range stalkers," he said, walking away. "ST1 Herbert is convinced this contact came into detection range above the layer, either snooping for electronic signatures or receiving updated orders. The submarine just descended below the layer."

"Does sonar have any idea what we're looking at?"

"They're still trying to classify the contact."

"So this could be surface noise caught in a convergence zone?"

"They don't think so. The signature is too distinct to have crossed the layer and bounced around for hundreds of miles. Plus, it appeared too suddenly."

She nodded and followed him through the dimly lit CIC to the sonar control room. Beyond the curtain separating the two spaces, several men and women huddled around the AN/SQQ-89 Integrated Anti-Submarine Warfare Display. They quickly made room for her.

"What do we have, Herbert?"

"Ma'am, if I had to guess before the analysis was finished, I'd say we're hearing reactor equipment."

"A boomer?"

"I can't say, ma'am. Could be a fast-attack boat," replied the petty officer.

"Not a surface contact?" she pressed.

"Negative, Captain. Guardian just lit up our sector. No surface tracks."

Shit. The presence of a nuclear-powered submarine was bad news, regardless of the type. It meant Russian or Chinese nuclear assets had been sent closer to the U.S. mainland; a move deemed unacceptable by the National Security Council and Pentagon planners. *Gravely*'s orders were specific: Hunt and kill any subsurface contacts in their operating area.

The problem they faced was localization. The towed array gave them a direction, but no distance. Their first tactic would be to send an aircraft down the line of bearing from *Gravely*, hoping to detect the magnetic disturbance caused by the submarine's metal hull. Unfortunately, this tactic wasn't an exact science and could last for hours. Despite the sheer volume of math and science behind antisubmarine warfare operations, luck played an almost equally important role.

To expedite the process, they'd utilize Guardian's extensive supply of passive sonobuoys along the detection bearing to fix the location of the sub. Easier said than done against a moving target that could be anywhere along a thirty- to fifty-mile line.

"Very well," said Thompson, backing up a few feet. "TAO, report this as a POSSUB, high confidence, and request that Guardian remain on station to assist. We're going to need their sonobuoys. Set flight quarters for Spotlight One-One. I want the flight crew briefed and the helo in the air within thirty minutes."

"I'm on it," said Mosely, disappearing through the curtain.

"And TAO?" she said. Mosely reappeared. "Energize the Aegis system. Once the sub figures out we're prosecuting them, they might do something desperate. I don't want anything slipping through our net."

"Yes, ma'am!" he said enthusiastically.

Thompson turned to Petty Officer Herbert. "How long until we've resolved the bearing?"

"It'll take the towed array at least fifteen minutes to steady on our new course. We'll have a solid bearing to pass on to the helo at that point."

"I want to know what we're up against before the helo is airborne," she said.

"If this submarine type is in the catalogue, we'll get it classified within ten minutes," said Herbert.

"Excellent," she said. "Nice work. All of you."

Lieutenant Commander Thompson left the cramped space and caught up with Lieutenant Mosely.

"I'll be on the bridge. Let me know as soon as sonar classifies the contact."

She barely heard them announce her presence on the bridge. Thompson settled into the captain's chair and closed her eyes. Her head swam with scenarios and contingencies. Once Lieutenant Mosely passed the report, there would be no going back. Atlantic Fleet commanders would commit *Gravely* to the fight. Kill or be killed. A seasoned submarine captain versus—*don't go there*. She knew *Gravely*'s combat systems inside out, and so did her crew. They were ready for anything.

Chapter 5

"Guardian" P-8 Poseidon Aircraft
37 miles southeast of USS **GRAVELY**

Lieutenant Commander Kyle West scrutinized the tactical action display in front of him. Seated in a row on the port side of the aircraft's cabin, four additional operators monitored the aircraft's sensors and surveillance feeds, making sure his display had the latest data from all transmitting units. The seat pitched downward, pulling his stomach with it. A few more of those, and he might lose his midnight snack. The P-8 was a militarized version of a Boeing 737, not exactly the ideal passenger aircraft for low-altitude submarine-hunting maneuvers. He took a few deep breaths and tried to ignore his worsening stomach situation.

"Sonobuoys Kilo-Three and Kilo-Four picking up the track," announced one of the enlisted operators in West's headset.

He pressed a button and replied, "Got it. Track hooked."

Unable to get a MAD reading from *Gravely*'s helicopters, Guardian and Sentry, another P-8 aircraft launched from Naval Air Station Oceana and started deploying passive sonobuoy patterns ahead of the reported bearing line in a "hail Mary" attempt to find the submarine. After exhausting more than three-quarters of their sonobuoy load out, they got lucky. A subsurface contact passed through one of the patterns, ten miles away from the helicopter. While Guardian swooped down to deploy more sonobuoys, Spotlight One-One closed the distance to the submarine, hovering nearby with two armed torpedoes.

So far, the Type 093 Chinese submarine had maintained course and speed, heading toward the Delaware Channel at ten knots, a relatively quiet, but urgent running speed. All of that was about to change. They needed to fine-tune the submarine's position for a deliberate torpedo attack by the helicopter. He expected all hell to break loose underwater once the submarine was pinged by the active directional sonobuoys.

"Go active on Oscar-Four and Oscar-Five," said West, switching channels. "Spotlight One-One, this is Guardian. Oscar-Four and Oscar-Five just went live. Confirm link to these sonobuoys."

A garbled, but readable voice responded, "Copy. Links are active. Bingo! I'm showing active bearings to target."

The submarine was as good as dead at this point.

"Spotlight, do you require further guidance to target?" asked West.

"Negative. I have a strong link to your sonobuoys. Moving into position to attack."

"Give 'em hell, Spotlight," said West.

He turned to the officer seated next to him, making sure his headset wasn't transmitting. "That should teach those Commie fucks a lesson."

"A cold, wet lesson," said the lieutenant.

"They probably won't feel a thing," added the radar operator two seats over.

"Too bad," said West, leaning back in his seat to

watch the digital battle.

"New radar contact, bearing two-five-five! Correction. Two new contacts—shit, these things are moving fast!" said the radar operator.

West stared at his screen, watching the new contacts speed away from the submarine's location, hoping that Spotlight One-One's link-track didn't disappear. The new contacts and the helicopter merged on his tactical screen.

Chapter 6

USS **GRAVELY** *(DDG-107)*
Off the coast of Delaware

Chief Fire Controlman Jeffries was hovering behind the ship's Anti-Air Warfare (AAW) console when Petty Officer Clark screamed in his face.

"TAO! New air tracks 1025 and 1026. Bearing zero-three-three. Distance forty-five miles. Heading two-niner-three. Speed three hundred knots and increasing. Altitude four hundred feet and rising!"

The sailor seated at the AN/SLQ-32 Electronic Warfare console on the other side of CIC called out what Jeffries suspected.

"I have no fire control radars or missile seekers along that bearing."

The new targets did not emit an electronic signal, which meant they were either land-attack cruise missiles dependent on GPS and terrain comparison to reach their targets, or anti-ship missiles in booster phase. *Gravely*'s response to each scenario would be the same.

"Stand by to take those tracks, Clark," he whispered in the petty officer's ear before turning to gauge Lieutenant Mosely's reaction.

Lieutenant Mosely stood behind his station, staring at the bank of raised flat-screen displays at the front of CIC. One of the screens showed the direction of the air tracks superimposed on a digital map overlay of *Gravely*'s assigned area of operations. The missiles fired by the Type 093 Chinese submarine were headed toward the Washington, D.C., area. Captain Thompson stood next to Mosely, reaching the same conclusion. She nodded at the TAO, who issued the orders.

"Fire Control, kill air tracks 1025 and 1026. I don't care what it takes. Spotlight One-One is weapons free to conduct a deliberate torpedo attack. I want that submarine dead," he uttered.

The Anti-Submarine Tactical Air Controller (ASTAC) two seats over from Clark responded. "Passing the order to Spotlight One-One. Weapons free."

Jeffries watched as the Combat Information Center flawlessly executed the multi-contact engagement. The Aegis combat system had been designed for a nearly automated engagement of enemy targets. By the time he turned to face the Anti-Air Warfare console, Clark had assigned three SM-2 surface-to-air missiles to each track. He patted the sailor on the shoulder.

"You know what to do," said Jeffries.

Clark pressed a series of buttons authorizing the salvo firing of six missiles. The ship rumbled against the pitch and roll of the sea, their only physical indication that the Vertical Launch System (VLS) had released the missiles. One of the screens in front of the captain and TAO flashed to a green image of the forward VLS battery. The dark green scene flashed white six times in rapid succession. A hollow voice echoed through one of the speakers.

"TAO, this is the OOD. I confirm six birds away."

"Confirmed by Fire Control," yelled Petty Officer Clark. "Six birds clearing booster phase. Looking good!"

"Time to impact?" said the captain.

Clark took a moment to examine his data fields. Jeffries refrained from helping the young sailor find the information. Coddling his sailors had never been part of the chief's training philosophy.

"Time to first impact in thirty-nine seconds, Captain."

Jeffries nudged him.

"Three niner seconds, ma'am."

"Very well," said Captain Thompson, nodding her approval at Jeffries.

"Torpedo away!" announced the ASTAC. "Spotlight One-One is maneuvering for re-attack, Captain."

"Don't make your reports to me. Lieutenant Mosely is fighting the ship," said Thompson.

"Aye, aye, ma'am," said the petty officer. "TAO, Spotlight One-One—"

"Got it, make sure Spotlight drops a sonobuoy for battle-damage assessment," said the TAO.

"Already in the water, sir. Sonar reports active torpedo pinging. It's just a matter of time," said the ASTAC.

Several seconds later, Clark gave them an update.

"Missiles entered terminal-guidance phase. Revised time to target estimate is one five seconds. Aegis shows a solid lock on the targets."

Jeffries mentally counted down the seconds. He reached twelve when Clark announced their arrival.

"Splash tracks number 1025 and 1026. Aegis is picking up nothing but falling debris from the tracks."

"Copy. Splash tracks," said the TAO, among a chorus of cheers.

Moments later, it was the ASTAC's turn to pass on some good news.

"TAO, all acoustic sources confirm an underwater

detonation. The torpedo has stopped pinging. Sonar assesses a hit. They're processing more data from the sonobuoy and towed array feeds to assess the extent of the damage."

Everyone cheered except for the captain, who whispered something to Lieutenant Mosely. He nodded before abruptly interrupting the celebration.

"Keep it down! This isn't over! ASTAC, order Spotlight One-One to re-attack the target with its second torpedo," said the TAO.

The order quieted the crew. The captain wasn't taking any chances with the submarine, which had very likely fired two nuclear-tipped cruise missiles at the capital—and could fire a whole host of antiship missiles on *Gravely* if it survived the first torpedo. Jeffries suspected that Guardian and Sentry would continue to drop torpedoes until they heard the Chinese submarine break apart underwater.

Chapter 7

15 miles northeast of Guangzhou, China
Early December 2019

Staff Sergeant Chen Tang-shan sat on the cold ground next to his assigned tent, peering through the fence at the orange aura visible over the darkened hilltops. Based on the distant glow, he knew the camp was due east of a major industrial area, but he couldn't be sure where. They could be outside one of several dozen Chinese cities, coastal or inland. The truck ride from the pier in Xiamen had lasted several hours by his guess. He wasn't sure, because his watch, along with the rest of his personal items, had been confiscated a few hours after his capture on Penghu Island.

As a Republic of China (ROC) Marine, he had devoted his career to preparing for this invasion, an unsurprising continuation of a youth spent under the constant threat of a breakdown in "cross-strait" relations. They had always understood the odds stacked against them, even with the prospect of American intervention. When the United States started to withdraw its military forces from the western Pacific theatre of operations, the Taiwanese government took immediate steps to safeguard the people. Chen's battalion was ferried from the Taiwanese mainland to Penghu, a small archipelago in the Taiwan Strait.

To what end? He'd spend the rest of his life in labor camps, with an occasional stint in a re-education facility. If he showed promise, and no signs of aggression, he might be returned to his family on Taiwan—if his family hadn't been moved to a labor camp in China. He wished he had been killed on Penghu.

Instead, his tank had been hit by an antitank missile fired from a Chinese attack helicopter within the first few minutes of the battle, killing the rest of his crew and disabling the tank. He spent the next seventy-two hours sprinting from one blasted structure to the next with a Marine infantry squad, occasionally stopping long enough to fire on an unsuspecting Chinese patrol. Chen and the two remaining Marines were captured at night on the third day of the invasion while swimming across Magong Bay to an outlying island.

They had hoped to find a serviceable boat on one of the islands so they could retreat to the mainland. They felt useless on the island. At night, they saw flashes across the channel between Taiwan and Penghu. The battle for Taiwan raged on while their fight dissolved into a pointless game of hide and seek with the Chinese. Their families needed them.

His wife and children lived in the West District of Chiayi City. They would no doubt see heavy fighting as the Chinese fought their way east through the city to the provincial government complex. Chen had seen the Army Reserve battle plans for defending the mainland. It would be a fight to the bitter end for the regular and reserve units assigned to defend the city, and the civilians caught in the middle.

They hadn't been the only ROC Marines with the same concern. The Chinese patrol boat that pulled them out of the water held several Marines from the 66th Marine Brigade, all plucked out of the jet-black water. Less than twenty-four hours later, he was deposited at Camp 78 with the clothes on his back and a pair of cheap plastic sandals. Made in China, no doubt.

Chen shivered, knowing it was time to return to his overcrowded tent and the worn bamboo mat so graciously "loaned" to him by the "people." The propaganda had started immediately. *People's* this and *people's* that. Intolerable on every level.

Headlights appeared in the hills, approaching the camp. One pair turned into several, as the road turned gradually toward the entrance on the northern side of the camp. More prisoners. Just what they needed.

A high-pitched noise drew his attention away from the trucks. The sound grew louder over the next few seconds, resembling a jet engine. He caught movement in his peripheral vision and jerked his head left—just in time to see a long, dark object fly over the eastern half of the camp. The sound rapidly faded as Taiwanese prisoners streamed out of the tents, cheering at the sky. Like Chen, many of them knew exactly what had passed overhead: a cruise missile.

Moments later, the watchtowers lining the camp bathed the prisoners in blinding light. Whistles blared, and amplified voices ordered them back to their tents. A few bursts of automatic fire emphasized the guards' urgency to restore order to the "people's camp." Chen wondered where the missile was headed, and if it signified anything beyond a random, desperate, retaliatory shot fired by one of their submarines or destroyers. He hoped so.

Chen had barely settled onto his mat when the tent

went dark—the intense light from the watchtowers no longer penetrating the thin brown canvas. The sudden change quieted the tent, only a few whispers penetrating the silence. Absolute silence. Something was wrong.

He scrambled to the tent flap on his knees, pushing through a sea of huddled prisoners. He crawled out of the tent and lay still in the rocky dirt. Aside from a few flashlight beams sweeping across the fence line in front of the closest guard barracks, the camp was completely dark. Only the lights on the inbound trucks penetrated the night—but the trucks had stopped moving. He stood up, fixated on the lights.

Why the hell would they stop in the open?

The guards in the tower to his right started shouting at him. Chen heard the words "last warning," so he raised his hands above his head and nodded.

He turned toward the tent, noticing something he had missed a few moments ago. Chen stopped and stared beyond the trucks.

Impossible.

He hoped his eyes weren't playing tricks on him. The prominent orange glow above the hills had vanished. The trucks. The camp's lights. The city. It all made sense. Someone had just thrown the switch over part of the People's Republic of China. Why had the Americans waited so long to strike back? It didn't matter. He was deeply satisfied knowing that the *people's* lives had been permanently cast into darkness.

Fuck the people.

Chapter 8

KJ-3000 Airborne Early Warning aircraft
153 miles east of Guangzhou

Major Xhua Hua stabbed at the button next to the console's trackball, locking the target in the system. A flurry of voices and movement erupted around him as equipment operators scrambled to report the target to a dizzying array of People's Liberation Air Force units on the ground. He swiveled his chair to brief his commanding officer, who had already crisscrossed through the maze of consoles to reach him.

"Colonel, I have an unidentified air track eighteen point two miles north of Guangzhou. Altitude 600 meters and rising. Speed 700 kilometers per hour. Zero horizontal trajectory. Zero squawk. Designating track number eight-five."

"Where did it appear?" asked the colonel, leaning in to view the screen.

"Here," said Xhua, pointing at his wide-screen display. "Eighteen point two miles north of Guangzhou."

"It's flying straight up?"

"Affirmative, sir. Altitude eleven hundred meters."

"It can't be a missile or a rocket. It's too slow," said the colonel, shaking his head. "And there's nothing listed on the ground in that area."

An officer behind them interrupted. "Colonel Jin!

Southern Air Defense Command demands a personal report on the contact!"

The colonel's face tightened, and he nodded stiffly to the junior officer before scrambling back to his station toward the front of the aircraft. Xhua turned his attention back to the display and watched the baffling contact profile.

"Altitude twenty-one hundred meters. Speed steady at seven hundred!" he yelled to the colonel.

This was a first for Major Xhua. He'd been assigned to airborne early warning aircraft since he joined the People's Liberation Air Force, rising through the ranks to the second-most senior position in the command and control center aboard the PLA's premier air defense platform. Only Colonel Jin and one of the pilots outranked him. In all of his eighteen years, he'd never tracked a straight-vertical contact this low to the ground. Military jet aircraft occasionally pulled this kind of maneuver during combat training, but in every case the aircraft started the steep ascent from a two- to three-thousand-meter altitude. Nothing about "eight-five" made sense. Another five seconds passed.

"Altitude thirty-two hundred meters. Speed holding," he said. *Three kilometers.*

"Review the feeds and confirm that we didn't miss anything prior to detection!" yelled Colonel Jin.

"Yes, sir!" he yelled, looking between the consoles behind him to assign the task to one of his junior officers.

"No! *You* review the feeds!" screamed the colonel.

Here we go. Southern Air Defense Command had started their inquisition. He wondered if the phased array ground radars situated further inland had seen anything different. Doubtful. They were focused on higher

37

altitude, over-the-horizon threats. He nodded and opened a separate command window on his screen.

"Captain Wu, stand by to assume primary tactical actio—" *What is this?*

The data window for track eight-five couldn't be correct. Altitude seventy-three hundred meters? Speed twenty-nine hundred kilometers per hour? Supersonic?

"Colonel! Track eight-five has increased speed to Mach two point three. Eight thousand meters!" said Xhua.

Colonel Jin snapped his head in Xhua's direction, but didn't respond. He kept nodding in acquiescence to the generals undoubtedly screaming at him through his headset. Xhua watched the altitude climb. Nine thousand. Ten thousand. Nearly a thousand meters per second. *What the hell is this?* A chilling thought entered his mind. ICBM? Second Artillery Corps certainly wouldn't disclose the location of their mobile launchers, so the area would appear empty to conventional PLA forces.

It was the only thing that made sense to him. The Americans had responded to the invasion of Taiwan with nuclear weapons, and China was retaliating. He resisted the urge to get up from his seat. He had nowhere to go and nothing to do except wait.

"Southern Air Defense Command confirms your data!" said Colonel Jin. "I have been assured there is nothing in the area."

"Retaliatory strike?" asked Xhua, silencing the command and control center.

Jin stared at him with his mouth agape for a moment before shaking his head.

"No. We would have an inbound warning by now," said Jin, the confidence in his voice fading.

"Twenty-one thousand meters, sir," said Xhua, grimacing.

What else could this be? A UFO?

"Guangzhou Air Base has scrambled a flight of two J-10 fighters!" yelled one of the console operators.

"I hope they brought space suits," said Xhua. "Because the contact will be in low Earth orbit before they reach it."

The colonel cursed and spoke forcefully into his headset, never breaking the steely-eyed glare at Xhua. *Message received. Quit speculating about nuclear weapons—do your job.* He turned to the screen. Twenty-three thousand. The altitude continued to climb while Jin talked to the Southern Air Defense Command. Thirty-two thousand. It had to be an ICBM.

At sixty-eight thousand meters, the track disappeared—followed immediately by the picture on his display. The cabin lights blinked and the plane shook violently, throwing Xhua against his seatbelt harness. The engines whined through the hull before settling into a stable pitch. The crew erupted in a cacophony of reports punctuated by cries of pain. He looked around and saw four members of the crew sprawled over the consoles and deck. They all appeared to be moving, which was a good sign. Panning toward the front of the cabin, he saw that Colonel Jin hadn't been so lucky. Jin's lifeless eyes stared at him from the rubber-matted deck, his head and neck jammed at an unsightly angle against the aircraft's mid-cabin door.

He flipped a switch to talk to the flight deck, but couldn't get the pilots to answer. His display screen reappeared with a prompt that told him that the system was in the reboot phase. The southern air defense zone was temporarily blind. He unbuckled his seatbelt and made his way to the cockpit door, grabbing anything sturdy in case the aircraft hit another patch of turbulence. Glancing down at Colonel Jin, he realized it wouldn't matter. He couldn't hold himself steady if the aircraft shook again. He knocked on the door, which opened before he lowered his hand.

A bloodied flight officer stood in the opening, his gray helmet cracked down the middle. He wiped the blood from his face and glanced at Colonel Jin's legs, which protruded into the aisle.

"Jin's dead. What is the status of the aircraft?" said Xhua.

The pilot pulled him into the spacious cockpit, taking Xhua by surprise.

"One of the engines is down, but the aircraft is stable—for now. We're running a diagnostics check on the main systems. What the hell happened?"

"I don't know. We were tracking a target headed straight up. It reached sixty-eight thousand meters and vanished right before the system shut down."

"Sixty-eight thousand? What was it, a missile?" asked the lead pilot.

"We don't know, sir," said Xhua.

"You don't know?" replied the pilot. "I'm taking us back to base."

"I need to get authorization from South Air Defense Command to end the mission," said Xhua.

"The mission is over."

"Negative, sir. We can't come off station without their permission," said Xhua.

The copilot interrupted the argument. "Both of you need to see this. Look toward the ground."

Xhua pushed past the dazed flight officer and leaned between the pilot and copilot seats, craning his head to see through one of the side windows.

"I don't see anything," said Xhua.

"That's the problem. The lights are out—everywhere," said the copilot. "Consistent with the equipment fluctuations, I'd say we've been hit by an EMP."

"I don't see how," said Xhua. "We would have been notified of an incoming ICBM."

"It doesn't matter. I'm declaring an emergency and landing this aircraft," said the pilot. "It's only a matter of time before we have a catastrophic equipment failure."

"Yes, sir. That's probably…the best course of action," he said, backing into the cabin, not sure what to do next.

The tactical situation over southern China had drastically changed, and not for the better.

Chapter 9

Sky View Tower
136th Floor
Pudong District, Shanghai China

Huan Xiao swiped the air a few inches from the ample touchscreen of her Jianyu smartphone, activating the device. Responding instantaneously, the screen displayed a picture of her family posing in front of a tranquil, azure bay in the Maldives. Her boys, ages five and seven, grinned widely at the photographer. Her husband displayed a forced smile, his thoughts thousands of miles away at Jianyu Tower.

She stole a glance out of the two-story, floor-to-ceiling window, the centerpiece of their 9,200-square-foot residence, at the zenith of Shanghai's tallest building. Across the Huangpu River, the warm, distant lights of the Bund waterfront beckoned over the cramped array of Technicolor towers jammed into Pudong. Jianyu Towers rose among them, displaying a dizzying array of brilliant colors that slowly shifted from dusk until dawn. Huan was thankful that she could still see the Bund. She was thankful for many things, mostly her two children, who were sound asleep.

Huan flicked her head a few centimeters left, clearing the screen with the nearly imperceptible movement, the device having already verified her identity through a subtle retinal scan. She had to admit, her husband's company's latest device was slick. Jianyu Industries didn't invent gesture-guided screen technology, but they had nearly perfected it. With a little practice, the features performed flawlessly, freeing a hand to hold a cappuccino or shopping bag. Another technological marvel designed to enable an upwardly mobile lifestyle. At least that's how they were selling it—or trying to sell it.

What should have been a breakthrough for Jianyu Industries, and the Chinese economy, had been hampered by another round of international trade setbacks. The launch was already three months behind schedule. The European release date, scheduled for early September, was inexplicably pushed back to November, followed by another delay in late November.

She suspected the problem stemmed from the brewing conflict with Taiwan. After the Americans withdrew their ships from the region, the Taiwanese government and military escalated their aggressive stance toward the Chinese. Rumors had spread through underground news agencies that Taiwanese Special Operations teams had been captured near Shantou, scouting the South Sea Fleet Naval Base. Whatever was happening, her husband knew more than he was willing to tell. He'd grown edgier by the week since the announcement of the November delay.

The scene beyond the reinforced, quadruple-paned windows vanished, leaving an impenetrable blackness—everywhere. Her phone's screen cast the only light she could detect inside or outside of the residence. She stopped breathing, listening to the unfamiliar stillness around her. Something must have gone wrong with the auto-tinting windows. But why would the entire suite go dark?

"Wei?" she said, calling out to her husband.

He was on the second level, in his study, just beyond the balcony. A light illuminated the windowpanes of a double set of French doors above her. She heard them click open.

"Wei? Something is wrong with the windows," she said, standing up in the darkness.

"It's not the windows!" he barked. "I just lost power to everything. Not even my laptop works!"

"How is that possible?" she said.

"It's not. The building has its own backup power system. The residence has its own backup system. This is bad news, Hu," he said, using his phone's built-in light to make his way to a spiral staircase.

Instead of heading toward her, Wei drifted to the center of the massive window. She stumbled across the marble floor to join him. Small lights flickered across the river, pinprick signs that the darkness wasn't a mirage caused by the high-tech, light responsive glass. Huan peered at the horizon, finding it devoid of Shanghai's endless sea of lights.

"Nothing," she said. "How could the power fail for the entire city?"

He took deep breaths, but didn't answer her. Wei was acting way too calm, almost like he had expected this to happen.

"Wei, what's happening?" she said.

"We need to pack up and get out of here," he said, putting both of his hands on the glass.

"What are you talking about?" she said, grabbing his shoulder and spinning him to face her.

She held her phone in the other hand, with the screen facing up. The light washed over his face, exposing a frighteningly detached look. He swallowed hard before turning his head and staring blankly past the glass.

"It won't be safe for the children in the city," he muttered.

"Wei! You're scaring me! Why won't it be safe here?" she pleaded, her hands trembling.

"Twenty-two million people live here, half of them migrant labor from the interior. We don't stand a chance," he muttered.

"In a power outage? You're not making sense," she said, shaking him.

He looked at her with wild eyes.

"The power isn't coming back on, Hu," he said.

"Of course it is," she said, cocking her head. "Why wouldn't it?"

"The rumors were true," said Wei.

"What rumors?" she demanded.

"Nobody thought they would retaliate," he said, ignoring her.

"I'm taking the kids to my parents," she said, walking away from him.

Whatever he was saying about the lights sounded like the ramblings of a madman on the verge of a breakdown. It wouldn't surprise her given his odd behavior over the past few months. The delayed launch of their flagship product had obviously been too much for him to handle. She'd check into the hotel on the seventieth floor of the tower, just to put some distance between them until the city restored the power. She sensed his presence close behind and whirled to defend herself if necessary.

"Sorry, Hu. This is just...this is like a bad dream," he said. "I don't think we'll be able to cross the river to get to your parents—and we need to be moving away from the populated areas."

He sounded normal again, but she still didn't understand what had him so spooked.

"I still don't understand why we can't stay," she protested. "The tower has its own security. Its own grocery stores. We have everything we need right here."

"Sky View is home to ten thousand residents. The stores will be emptied within minutes once people realize that the lights are out for good. Then they'll turn their attention to us, at the top of the building. That's how it works. The building will devour itself from within, and whatever's left will be devoured by the millions of people living in the slums we created. Our only chance of survival is to get out of this building—immediately," he said.

"We should just wait for the power to be restored," she said. "It's too dangerous to travel in a blackout."

"Hu, my love, this isn't a blackout. Can't you see? Nothing is functioning here," he said, gesturing around the deathly still residence. "The residence is on backup battery power, but nothing works."

She stared at him, still not grasping what he was trying to say.

"This is a retaliatory EMP attack. It all makes sense now. The trade restrictions, bogus underground news reports, travel bans—they've been keeping us in the dark. Ha! Did you hear that? In the dark. Now we're really in the dark," he said, laughing.

He was starting to sound crazy again. Huan backed up slowly, bumping into an end table and knocking over a lamp. The room brightened momentarily, an orange fireball fading on the southwest horizon. They ran to the window together, pressing against the cold panel.

Something big had exploded on the outskirts of Pudong. The metal chandelier above them rattled, followed by a vibration through the floor and glass. She recoiled from the glass, feeling completely exposed twenty-two hundred feet above the ground.

"I better wake the kids," she said.

"I'll take an inventory of our food and supplies. We won't be able to carry much," said Wei.

"What do we tell the kids?" said Huan.

"We're going on a bike trip. That's all," he said, lowering his voice to finish. "A bike trip as far away from the city as possible."

"The New Caliphate"

Chapter 10

Michael Atlee tightened his royal blue tie and examined his thick brown hair in the full-length mirror in his private bathroom. Impeccable. He was scheduled to meet with the Prime Minister at 10 Downing Street in a half-hour—just a five-minute car ride away. Unfortunately, the security procedures required to transport him one bloody kilometer could last twenty minutes. He could walk there in less time, which wasn't a bad idea. A little fresh air might do him some good.

Atlee still felt flush, his heart racing at the prospect of the sudden request for an audience. The mass emigration had finally drawn enough attention to warrant a cabinet meeting to discuss a strategy. He had his own opinion on the matter, but he'd wait to see what the "decision makers" had to say. So far, the Home Office had simply tracked and observed the growing trend, reporting the details to the Prime Minister's office.

He opened the bathroom door and stepped inside his spacious, modernist office, hoping to review a few emails before his security detail arrived. A knock at the door stopped him before he reached the desk. He hated when they came for him early. A few minutes shaved off his

51

day, here and there, landed him woefully behind schedule. Glancing at his watch, he sighed.

"Come in," said Atlee, the door opening immediately. "I was just—"

Two men he instantly recognized stepped inside and closed the door. David Wilson, Deputy Prime Minister, and the Right Honorable Malcom Straw, Secretary of State for Foreign and Commonwealth Affairs, both senior Cabinet members like himself. Something was seriously amiss to draw two of the most powerful government figures in the United Kingdom out of their offices—unannounced.

"Gentlemen, please," he said, gesturing to the Scandinavian-style furniture surrounding an art deco coffee table. "Shall I have Mary bring tea?"

Malcom Straw consulted his watch. "I would suggest something stronger, if it weren't ten thirty in the morning."

"Let's not cross the possibility off the list," said the Deputy Prime Minister, cocking an eyebrow. "Sorry to ambush you like this, Michael, but we thought it might be best to put some…distance between 10 Downing and our conversation."

Atlee strode to the cherry-top bar cabinet behind the dark yellow leather couch.

"Sounds like we could all use a nip, if this conversation is headed where I suspect," said Atlee.

The two well-dressed men agreed, sitting across from the couch on matching chairs.

"Ghastly furnishings, Atlee. What have they done here?" said Straw.

"Ghastly indeed. The entire building is an affront, if you ask me," said Atlee.

"A far cry from Whitehall," said Wilson.

"Neat, I presume?" said Atlee, removing three crystal tumblers.

"Sounds good. No need to get complicated," replied Straw.

"Agreed," said Wilson.

Atlee greeted the men with three glasses, each holding a generous, dark amber pour of a rare Highland Scotch. With tumblers in hand, they toasted the Queen and took liberal drinks.

"So, I've been given some direction regarding the startling rise in Muslim departures," started the Deputy Prime Minister.

Atlee knew it. His report had stirred up a mess. He wasn't surprised. Conservative estimates put the number of Muslim males departing the U.K. at more than five thousand per day—with the figure increasing steadily. The Mullahs' call to form the New Caliphate resonated within the Muslim community here and on the Continent. The sudden withdrawal of United States military forces from the Arabian Gulf region tipped the balance of power in favor of the rising Caliphate. The last European units departed three weeks ago, scuttling their equipment in northern Iraq to prevent its use by the swiftly approaching militant army.

"This is guaranteed to stir up controversy," said Atlee. "Not to mention the possibility of upsetting an already tenuous peace."

"The Prime Minister just departed a meeting with the French Prime Minister and German Chancellor. They've agreed on a political strategy to bring the rest of the European Union onboard with the plan," said Straw.

"I meant here in the U.K.," said Atlee, posing a

quizzical look. "That's not what you're talking about—is it?"

Straw and the Deputy Prime Minister shared a glance, Wilson breaking a tight grin.

"Far from it. The Prime Minister wants to expedite their departure. Encourage it," said Wilson, belting the rest of his Scotch. "Even enable it."

They studied his reaction, like best friends proposing something unthinkable to test each other's loyalty.

"And the rest of Europe plans to do the same?" said Atlee.

"France and Germany see this as a chance to start over. The rest will follow suit," said Wilson.

"Good God," Atlee muttered, unable to suppress a growing smile.

"Something amusing?" said Straw, casting a doubtful look his way.

"Not at all. This is like a dream come true, though it will be a mess to implement," said Atlee.

"A little mess now to prevent a bigger mess later. Just so we're clear, once they leave, they will never be readmitted. This is a one-way ticket," said Wilson. "That's where the Home Office earns its money."

"What about the families remaining here?" said Atlee, finishing his Scotch.

Wilson shrugged his shoulders and threw back his tumbler. "One step at a time, Michael."

Atlee contemplated another drink while countless thoughts and questions emerged. He hadn't expected this at all. Not in the current political climate. This would take some serious maneuvering in Parliament, although the general public would overwhelmingly support the measure. A thought stopped his reverie.

"I can't imagine Israel will appreciate the sudden, uninvited deposit of several million radical Islamic recruits at their doorstep," he stated.

"I'm told the Foreign Office already worked out the details," said Wilson, turning his head toward Malcom Straw.

"I don't have the foggiest idea what you're talking about," said Straw, smiling wryly.

Atlee got the message. The fewer people privy to the full plot, the better. A sense of dread dampened the elation that had energized him minutes ago. His eyes drifted to the half-filled decanter in his peripheral vision. Something told him he'd need to refill the crystal vessel before the week was up.

Chapter 11

10 miles south of Mosul
Islamic State of Iraq and Syria (ISIS)

Captain Harrison McDaid lowered a pair of powerful binoculars onto the sand-colored, cloth mat in front of him and rubbed his eyes. Nothing had changed on the highway leading out of Mosul. Large convoys departed the city hourly, ferrying fresh recruits south to the training center outside of Ramadi. A mix of sedans, civilian pickups and Soviet-era, open-back diesel transports, he estimated they carried nearly a thousand jihadists an hour south. An equal number of vehicles streamed north along the sand-swept road, returning from the long journey to deliver recruits. Highway One fed the Caliphate's push against Israel, and there was nothing they could do about it.

His mission was to observe and report ISIS movement south of Mosul—and that's all his team had done for the past seventy-two hours. They established a hidden observation post in the rocky hills a few kilometers from the highway, guided by a pair of Peshmerga Special Operations soldiers who joined the team in Arbil. The Peshmerga had been essential to their undetected navigation through the badlands southeast of Mosul. He felt safer with them around, their hatred of ISIS nearly palpable.

The Kurdistan government had a vested interest in keeping a close eye on the rising extremist menace to their west. ISIS incursions into the autonomous region had been limited, stopped by the same Peshmerga brigades that had fought them to a standstill on the Syrian/Kurdistan border a year earlier. The Caliphate settled for Mosul, temporarily ignoring the oil-rich lands in Kurdish hands. They had a more pressing duty, or jihad, on the front burner.

The prospect of pushing Israel into the Mediterranean Sea was too tempting for Caliphate leadership, fueling an unprecedented recruitment surge. Conservative estimates put the number of jihadists gathered near Ramadi at 1.2 million. The recruit-processing center in Mosul was the largest feeder into Ramadi, funneling European Muslims from the Turkish/Syrian border to the sprawling training center.

Based on what he had seen over the past few days, the numbers would likely double in less than a month. Possibly half that time, if reports filtering out of Umm Qasr and Kuwait City were accurate. Merchant vessels arrived daily, carrying military equipment and fresh recruits from outside of the Arabian Gulf.

McDaid shook his head and yawned. He had no fucking clue why coalition forces were taking a wait-and-see attitude here. One million jihadists was more than enough to force Israel into a strategic withdrawal of their population. Two million was enough to rapidly overwhelm their armed forces, putting them at risk of a second genocide. What they needed to do was turn this road into another "Highway of Death," like the first Gulf War.

He patted Sergeant Harrow on the shoulder. "Going to stretch my legs for a minute."

"Take your time, sir. Next convoy leaves in thirty minutes," said the soldier.

"I'll bring us some hot coffee," said McDaid.

"Sounds grand, sir," he said, scanning the distance through a sand-colored, tripod-mounted spotting scope.

McDaid slithered backward, clearing the desert camouflage net stretched over them. Once outside of the two-man hide site, he turned onto his back and slid down the back of the rocky outcropping toward a larger net staked between an irregularly dispersed pattern of half-buried boulders. Two smaller nets, hidden among the boulders, protected the flanks of the SAS position from unwelcome guests. They had a tidy, well-concealed position, unlikely to be disturbed—unless they were spotted from the road.

His feet struck the hardened sand next to the net, rousing one of the resting soldiers from a nap. The outline of a head and hand appeared through the tightly woven netting as McDaid ducked inside the partially shaded enclosure. Lieutenant Murray Osborne squinted at him, his hand a few inches away from his face. The officer lay in a tan sleeping bag next to one of the Peshmerga, who he suspected was not sleeping either. Nobody slept well out here.

They stole whatever sleep they could, spending most of their time awake—hoping the men on the perimeter didn't fall asleep. This cruel, almost ironic cycle continued until their bodies simply forced them to sleep, often for extended periods of time. They were about forty-eight hours from reaching that point. That's when life at an isolated observation post got interesting.

"Time to swap already?" he croaked, not bothering to check his watch.

"Negative. You have a few more hours," said McDaid, fiddling with a small portable stove set on a flat rock. "Thought I'd brew a cup."

The young officer pushed his sleeve down to examine his watch.

"Might as well join you," he said. "I can't sleep a wink in this cold. Who'd have thought we'd hit freezing temperatures out here?"

"I've become convinced that January anywhere outside of the tropics is miserable business," said McDaid, igniting a small stove perched on a flat rock next to the team's backpacks. "Cheer up. It'll be sunbathing weather by one in the afternoon."

"Just in time to cook us," said the lieutenant.

The headset concealed beneath McDaid's shemagh crackled. "Captain, you need to see this. I have military-grade vehicles headed north along the highway."

"Copy that. Be right up," he said, turning the stove off.

Lieutenant Osborne unzipped his sleeping bag and sat up, tapping his earpiece.

"Need me up top?" he said.

"Not yet. Wake Besam and prep for withdrawal—just in case," said McDaid.

"I'm awake," said the Kurdish soldier, holding a thumbs-up out of his sleeping bag.

McDaid scurried under the netting, transmitting to the two sentries watching their flanks.

"Nari and Hughes, did you copy that last transmission?"

"Solid copy. North by northeast clear," said Staff Sergeant Hughes.

"All clear, south by southeast," said Nari, in a thick, almost indecipherable accent.

"Roger. Prepare for immediate withdrawal," said McDaid.

He crawled up the hill to the primary observation post, nestling into position next to the soldier watching through the spotting scope.

"Care to take a look, sir?" said Sergeant Harrow, sliding over to make room for him.

"What do we have, Harrow?" said McDaid, adjusting the scope to examine the lead vehicle.

"If I didn't know better, I'd say Humvees," said Harrow.

Harrow was right. A line of turret-equipped, armored vehicles, similar in size and shape to the American Humvee, raced toward Mosul. For a brief moment, he wondered if this was some kind of raid against the ISIS recruitment center. The confused thought vanished when he was able to magnify one of the turrets. He recognized the Type 85 heavy machine gun first, followed by the standard black garb worn by ISIS regulars.

"Looks like the Caliphate got an upgrade. Mengshi tactical vehicles. Humvee knockoffs—and damn good knockoffs at that," said McDaid, searching for vehicle markings.

"I don't see any identification. Could be from Pakistan or Indonesia. Both countries have ordered more than twenty thousand of these from our friends in the People's Republic."

"Could be from China, given the circumstance," said Harrow.

"True. Regardless of the source, this does not bode well for any of the Caliphate's neighbors. What else are they offloading in Basrah and Umm Qasr?" said McDaid.

"That's for a different troop to worry about, sir. I'll call this in. I guarantee our boys will be interested in this development—along with the Kurds," said Harrow.

"Very interested. Might prompt them to do something about this rubbish," said McDaid, staring at the black ISIS flag fluttering above the armored vehicle.

Chapter 12

140 Miles east of Jerusalem
Highway 10, Jordan

Aariz Khalid bounced against the rough wooden bench, gripping the canvas top's metal frame to stay upright. His other hand clutched the automatic rifle he had been issued in Ramadi. The ride had been smooth until they reached portions of the highway that had been purposely bombed by Jordanian Air Force pilots. Periodically, the convoy slowed to avoid the charred hulk of a truck bearing a frightening resemblance to the one transporting him to the Safawi staging area. The pungent smell of burnt flesh mixed with diesel fumes reinforcing the severity of his situation.

He'd gone from attending classes at Birmingham City University to an ISIS training camp within the span of three weeks, a radical transformation for a twenty-year-old more interested in chasing girls on campus and playing video games than attending daily, let alone weekly Mosque. There had been no choice, really. He'd joined his friends out of fear. Not the fear of letting them down, but out of true fear for his family's safety. When the American-led coalition pulled its forces out of the Caliphate's way, many of his university and secondary school friends changed overnight.

Their hushed rhetoric and restrained preaching exploded, yielding an unapologetic, unrelenting barrage of threats against both him and his family. After his youngest sister was cornered walking home from school by a group of young men turned "religious police," he relented. Three days later, he was on a merchant ship headed to Turkey. Five weeks after that, he was riding in a canvas-covered coffin, on a flat, exposed road less than a few hundred miles from their "greatest enemy."

He looked around the dusty compartment in the fading light, reading the faces of his platoon. Some of them looked at peace with their fate. Most appeared nervous, their eyes furtively glancing from side to side, widening with every bump or unfamiliar noise. Others stared into the middle distance, trying to come to grips with the battle ahead. He wondered how many of them had been bullied into their seats on this truck. None of them dared to say anything about their predicament. Recruits stupid enough to complain about their treatment or request a return to the U.K. had been executed on the spot in Turkey. The killings stopped after Mosul, the message now crystal clear. There was no turning back.

The truck rapidly decelerated, pushing Aariz against the middle-aged man to his right. The man to his left slammed into him, knocking both of them to the metal floor. A rifle barrel hit him in the left temple as half of the truck's occupants tumbled off the center-facing benches. The shrill voice of their platoon commander, a hardened ISIS fighter, pierced the chaos. Aariz peered through the tangle of legs and arms to see him waving them out of the truck. Through the din of yelling and curses, he heard the word "helicopter," followed by an ominous deep thumping.

The men responded to the sound and its obvious implications, scrambling out of the truck. By the time Aariz hit the pavement, the whoosh of a rocket reached him. A sharp explosion vibrated the convoy, followed by a concussive blast wave. Turning his head in the direction of the blast, he saw several black-clad men land in smoking heaps on the side of the road. Cracks filled the air and the asphalt disintegrated next to Aariz, drawing his attention to three squat-looking objects spaced evenly over the low hills north of the convoy. Apaches. He sprinted away from the truck, diving to the ground as the air exploded with cannon fire.

He put his hands on the back of his head and pressed down, trying to present the smallest target imaginable to the gunners in the helicopters. He'd seen enough Apache footage online to know that he couldn't hide from their thermal cameras. His only hope was to become a much smaller target than the rest of the jihadists. A hand gripped the back of his ammunition vest, yanking him off the ground.

"Get on your feet and honor Allah," his platoon commander screamed.

Aariz twisted free, ending up on his back. The bearded militant snarled and reached down to grab him, disappearing in a scarlet burst of gore and pieces. He stared at the suspended remains of the man's body, vaguely aware of his truck exploding in the background. The detonation shook the sand, knocking the shredded corpse on top of him. He lay in complete stillness, praying for mercy, as the helicopters strafed and rocketed the convoy.

Nor did he move after the attack when the men prodded his blood-soaked, body-part-covered "corpse."

He stayed there until dark, long after the convoy departed. Rising slowly, he scanned the dark road next to the closest smoldering truck. Several dark lumps littered the ground, giving him hope. The men sent to examine him hadn't been interested in the sustainment pouch attached to his vest—only the rifles.

His first priority would be to search the bodies for food and water. They had been issued two bottles of water and a vacuum-sealed, Chinese meal upon boarding the trucks in Ramadi. He saw five more wrecks spread out along the road, each likely surrounded by more dead fighters. Aariz planned to load up and get off the road. He'd head east toward the Mediterranean, hoping to run into a true Arab brother—if they hadn't all been wiped out by the Caliphate.

Chapter 13

West of Ramadi, Iraq

Major Ilan Katz watched the featureless, purple-gray landscape race below his F-15E Strike Eagle.

"Sixty seconds to maneuver point alpha," said Captain Jacob Eshel, the aircraft's Weapon Systems Officer. "ESM is clear. Spotlight One reports radar clear to target."

An Airborne Early Warning (AEW) aircraft circling over the empty desert fifty miles south kept a close eye on their approach. ISIS had no known aircraft-intercept capability, but the quality of military equipment arriving in Iraqi ports left mission planners nervous. The nations backing these extremists had deep pockets, and it was only a matter of time before their commitment to the Caliphate started to include trained pilots.

"Very good. Run final weapon diagnostics," said Katz.

"Running diagnostics now," said the captain.

The aircraft rumbled, hitting an early evening temperature gradient common to low-level desert flying. With the sun below the horizon, the ground radiated heat into the cooling air. Evenly distributed near the ground, it didn't create a problem, but the temperature differentials occasionally concentrated in a single location and created a "bump." *Nothing to get worked up about.*

"I have a clean diagnostics check. Ready to arm the weapon," said Eshel.

"Stand by," said Katz, opening the designated command and control frequency.

"Forge, this is Hammer One. Approaching maneuver point alpha. Request failsafe instructions. Over."

Failsafe was the point of no return for the mission. Once the weapon left the aircraft, they couldn't take it back. He was giving them one last chance to call off the mission.

"Hammer One, this is Forge. Proceed with Clean Sweep," said a voice through his helmet speaker.

"This is Hammer One, copy proceed with Clean Sweep," he replied, switching back to the cockpit communications circuit. "Jacob, arm the weapon."

"Weapon armed," said Eshel, moments later. "Toggle the consent-to-fire switch, and the fire control computer does the rest—except fly the aircraft."

"Eventually, they will fly themselves for missions like this," said Katz.

"Let's hope there are no more missions like this," replied Eshel.

Katz saw the status of the weapon change on his helmet-integrated HUD. He selected "Special" with a toggle switch on the center control stick and changed the status to "Consent Release." All he truly had to do from this point forward was follow the maneuver pattern calculated by the computer.

"Maneuver point alpha in five, four, three, two…here we go," said Katz, easing the control stick back and increasing the throttle.

His G-suit responded immediately, squeezing his lower extremities. The maneuver wasn't extreme, but the aircraft's computers were programed to counter the G-forces diverting blood and oxygen away from his brain. He steadied the Strike Eagle in a forty-degree climb, watching the altitude rapidly increase. A dark orange sun appeared over his left shoulder, bathing the cockpit instruments in a rusty glow.

"Fire control radar detected bearing zero-niner-three," said Eshel.

Hundreds of black-clad jihadists were no doubt scrambling to ready their shoulder-fired, surface-to-air missile launchers, in case his jet stumbled into missile range—which it wouldn't. Their payload would be released far outside of ISIS's surface-to-air missile range. Satellite imagery and agents stationed in the ports reported nothing more sophisticated than short-range missile systems mounted to several of the new armored tactical vehicles rolling off Chinese-registered merchant vessels.

Katz maintained the climb, keeping an eye on the fire control computer indicator. He was well within the parameters for a successful release. Fifteen seconds into the pop-up maneuver, his HUD flashed "Special Released." He never felt the bomb detach, which wasn't unusual.

"Confirm weapon release," said Katz.

If the bomb remained attached to the aircraft, they would be forced to abort the mission, and a second aircraft ten minutes away would take their place.

"Visually confirmed," said Eshel, who had access to a camera view of the aircraft's weapons pylons.

Katz rolled the Strike Eagle starboard and dove for the deck, maintaining a tight turn. His G-suit fought the maneuver as his facial muscles rippled from the extreme

G-forces. A few seconds later, he steadied the aircraft at one thousand feet, heading southwest. He'd take a circuitous route over northern Saudi Arabia, steering clear of Safawi.

Hammer Two, piloted by their squadron commander, would release a smaller yield, precision-guided nuclear bomb in less than two minutes—erasing ISIS's forward staging area. He increased the throttle, breaking the sound barrier and continuing to Mach 1.5. They needed to put as much distance as possible between Ramadi and the aircraft.

"Time to target?" said Katz.

"Thirty-two seconds. At this speed, we'll have a twenty-one-mile buffer. We're good," said Eshel, easing both of their fears.

The 700-pound, GPS-guided nuclear bomb had been tossed on a trajectory toward Ramadi, where it would detonate six hundred meters above the center of the fully exposed ISIS training camp—at the optimal height to unleash the full damage potential of a twenty-kiloton blast against ground targets. They flew in silence, the gravity of the act weighing heavily on their consciences. The immediate death toll would be in the hundreds of thousands, stretching close to a million within a few days.

Ramadi and Fallujah would essentially cease to exist, along with the imminent threat to his motherland. He could never forget that. The use of nuclear weapons had been a last resort—the unavoidable response to a planned invasion by millions of crazed fanatics. The Caliphate had been days away from launching the first wave of an attack that would have assuredly destroyed the State of Israel.

The dark blue sky brightened, a flash momentarily revealing the khaki terrain as far as he could see. The artificial light faded just as quickly, returning the darkness. He activated his helmet's integrated night-vision system, regaining the horizon. Katz resisted the temptation to look back. He absolutely didn't want to see it.

"Detonation visually confirmed," said Eshel, sounding less than enthusiastic.

"Copy and concur," said Katz, opening the command and control channel.

"Forge, this is Hammer One. We visually confirm detonation of the weapon."

"This is Forge. Satellite feed confirms detonation on target. Stay thirty miles south of Safawi. Forge, out."

That's it? Just a standard radio transmission? He supposed that was all the situation warranted. He hoped that was all it warranted. No celebration back at base. He'd be happy if nobody mentioned the mission again, in any context. Colonel Ilan Katz wanted nothing more than to turn his aircraft over to the on-duty maintenance team and drive home to his family—secure in the knowledge that their home was safe. That Israel was safe.

"Talk of Secession"

Chapter 14

Belfast, Maine
February 2019

Lieutenant Colonel Sean Grady took a sip of water from the CamelBak hose clipped to his shoulder, swishing the over-chlorinated liquid around his mouth. That's how he brushed his teeth these days. Toothpaste hadn't been a high-priority stockpile item, and the limited quantity uncovered in the storage buildings had been delivered to the FEMA camps in New Hampshire.

The younger Marines joked that the toothpaste was meant to supplement camp rations. Not everyone laughed at their sophomoric attempts at "keeping it real." The sprawling camp system had struggled to keep up with the constant influx of refugees throughout the winter. There might be some harsh truth to their raw humor, and most of the Marines didn't want to picture anyone eating toothpaste to stay alive.

Little had gone right once the weather turned bitter cold. Less than ten percent of required camp capacity had been constructed. Regional Recovery Zone leadership had refused to assign security or border units to civil engineering tasks. The militia scare in September left the bureaucrats skittish, afraid to venture out of their compound at Sanford International Airport.

Instead of solving the problem with a few thousand well-fed, structured soldiers, Governor Medina let a hundred thousand severely malnourished and categorically disorganized refugees assemble the camps from scratch. What should have taken two weeks in late September, lasted until December. Countless thousands died of exposure and related sicknesses while building the camps. It had been the closest Grady had come to storming the RRZ compound and putting an end to the endless stream of indecision and incompetence.

Two things kept him from crossing that line, and they were both intimately connected. Family and Corps. He had a duty to protect his Marines, which extended to their families. If he acted on his instinct to mutiny against the RRZ, he'd jeopardize the safety of his Marines and the families successfully relocated to Fort Devens or Westover Air Force Base. He had no idea what would happen to the families if 1st Battalion, 25th Marines was declared a domestic terrorist organization, and he had no intention of finding out. He owed that much to the Marines under his command, though he wasn't sure how much longer he could keep that promise. There was a good chance he might break it today.

He sat in the lead Matvee of a heavily armed eight-vehicle convoy sent by Governor Medina to secure the Searsport Marine Terminal. "Capture" it was a more accurate description of his mission. Elements of 3rd Battalion, 172nd Infantry Regiment, a Maine-based National Guard unit aligned with the Maine state government, had been reported at the terminal. Satellite surveillance indicated a small garrison of soldiers at the facility. Nothing larger than a platoon.

The garrison was established after hostilities flared

between RRZ officials and state government representatives over the use of state infrastructure assets. The RRZ wanted everything funneled south to support the security zone, while the state backed a wider approach to the disaster-relief efforts. It was clear from the beginning that the two sides would never reconcile this difference, and it certainly didn't help that the state governor refused to acknowledge the RRZ's authority. The disagreement created more anxiety than either side needed in the aftermath of the event.

The low-intensity political contest between the two entities hadn't progressed past threatening words and a few tense blockades of military convoys headed into central Maine. He guessed that was about as far as the state government was willing to take it. Actually, he prayed that was the case, because Governor Medina's light-handed response to the issue had nothing to do with diplomatic savvy. The RRZ had its hands full securing the border and administering the various programs associated with the refugee camps. That was about to change, which was why Grady had been sent north with two platoons of Marines, supported by four UH-60M Black Hawks. He hoped this could be resolved without incident. The last thing any of them wanted was a fight.

A snow-shrouded house tucked between a stand of thick pine trees caught his attention. The long driveway leading to the house had been recently cleared. The barrier of snow left at the bottom of the driveway after the last storm had been pushed into the road to melt. He could tell they had shoveled it by hand based on the clean shave they had given the asphalt. Snowblowers left a quarter of an inch, along with the telltale, even track marks. They must have a working vehicle. Nobody would go through that much trouble without a good reason.

The number of houses along the road increased as they approached Belfast. According to the command tablet attached to the dashboard in front of him, they were less than a minute from reaching Route One, where they would turn north for Searsport. He would have preferred to take a less conspicuous route, avoiding towns like Belfast, but only two approaches to the marine terminal area were kept clear of snow, one leading north and one leading south. The trucks delivering refined petroleum products and supplies to the various state and RRZ entities used the routes to reach Interstate 95, where the vehicles could range the entire state.

"Follow the signs to Route One north. Should be coming up," he said to the driver, switching to the primary tactical channel monitored by the vehicle leaders.

"All Raider units, this is Raider Lead. We're ten minutes from the objective. Raider will remain in a weapons hold status unless changed by Patriot. Defensive fire is not authorized in response to small-arms or crew-served heavy-caliber fire. Only the confirmed presence and clear intent to employ anti-vehicle weapons justifies defensive fire. Remember, these are Americans. Brothers and sisters in arms. We don't give them any reason to think otherwise. Out."

"Turn coming up, sir. Looks like we have to cross over Route One and drive through the town to reach the on-ramp," said the driver.

"Roger. Keep us moving through the town."

Grady called the lead helicopter on a separate, dedicated UHF radio channel.

"Night Train this is Raider Lead, over," said Grady.

"This is Night Train."

"Raider is ten mikes out from objective. Request Night Train on station in fifteen mikes."

"Copy fifteen mikes," said the staticky voice.

"Roger. Weapons hold unless otherwise ordered," said Grady.

"Copy weapons hold."

Grady replaced the handset and shifted in his seat, making room to move his rifle. He expected no trouble in Belfast, but he'd learned never to make assumptions about the perceived threat level. The driver crossed the overpass and turned right on a snowplowed, two-lane road paralleled by a string of telephone poles. The town turned out to be little more than a tighter collection of houses. They passed a VFW hall on the right side of the road. An American flag over a Maine state flag sat motionless at the top of a flagpole in front of the cleared parking lot. It looked like the VFW was in business.

He wished they could settle this business inside the hall over a few draft beers. Grady was sure they could reach some kind of agreement if they sat down as fellow service members, instead of pawns in a dangerous power play.

The Matvee turned onto High Street, bringing them to the Route One North on-ramp. On-ramp seemed like an overstatement, since they transitioned from a two-lane road to a slightly better built two-lane road. Quintessential Maine. The driver slowed the vehicle as soon as they straightened on Route One. Two up-armored Humvees blocked the entrance to the flat bridge less than three hundred feet ahead. He should have guessed this wouldn't be easy.

Son of a bitch.

"Raider units, we have a roadblock at the west end of

the bridge. Raider Two-Zero, pull alongside Raider One-Zero. We're going to approach slowly as two columns. Stop on my mark," said Grady.

"Two-Zero copies. Moving up."

The fifth vehicle in the column swung into the empty oncoming traffic lane and pulled parallel to Grady's vehicle. The rest of Raider Two-Zero's vehicle troop followed, creating two columns of four vehicles and filling the road. Grady stopped the formation fifty feet in front of the blockade, examining the scene.

He counted eight soldiers on the bridge and two turret gunners. The turrets contained M240 machine guns, useless against his Matvees. This appeared to be more of a symbolic show than anything—he hoped.

"Raider units, this is Raider Lead. I'm heading over for a chat. Stay alert. Out," said Grady. "I'll be right back," he said, getting out of the vehicle.

The cold air stuck to the inside of his nose as he shut the door to the toasty cabin. He slung his rifle over his shoulder and motioned for the vehicle leader behind him to join the greeting party. Staff Sergeant Taylor stepped onto the asphalt next to Raider One-One and nodded. They met next to Grady's rumbling vehicle.

"What are we looking at, sir?" said Taylor.

"Looks like more of a welcoming committee than a serious attempt to stop us," said Grady.

"What if they refuse to move?" asked Taylor.

"Then we'll have to push them out of the way. We outweigh them by about twelve thousand pounds," said Grady, patting the hood of the Matvee. "Let's get this over with."

As they approached the Humvees, a major dressed in digital ACUs, carrying a short-barreled M-4 carbine, stepped between the vehicles. The officer scrutinized Grady's uniform for a moment before snapping a crisp salute. Grady returned the military courtesy, eyeballing his name patch.

"What am I looking at here, Major Richards?" he asked.

"Hopefully nothing, Colonel," said the National Guard officer, looking past the Marines at the column of Matvees.

"Nothing would be a clear road to Searsport. This doesn't look like nothing to me," said Grady.

Despite his sympathy for the local government, he had a duty to safeguard his Marines. The best way to do that was to project a strong, uncompromising presence.

"Searsport has adequate security, Colonel. 3rd Battalion, 172nd Infantry Regiment has a company of soldiers guarding the facility."

Grady stared at the major, sensing his unease with the situation.

Platoon, but I'll give you credit for the bluff.

"The RRZ would like to free those soldiers for other duties in the state. We're a little overstaffed down south," said Grady.

The major nodded. "Would the colonel entertain a meeting with the state governor?"

"Susan Dague?"

"Yes, sir. She's at the Searsport facility."

"How much warning did you have about our visit?" said Grady.

"Enough to bring a company of soldiers and all of the battalion's armored vehicles. Searsport is a secure facility, sir," said the major.

Maybe the major hadn't been bluffing.

"You're not planning to put bags over our heads for the trip, are you?"

The major almost laughed. "Negative, sir. This is more of a site visit, so you can assure the RRZ folks that we have adequate security at Maine's only fully operational marine terminal."

"I'd love nothing more than to assure them that the situation is under control, and that the Searsport facility will continue to fulfill the RRZ's requirements," said Grady.

Chapter 15

Searsport Marine Terminal at Mack Point
Searsport, Maine

Grady accepted a ride in one of the National Guard Humvees after briefing Captain Williams, the senior officer remaining with the Marine convoy. He reluctantly left Staff Sergeant Taylor behind, suspecting that Governor Dague had more than a tour of the security arrangements in mind. His gut instinct told him that this would be an executive-level negotiation that would likely result in a status-quo arrangement. He wasn't sure how Taylor would respond to Grady's dismissal of the RRZ's directive to "secure the facility—using force if necessary," and he didn't want to put the staff sergeant in a position to question the decision.

The first thing he noticed when they arrived at the gate was a series of HESCO barricades anchoring an armored guard post. Two up-armored Humvees were parked behind a long stretch of fence to the right of the entrance, overlooking the Jersey barriers funneling traffic into the facility. He saw no sign of any weapons heavier than the 7.62mm M240 machine guns, which matched their intelligence briefing. 3rd Battalion, 172nd Infantry Regiment's Category Five Response load out hadn't included MK-19 grenade launchers or M2 .50-caliber machine guns. Since the unit wasn't located in a critical, high-population area, Homeland planners thankfully hadn't seen a need to include heavy firepower.

They passed through the gate and drove a few hundred yards to a parking lot in front of a two-story, corrugated aluminum building. At least twenty Humvees were parked in the lot, facing outward, their crews standing around the vehicles. If this was the extent of their show of force, the RRZ had little to worry about. Unarmored Humvees and lightly armored soldiers posed little threat to his Marines, and even less of a threat to armored elements of the 10th Mountain Division. If the RRZ wanted the facility, they could take it.

Why didn't Medina send a Stryker company to take care of this?

He knew the answer; she didn't care for Grady, so she sent him to do the RRZ's dirty work.

Major Richards nodded as they parked. "Governor Dague is in this building."

"This is the extent of the battalion's armored vehicles?" asked Grady.

"We had a limited motor pool to start with at the reserve center. Older stuff, non-EMP hardened," said Richards.

Grady shook his head. "This can't be all of it. This is barely enough to transport a company of soldiers."

Richards ignored the comment and opened his door. The soldiers were called to attention when Grady exited the Humvee.

"Carry on, soldiers," said Grady.

Grady made a few observations as they crossed the parking lot. Overall, the soldiers looked healthy. They were dressed in the latest generation ACU-patterned Extreme Cold Weather Clothing System (ECWCS) and half of them carried Bushmaster ACRs. He was surprised to see the Adaptive Combat Rifle. The rifle had seen limited distribution throughout the various services, despite rumors of sizable Department of Defense purchase orders. Mystery solved. Just like the thousands of ROTAC satellite phones that had been reserved for Category Five disaster response. Strangely enough, he didn't see any radios resembling the ROTAC.

He studied the vehicle markings on the hoods of the Humvees, possibly confirming Richards' statement. He saw a wide representation of various company and platoon unit designations. Grady found it odd that Homeland planners hadn't included additional vehicles in their load out. Maybe the battalion's allotment had been reduced to fit the perceived need in central and northern Maine.

"How many Humvees do you have out of commission?" Grady asked when they reached the door to the building.

"More than half," said Richards.

"We need to get that fixed. Should be relatively simple with the right parts," said Grady.

"That's the problem. We don't exactly have access to the Army supply system," said Richards.

"I might be able to work something out," said Grady, stopping at the door. "Is your commanding officer present?"

"You're looking at him, sir. Major Don Richards. Former battalion S-3," said Richards. "Our CO was on vacation with his family in Colorado. Camping trip. The XO was at a family reunion in Wells. They rented two big houses side by side on the beach. We haven't heard from either of them."

Grady shook his head.

"Everything between the beach and Route One in Wells was swept inland by the tsunami. Few survived."

"That's what we heard. The governor officially appointed me as battalion commander a few days after the event," said Richards. "We've been scrambling ever since."

"So…what am I walking into here, Major?"

"The governor has no intention of recognizing the RRZ's authority in the state."

"That's not really a debatable point. The president activated the National Recovery Plan, which clearly establishes RRZ authority over local government and defines the roles for each entity," Grady explained. "Security is an RRZ function—like it or not."

"She doesn't recognize the 2015 Defense Authorization Bill. Her staff will argue that your presence—the RRZ's presence— is a violation of the Insurrection Act," said Richards.

"It's a little late for that argument," said Grady. "I hope there's more to this meeting than a constitutional debate."

"There is," said Richards. "Though I can't guarantee you'll like what she has to offer."

"Offer?" asked Grady, opening the door. "This should be interesting."

Governor Dague was waiting for them in a small conference room on the ground level. The governor was dressed in a thick red winter jacket and winter cap, sporting a worn pair of waterproof boots made famous by one of Maine's premier outfitter companies. She looked like someone you'd expect to find ringing a Salvation Army bell in front of a grocery instead of a state governor, but looks could be deceiving in Maine. Dague, a career state prosecutor, was rumored to be hell on wheels in a negotiation, and downright cutthroat when the cards were stacked in her favor.

Grady walked around the conference table to shake the governor's hand.

"Lieutenant Colonel Sean Grady, ma'am. It's an honor and a surprise to meet you," he said.

"Not a pleasure?" she asked, shaking his hand firmly.

"Under the circumstances, that remains to be seen," said Grady.

"Please take a seat, gentlemen," she said, pulling a chair out for herself.

"I can see my breath in here. No heat in this building?" said Grady.

"Every drop of fuel that comes into this port goes to the people of Maine. Hospitals, shelters, health clinics, and public safety. This has been my top priority as governor," she said. "RRZ fuel demands have severely undercut these efforts. It's too early to tell, but we estimate that thousands of Mainers died of starvation or exposure during the winter. It's hard to explain why homes couldn't be heated and food wasn't distributed because the federal government needed to maintain twenty-four-hour helicopter coverage over FEMA camps in New Hampshire. Camps receiving food originating in Maine."

"Ma'am, your reputation precedes you, so I'm not even going to pretend you don't know that our helicopters, along with all of our vehicles, run on JP-8, not home heating oil," said Grady.

"Nice try, Colonel, but I know JP-8 is essentially a kerosene-based fuel and can be used in kerosene heaters.

I've seen studies suggesting it can be safely used in heating boilers. I believe the Air Force looked into this in the early nineties. We're pretty savvy around here when it comes to heating solutions," she said.

Grady realized he wasn't going to win a debate with Governor Dague, though he couldn't help continuing the discussion.

"JP-8 has a lower flashpoint than heating oil, which requires mechanical adjustments and constant monitoring, unless you want to potentially run your system into the ground. Maybe if the Maine legislature had supported your efforts to convert the state to natural gas, we wouldn't be in this situation. The Maritimes and Northeast Pipeline from Nova Scotia is fully operational, and could provide enough natural gas to heat every home in the state. Instead, that pipeline is heating homes in Massachusetts and Connecticut."

"Touché, Colonel. You've done your homework," she said, appearing to seriously contemplate her next statement. "I'll come right out and say it, Colonel. The Searsport terminal is operating at full capacity, and RRZ shipments are monopolizing terminal intake. From what I can tell, and from what the people in southern Maine can tell, most of the RRZ's *take* is being spent on efforts outside of the state."

"The RRZ is paying for every shipment that comes into the terminal. The last time we checked, the state of Maine had no cash reserves. Everything that comes into that terminal is owned by the RRZ and given to the state. We're barely maintaining the necessary levels to sustain operations within the New England North zone," said Grady.

"My sources indicate that you're stockpiling fuel and

supplies. This puts me in an awkward position," she said.

Grady took a deep breath. She was forcing him to skirt around the authority issue. He wasn't sure if she was doing it on purpose, or if the natural course of these discussions inevitably led down that path. She had to know. Maybe it was time to embrace the subject.

"Ma'am, I don't know what to tell you. I have my orders, and right now, a company of soldiers is sitting on my objective. Your recent communication with the RRZ, along with some fiery rhetoric over several HAM radio channels has called into question the security of the RRZ's supply line."

"Searsport is in good hands," said Dague. "Major Richards' battalion is more than capable of securing the facility."

"I haven't called into question 3rd Battalion's capabilities. You're deflecting the issue, ma'am."

"I'm well aware of that. You've been respectful and polite, Colonel, but you haven't addressed me by my title—why is that?"

Here we go.

"Nothing more than an oversight on my part, Governor," said Grady. "Here's what I propose. In an effort to free up some of Major Richards' soldiers to assist the state with other recovery tasks—at your discretion—I'll garrison four vehicles and two squads of Marines at the Searsport facility," said Grady.

"How generous," she said, her eyes narrowing. "I'll have to decline the offer."

"You should seriously reconsider, Governor Dague," said Grady. "Leaving Marines gets the RRZ off your back. I can't go back to my vehicle and report the status quo here. You've taken that option off the table by threatening to take control of the Searsport terminal."

"I never threatened to do that," said Dague.

"You hinted at it, ma'am, and that's as good as a threat these days. A threat to the entire RRZ. This isn't just about Maine. The New England North recovery zone is responsible for several states, and this is the only functioning terminal," said Grady.

"Nobody believes that," she said.

"It's a fact. Three Connecticut maritime terminals deep inside the Long Island Sound survived the tsunami waves from the second strike off Long Island. Stamford, New Haven and Bridgeport. Unfortunately, nothing will be delivered to these facilities, because we can't guarantee safe passage through the sound or secure docking at the terminals. Searsport is the only show within the RRZ, and frankly, the state of Maine is getting a disproportionate amount of the fuel flowing into the region. Governor Medina has been putting up with it because she's had her hands full keeping a few hundred thousand refugees from rampaging your state. Trust me, you can handle the bad press of accepting a joint security arrangement in Searsport. It beats the alternative."

"That sounded like a threat," she said.

"I carry out orders, Governor Dague. In this case, I'm making a notable exception."

Dague looked out of the window next to her seat. She waited a few seconds before responding.

"The rumor circulating around Sanford is that you don't care for the way the RRZ is being run," she said. "From what I've heard, this isn't the first time you've taken liberties with your orders."

"Disagreement between military and civilian leadership working in close proximity is nothing new. I've been through this before. In my experience, as long as the end result is the same, civilians tend to overlook the means. Shall I make arrangements to garrison my Marines at the terminal, or would you prefer Governor Medina gets directly involved? She sent me up here expecting failure. I'd prefer not to give her what she wants."

"If Major Richards could use some assistance handling the security arrangements in Searsport, I don't have a problem with it," said Dague.

Grady turned to the major, raising an eyebrow.

"I see no reason why this can't work to everyone's benefit," said Richards.

"Exactly. The longer we keep the RRZ authority happy, the better for everyone. The situation will gradually improve for Maine. Repairs on the pipeline facilities in Portland are nearing completion, along with the harbor-dredging project. If all goes well, they'll reverse the flow of the pipeline and start moving product down from the refineries in Montreal."

"If the RRZ doesn't take it all," said Dague.

"I don't see that happening. The recovery plan starts with Maine and radiates outward. Unfortunately, none of the Category Five scenarios included a tsunami wiping out port facilities up and down the New England coast. You have to believe me when I say that we've barely kept up with refugee camp management. If Portland harbor opens for business, the RRZ can stabilize Maine and start moving outward," said Grady.

"A lot of Mainers don't trust these RRZ folks," said Dague. "Myself included."

"Mainers don't trust anybody from out of state, Governor," said Grady. "Which is why I like it up here. I know exactly where I stand at all times."

Governor Dague laughed at Grady's statement, patting him on the arm.

"We might make you an honorary Mainer after all," she said.

"Don't take this the wrong way, ma'am, but I truly hope I'm not here long enough to earn that title," said Grady.

She laughed again. "No offense taken, Colonel Grady. The sooner you're out of here, the sooner things go back to normal."

"I'm not sure they'll ever go back to normal—not after this," said Grady.

PART II

"Little Picture"

Late April 2020

Chapter 16

Belgrade, Maine

Alex pulled the snow-encrusted wool cap tighter over his head and grabbed the four-foot-long, wildly flapping sheet of ripped plastic. Reaching into one of his cargo pockets, he fumbled to remove the industrial stapler. A stinging gust of wind tore the clear film from his gloved hands before he could kneel to reaffix the plastic to the raised wood frame. Seizing the sheet, he pulled it downward, hoping to quickly staple it against the lip of the garden frame before another gale-force blast crossed the frozen lake.

"Son of a mother..." he mumbled, getting a close look at the inside of the garden box.

The storm had intensified overnight, packing the ten-foot-by-five-foot box with at least a foot and a half of snow. So much for the cold-frame starter boxes. Surveying the backyard, he saw that all of the boxes they had built in the fall had suffered a similar fate. Plastic either missing or torn, snow drifts inside the frames. He sensed a presence and looked up to see Charlie standing a few feet away dressed in thick winter gear, shaking his head at the disaster.

"Looks like I fucked up," said Alex. "We started too early."

Charlie stepped forward, the snow already accumulating in a thin layer on his jacket and hat.

"We haven't had a storm this late in April for years—if ever," said Charlie, kneeling next to the box. He stuck his hands inside the frame, gently searching through the sticky snow for signs of the seedlings that had flourished under their vigilant care over the past few weeks. Wilted strands of green emerged. Charlie was careful not to sweep the plants away with the snow, but it didn't matter. They couldn't be salvaged at this point.

"I don't think there's any point bringing the rest of the crew out," Alex said loudly over the storm.

Charlie nodded. "We'll be fine. There's plenty of food to bridge the gap."

It was Alex's turn to nod—although he didn't share Charlie's outlook. Alex stood up and brushed the snow off his pants and jacket.

"We'll see you guys when this calms down. Figure out where to go from here," said Alex, realizing his statement sounded dreadful.

"This isn't the end of the world, buddy. It only set us back by a month or so," said Charlie, putting a hand on his shoulder.

"I know, I know," said Alex. "I was just hoping to eat something fresh for a change."

"Fresh is overrated, buddy," said Charlie. "Didn't you eat nothing but MREs and reconstituted rations in Iraq? This should be a walk in the park for you."

"The glass is always half full in the Thornton house," said Alex.

"Just trying to keep it together," said Charlie.

"You've been doing a good job," said Alex, glancing at the snow-filled planting frame. "Let's grab the plastic so we don't lose it."

Alex departed after rolling the thick plastic greenhouse film with Charlie, seeking the tracks he had left on the way in. He'd taken the road instead of the backyards, not wanting to push his luck with a skittish neighbor. The community had formed a loose association during the fall, mostly promising to stay out of each other's business. Forming this alliance had been a tough pill to swallow for Alex and his group, despite the fact that the neighbors adamantly denied plundering the Thorntons' cottage stockpile.

Two years' worth of food disappeared from Charlie's basement—enough to have guaranteed his group's survival next winter if the upcoming summer harvest didn't meet expectations. Forgetting about the theft wasn't easy, but Alex wanted above all things to be left alone at this point. Going door-to-door and forcing an armed search, like Charlie initially suggested, would prove far more damaging to their long-term survival prospects than simply letting it go. They had enough food to survive the first winter, and frankly, he couldn't blame them for taking the food.

Three of the families had been renting for the week and would have been caught with little more than a few days' supply of chips and hotdogs. Without a working car, they were more or less locked into place. The rest were a combination of full-time residents, mostly retired, and second-home owners caught at the lake during a late summer vacation week. Few of them would have kept a sizeable stockpile of food or emergency supplies, especially during the summer.

With Charlie's home standing empty for more than two weeks, and none of the other summer-home owners returning, they probably figured the Thorntons had been killed in the tsunami. The fact that nobody coughed up the supplies when they returned reinforced the decision. They didn't need eleven starving households conspiring against them during the middle of the winter. Charlie reluctantly agreed. They had been down that road before, and nothing good came from it. Alex wanted to avoid the mistakes he'd made on Durham Road, or at least play the game a little differently.

Isolation wasn't an option here, and he was the outsider. He couldn't forget that. Most of these people had lived here for years, some raising families on these shores. Six homes had been left vacant, Alex's family taking the largest of them. Nobody had been happy to see them, especially after the shootout with Eli's crew. He saw it in their stares during the first community meeting. Distrust. Resentment. Fear. He caught the gist of the whispers nobody dared speak too loudly. They quietly challenged his presence with weak protests of "not the owner" or "squatter." Alex understood their misgivings. He'd spent the winter of 2013 casting the same judgments—correctly and incorrectly.

Alex found his footsteps, already partially swallowed by the sideways snow, and trudged north toward his house at the end of Crane Road. He had about a quarter-mile hike to reach the post-and-beam home nestled into the trees. The house had proven spacious enough to move the Walkers out of Charlie's A-frame cottage. Kate opened the side door when he arrived.

"How bad is it?" she asked, shutting and locking the door behind him.

Alex threw his hat and gloves on a wide, rustic bench inside the mudroom, savoring the dry, radiant warmth cast by the kitchen's wood-burning stove on his hands and face.

"The wind tore the plastic off last night. The frames were filled with snow. A small setback. Not a big deal," he said.

Kate held out a steaming mug of coffee. "It sounded like a big deal when you left."

"The fresh air changed my perspective," he said, hanging his jacket on a row of hooks.

Alex took a sip and grimaced. Refiltered grounds. A step above dirty sink water.

"We'll refresh the grounds in a few days. Better than nothing," she said.

"Better than nothing," he echoed, forcing a smile and trying to shake off the setback.

"We'll be fine," Kate said, taking his hands and squeezing them.

"That's what everyone keeps telling me," he said, leaning in and kissing her.

She smelled like a campfire, like everyone and everything inside the house. He only noticed it now after coming in from the outside, when the odor lining his nostrils had faded enough to tell the difference. Alex held her for a moment, acutely aware that he could feel her ribs and shoulder blades. Like everyone, she'd lost a lot of weight.

"I'm just not sure I believe it. We've eaten through too much of our food, and that's on seriously reduced rations."

"We have nothing to do this summer except prepare for the winter. Losing a few cold frames filled with seedlings isn't going to make or break us," she said, taking a step back.

He nodded slowly—a default motion when he wasn't fully convinced. The food situation had turned out to be more tenuous than he'd expected. By abandoning the Limerick compound, they left behind more than three to four months of planted sustenance—challenging every facet of Alex's food plan. Grains, potatoes, root vegetables, corn, tomatoes, peppers, cabbage, fruit trees, row after row of dry beans...the list went on. Whatever they couldn't eat directly from the garden could have been canned or dried for winter months. Even in Limerick he had counted on digging into the prepackaged food to bridge the gap from late winter to early summer.

Thanks to the unexpected storm, they would burn through most of their prepackaged food by the time the first measurable meal could be served from the newly planted gardens. He shook his head. Alex couldn't envision a scenario that didn't put them in serious trouble by next January. Even if they had a bumper harvest, with no setbacks, they might be able to produce three to four months of food per family. Hunting and fishing might give them another month, if the area wasn't completely depleted by the fall.

The lake had been emptied of fish by late November. He had no idea if any of the native species would return in appreciable numbers. Ducks and geese would come through soon, returning again in the fall, but the lake would turn into a shooting gallery at the first sight of them. Last October's waterfowl season was cut decidedly short by the incessant gunfire. Worse yet, Charlie didn't seem optimistic about hunting game, especially with every household turning to the forest to procure food.

It wouldn't be enough.

"You're doing that nod thing again. What is it?" Kate asked.

"I don't know. Maybe we should revisit our plan to sail out of here."

Chapter 17

Belgrade, Maine

Kate Fletcher kneeled on the floating dock and lowered a red, three-gallon plastic bucket into the water. She waited until it completely submerged before pulling it onto the dock next to another full bucket of pond water. It was her turn to fill the toilet tanks. The two buckets represented four flushes, barely enough for the first round of early morning bathroom visits. She'd dump the buckets into the tanks and return for more, placing the filled buckets in the shower stalls. The last person to use the bathroom for more serious business would replenish the water and place the buckets outside of the door to the garage, where Kate would see them. She anticipated making at least three additional trips within the next couple of hours. All part of their new life without electricity.

She couldn't complain—they had easy access to water, and the house was hooked up to a septic system. Their primary sanitation needs could be met without power—indefinitely if the septic system didn't fail. Trudging back and forth to fetch water was a small price to pay to avoid using a medieval scheme of kitchen bags and receptacles to ferry human waste out of the house. A very small price.

Kate surveyed the lake. Growing pockets of slate-colored water competed with vast sheets of bleached ice that had receded from the shoreline. Long Pond would be "ice-out" within two weeks, maybe sooner if another late season storm didn't hit the area. She hoped they had seen the last of the snow. Alex was right about their food situation. They needed to replant the cool season vegetables immediately, so they could give the seedlings a head start and clear the way for the warmer season crops. Within a month, cabbage, kale, broccoli and cauliflower plants could be transplanted from the cold frames to the garden beds, making room for beans, peppers, squash, and other warm season crops.

Still, the unexpected late April storm wouldn't be the big deciding factor Alex dramatically portrayed. They couldn't plant the lost seedlings for another two to three weeks anyway due to predicted frost dates for this area. Their next-door neighbor, a perpetually swearing, umpteenth-generation "Mainah," warned against putting any exposed plants in the ground before the end of the third week of May. They'd lost a few weeks, not much more than that.

She suspected Alex's pessimistic outlook had more to do with the long winter and the prospect of enduring another. Kate shared similar reservations. It had taken them a few years of trial and error in Limerick to produce substantial garden and crop yields, with the help of commercially available compost, fertilizer and organic pest-control products. Here, they would have the benefit of the knowledge gained at the compound in Limerick— and that was about the extent of it. The vast beds of unamended soil they created in the fall would either support their farming efforts or thwart them. By the time they could make that determination, their packaged food stores might be depleted.

Preparing the boat wasn't a bad idea. She just wasn't sure leaving would improve their situation. Even if they could save enough dried food to reach South America, which was at least a thirty-day voyage under the best circumstances, there was no guarantee that the food security or political situation would be any better than the United States. The journey itself was fraught with risks and uncertainties. Storms, pirates, equipment malfunctions—they'd be on their own with no expectation of assistance until they reached Bermuda or the outer Caribbean islands, and no guarantee when they did. With the geopolitical situation continuing to deteriorate, there was no way to guess the true impact of the event abroad. They'd have to carefully weigh this decision. Something Alex didn't seem interested in hearing.

The dock creaked, drawing her attention to the shoreline. Tim Fletcher stood at the edge of the float, one foot on the platform, the other planted firmly on the sandy beach. He held two buckets in his hands. With less hesitation and a lot more balance than she expected from a seventy-two-year-old, Tim propelled the other leg onto the dock.

"Thought you could use some help," he said, setting the buckets next to hers.

"That's nice of you, Tim. Thank you," she said, lowering one of the buckets into the dark water.

"Alex is almost done with breakfast. Figured we could double up on this so we could eat together."

"What's on the menu this morning?" she asked, lifting the bucket onto the dock.

"Breakfast skillet. Yummy," he said, rubbing his flat stomach.

Tim looked the gauntest of everyone in the extended group. Age combined with minimum rations had pulled the skin taut across his face, exaggerating his sunken eye sockets. Like everyone, he complained of chronic exhaustion, but it seemed to have visibly worsened for him toward the end of the winter. He moved fine, but looked utterly drained. This morning he appeared pensive, almost brooding.

"Breakfast skillet number five-three-two-one-seven?"

"Negative. Number five-three-two-one-six. Ham and peppers," he said and winked.

"My favorite," she said, standing up.

Tim grabbed two of the buckets by their handles and lifted them off the dock.

"Just grab one. I can run back for the extra bucket," said Kate.

"I'm not that broken down, Kate."

"I know. Just be careful at the end of the dock," she said.

After they had helped each other off the dock and started across the backyard, Tim turned to Kate.

"I'm worried about Alex," he stated.

"He's worried about you," she said, wishing she had just shut up and listened.

"I could use another thousand calories per day, but so could we all. That's not what we're talking about. He's acting despondent, and it's starting to spread to the rest of the group. What's going on? And don't tell me PTSD. He was fine until we started planting the cold frames," said Tim.

She lowered her buckets next to one of the long

garden beds and pretended to examine the soil. They had removed the sod and tilled the soil in ten-foot-by-thirty-foot strips with the shovels last fall. The rows were oriented north-south so none of the rows would overshadow the others. The tallest plants would be placed at the northernmost end. They had spent entire days strategizing the garden during last September, and the rest of the fall diligently digging and preparing the beds. They treated it like the deadly business it would be next year.

"He's worried about next winter," she said.

"Already?" he asked, irritated.

"He's not seeing the garden and our natural surroundings as a viable scenario. Frankly, I'm starting to question it myself," she said.

Tim sighed, kneeling next to her. "I'm not sailing out of here on a boat. We're too old for that shit."

Kate stifled a laugh. "He's thinking of it as a contingency. Like last year. We'll do everything we can to make the garden work and assess the situation in September."

"Hurricane season."

"We'd start out as late in October as possible. Sail down the coast to Jacksonville and wait for a good stretch of weather. A few good days from there should put us below the southern limit of the fall gales."

"A lot can go wrong on a trip like that, especially for a crew that's never been more than ten miles offshore."

She couldn't argue with him. He was right on every count, and she wanted more than anything to stay in place. Ultimately it wouldn't be their decision. The ground under her fingers would make the final call. If the ground didn't yield enough food for nineteen people, they'd take at least four mouths out of the equation.

Maybe everything would be back to normal in the United States by the fall. However, that was doubtful.

"We might not have a choice," she said, running wet soil through her fingers.

"We'll cross that bridge when we get there," said Tim. "Until then, square away mister doom and gloom. He sets the tone for everyone."

Chapter 18

Belgrade, Maine

Charlie dipped his hands in a plastic bucket filled with a diluted bleach solution and opened the bathroom door. Alex stood in the front doorway, next to the kitchen, dressed in woodland camouflage pants and a gray, wool sweater.

"Make sure you rinse your hands in the bucket," said his wife.

"I know the procedure. I've been living the dream for eight months now," he said, trying not to sound annoyed.

"And shut the door!" yelled Linda, appearing to hand Alex a cup of steaming coffee.

"Jesus Christ, it's not that bad!" he said, pulling the door closed.

"Well, it hasn't gotten better, so do us all a favor," she said, turning to Alex. "Fresh grinds put him in the crapper earlier than usual."

Alex hesitated to sip the coffee.

"See! You've grossed him out, Linda. Sorry about that, Alex. I promise nobody crapped in your coffee mug."

His friend shook his head with a confused grin.

"I had never considered the possibility of...that. Until now," said Alex.

A few grunts and groans came from the sleeping bags

in the family room, the only signs of life from the group of five teenagers strewn across the floor in front of the wood-burning stove.

"Just kidding, buddy. What brings you over this early?"

Alex motioned for Charlie to join him outside and stepped through the front door, disappearing into the front yard. Charlie stepped into the dining room and nodded at Ed and Samantha, who had already taken Alex's cue and pushed their chairs back. The group of adults met halfway up the gravel driveway, waiting for Charlie and Linda. He walked slowly with his wife, who couldn't easily walk without a cane. None of the nearby hospitals could provide the level of orthopedic surgery she required to properly reconstruct her ankle. It was something she would have to endure until *things got back to normal.*

"What's up?" asked Ed, glancing anxiously at the trees and evergreen bushes surrounding the property.

"Nothing's wrong. Sorry about the secrecy. I just didn't want to get the kids involved right now," said Alex. "I wanted to talk to you about a contingency plan, in case the summer's harvest doesn't add up."

The smiles and squints in the early morning sun slowly faded to uneasy grimaces.

"I know I'm not the only one that's more than a little concerned about next winter," said Alex.

"Where's Kate?" asked Samantha.

"We've talked about this at length, and we're on the same sheet of music," said Alex.

"It'll be tight, Alex, but we've done the math," said Charlie. "I know some great hunting spots less than a half-hour away. Isolated places that people can't get to without a car. As long as we save some gas for the trip, we'll come back with a lot of meat."

"I think you're overestimating what we can bring in with hunting. The winter was a bust," said Alex.

"We just need to get far enough away from the lakes. Away from the people. One moose represents about three hundred pounds of meat."

"Good heavens," said Samantha, shivering.

"Don't knock it, Sam. Done right, moose is good eating. Right, Linda?"

"You've never dressed a moose…or shot one," said his wife.

"I'll figure it out if I bag one," he mumbled, knowing that the odds of finding a moose were slim to none.

"Anyway. I'm talking about a contingency plan, in case the math doesn't work out."

Another thought hit Charlie like a bolt of lightning. "We can use the sailboat for fishing, especially in the fall. I know how to cut and dry fish. That's how they used to survive the winters in Iceland and Norway."

"The contingency plan involves the sailboat," said Alex.

"I thought Kate talked you out of sailing to the Caribbean," said Linda.

"She did, after I talked myself out of it," he said.

"Then why the sudden one-eighty? We have a good plan. The storm set us back a little, but that three weeks isn't going to make or break us," said Ed.

"I agree, but if we have a serious shortfall from the harvest, the group will be better off with fewer people to feed," said Alex, stepping closer and lowering his voice. "And everyone remaining behind can squeeze into the other house."

"Why would we do that?" asked Ed.

Charlie understood immediately. "Damn it. You think of everything, don't you? I can't believe I missed that."

"Missed what?" Samantha demanded.

"So we can defend ourselves. This whole neighborhood's gonna run out of food!" yelled Charlie.

"Keep it down," hissed Alex, looking around the yard.

"Sorry. Sorry," whispered Charlie.

"Let's limit this discussion to the adults, for obvious reasons. Even if we manage a strong harvest and shoot a moose, I think we need to consider moving everyone into the bigger of the two houses. Possibly right after the last food comes out of the ground. Just to be safe," said Alex.

"Maybe we should have a community meeting. Try to encourage everyone to raise food, hunt, fish—whatever it takes," said Linda.

"That'll draw too much attention to our own food security efforts. I'd prefer nobody had a full picture of what we're trying to accomplish. We barely have enough seeds for our own gardens."

"It'll be hard to hide what we're doing. We'll probably have to triple the square footage of our current beds. We barely have a tenth of an acre tilled as it is. Homesteading wisdom dictates anywhere between a half-acre to an acre to feed one person for a year," said Charlie.

"We only have three-quarters of an acre between the two lots, anyway," said Ed.

"We'll keep to ourselves as much as possible," said Alex.

"What about the community watch idea? I still think we should post people at the entrance to the neighborhood. Probably another group along the lake as well once the ice clears. Our gardening efforts are likely to draw attention from the houses across the water," said Charlie.

"We'll have to put some serious thought into that. I like the idea of a shared security arrangement, but we simply can't extend that sense of community to our food. If security becomes an issue, we can move everyone over to our house earlier and post a sentry team to watch over the gardens here."

"It'll be crowded over there," said Ed.

"You won't notice the difference. If anything, you'll have a little more room and a lot more privacy," said Alex, nodding at the house.

He was right about that. Charlie's open-concept A-frame cottage appeared to be designed specifically without privacy in mind. The single bedroom loft was open to the family room below. Even a whispered conversation could be overheard from the lower level. The house Alex's family occupied had more of a traditional layout, with three bedrooms and two bathrooms. They could easily fit into the house without a problem. The logistics of feeding and keeping nineteen people busy in a confined space during the winter would be a challenge, but they'd work it out. They always did.

"Sounds like a plan," said Charlie.

"I hope we can stay together," Ed said, patting Alex on the shoulder.

Alex's distant look focused, and a warm grin broke through his ominous façade. It was good to see the old Alex shine through from time to time. He hadn't been the same since Boston.

"This is one hell of a group. I'd do anything for you guys. I don't want to leave, but it might not be my decision to make," said Alex. "We should draw up plans to dig more garden beds."

They immediately took his cue to change the subject.

Samantha asked, "Do we have enough seeds?"

Another round of silence enveloped the group.

"My dad says we have enough to replicate the gardens in Limerick," said Alex.

Charlie glanced at the patchy, light brown grass surrounding the driveway.

"We have a lot of digging ahead of us," said Charlie.

"This is going to kick our asses for the next thirty days," stated Alex. "The sooner we get started—the better."

"Shit. I thought gardening was supposed to be relaxing," said Charlie.

"It is when your life doesn't depend on it," said Alex. "Let's meet over at my house to start figuring out what we need to do."

After Alex disappeared behind a thick stand of pines lining the dirt road, Ed sighed.

"He doesn't look convinced that this will work," said Ed.

"I don't think he was ever truly convinced," said Charlie.

"Then why did he stay? Not that I'm suggesting anything was wrong with the decision," said Samantha.

Charlie knew why Alex had chosen to stay. He couldn't stop looking out for them. Alex's contingency plan was a thinly veiled continuation of his selfless leadership. Behind the rugged individualism and harsh pragmatic outlook, Alex's bond to the group was unbreakable—even if it meant physically leaving them behind.

Chapter 19

Belgrade, Maine

The mud sucked at his boots, drawing his thoughts to the security situation. With the snow gone and the roads passable, they'd have to be vigilant. Winter survivors would be out in force, foraging for food and supplies wherever they might find them. Homes would be the first logical choice. Charlie was right about posting a guard on the waterfront. A pair of binoculars in the wrong hands could put a threat at their doorstep, if they didn't already have one brewing in their midst.

He glanced at the house to his right. Maybe a neighborhood meeting was in order—to assess the situation. Thinking back to Durham Road during the Jakarta pandemic dampened his enthusiasm for the idea. He didn't have a good track record with neighborhood meetings. Maybe a door-to-door assessment was a better idea. Keep the neighbors from joining forces and ganging up on them. He hated thinking like this, but wishful philosophy didn't keep you alive.

The meeting had gone better than he had hoped. Deep down inside, they all knew he was right, even though nobody wanted to acknowledge it. He barely wanted to admit it. Who knew? Maybe they'd pull off a miracle, and the boat wouldn't be necessary. He sincerely doubted it, but planned to put one hundred percent of his energy behind trying. It was all he could do. The decision was truly out of his hands. Of course, this all depended on the boat.

His arrival in Belfast Harbor had undoubtedly attracted attention from stranded boaters and locals. He'd stripped the boat of anything useful and siphoned most of the diesel, but a thirty-eight-foot sailboat itself could be considered useful in midcoast Maine. The scarcity of fuel would renew interest in sail power, which was why the sails were the first things to come ashore with him. A trip to Belfast was in their very near future. If the boat wasn't an option...he didn't want to think about it.

"Captain Fletcher," someone whispered behind him.

He whirled around, dropping a hand to his holster. Nobody had called him captain since last fall, except for Ken Woods, who stood in front of him on the road with his hands in the air.

"Jesus, Ken. You shouldn't make a habit of sneaking up on ex-Marines. And please call me Alex," he said.

"That's why I waited for you to pass. Hey, once a captain always a captain to a staff sergeant," said Ken, stepping forward.

"You want me to start calling you staff sergeant?"

"You got me there. That was a long time ago. I got out a few months after the first Gulf War," said Ken, rubbing his long gray beard.

"My recent tenure as captain lasted about three weeks. I hadn't worn the uniform since 2004 prior to that," said Alex.

"Alex it is. Hey, I couldn't help overhear your conversation—"

"From your house?" asked Alex, wondering where this was going.

"Well, not exactly from my house. I saw you walk by, on the way to your friends. I thought I'd say hi, but by the time I got my boots on, you guys were already talking."

"So you decided to listen in?"

"I couldn't help it. It's a long winter talking to yourself," said Ken, avoiding eye contact.

"You don't have anyone else?"

"No. My wife got the cancer three years ago. I've been trying to tear myself away from the lake to move near the kids, but…"

Alex nodded, feeling the conflict in Ken's voice.

"It's a beautiful lake. Must have been a wonderful place to raise a family," said Alex.

"It was. Nearly impossible to leave," he said, barely getting the next words out. "I hope I get to see them again."

A few moments passed before Alex continued. "Where do your kids live?"

Ken looked up, a fierce pride glowing in his eyes. "Two boys. One's a family doctor out in Durango. The other runs an outfitting company in Troy, Montana. Taught them to fly-fish on the Kennebec just a few miles from here."

"During my brief stint as Captain Fletcher, I learned that the EMP bursts' effects weren't as pronounced out west. The orbital detonation likely occurred over the southeast. Tennessee or Kentucky would be my guess. Something tells me your boys are fine—and you'll definitely see them again."

Ken nodded, tears streaming down his face.

"Why don't you tell me a little more about your spying escapade?" said Alex, eliciting a brief laugh.

"I couldn't help but overhear your discussion about the gardens," Ken said, wiping his face.

"I'm sure you couldn't," said Alex, smiling.

"Right. Anyway, you're going to need a hell of a lot more acreage to feed your crew year round. Nineteen of you? You won't need an acre per person, but I think you're looking at quadrupling the acreage. If you work two or three acres properly, you could squeak by with some solid hunting, trapping, and fishing."

"I think the lake has been cleared out," said Alex.

"Maybe so, but some of the more isolated stretches of the Kennebec River should be productive throughout the year. We can try the Sebasticook and Sandy River if that fails. Most people don't have any way to get up to some of the best angling spots."

"I suppose you could show us where to find these spots?"

"It would be my pleasure. You can also add my property to your acreage count. I have about three-quarters of an acre. I won't use more than a quarter acre. That should help get you to your magic number, but it sounds like you're going to need more seeds. I'd give you some, but I barely have enough for myself. I save what I can from last season's garden and order whatever I need in the spring. I used to keep two seasons' worth of seeds on hand, but I've gotten pretty good at reclaiming them."

"We can probably work something out in exchange for the use of your land," said Alex.

"Don't worry about me. I have more than enough—" Ken paused, a look of discomfort spread across his face.

"Your secret is safe with us," said Alex. "Especially since you probably know most of our secrets."

"I really didn't mean to—"

"I'm just messing with you, Ken. It's a bad habit of mine," said Alex, extending a hand. "I'll take you up on your offer."

Ken looked relieved. He firmly shook Alex's hand, a sense of purpose flashing across his face. Alex saw a strong and loyal ally in Ken. A force multiplier in terms of survival, not another mouth to feed. If they could find a few more like him in the neighborhood, they'd have a much better chance at staying on the lake.

"Then we'll need to get our hands on more seeds. We have two major seed distributors in the Waterville area. One is co-op and gets most of their seeds from outside sources. The other produces their own line of organic seeds."

"Johnny's Seeds?"

"Exactly. I think we should pay them a visit," said Ken.

"I can't imagine they'll be selling seeds," said Alex. "The place is probably wiped out—or ransacked."

"I don't think anyone up here would ransack Johnny's Seeds. They've been a local institution for more than forty years. The question is whether they managed to keep the farm up in Albion operational during the fall. That's when they do most of the work. If they kept it running, they should have a good supply of seeds."

"I'll run this by the group and pick you up in about thirty minutes. How far away are their warehouses?" said Alex.

"The seeds are kept in Winslow, about ten miles from here, but it might be worth starting out in Albion, at their research farm. That's where they test seed germination and determine what they'll sell. If they're operational, we're in business."

"Let's hope so," said Alex.

Chapter 20

Waterville, Maine

Waterville felt a lot closer than it had looked on his map. They had crossed under the Maine Turnpike overpass within fifteen minutes of pulling out of the driveway, transitioning into an uncomfortably urban area lined with strip malls, fast-food chains, and car dealerships. The area still had a rural feel, like the outskirts of most Maine cities, but Alex couldn't shake the feeling that they were far more exposed in Charlie's neighborhood than he had originally estimated.

The streets were barren of cars. The only vehicles visible from the road sat in motel parking lots off Kennedy Memorial Drive, likely abandoned several months ago. They passed a large strip-mall parking lot on their right, anchored by a Harrigan's grocery store and a CVS. Ringing the empty lot, missing or partially shattered windows adorned the businesses.

"Looks like things got ugly in town," said Alex.

Ken stared at the eerie scene, not moving his head. "I think we should take the long way to Johnny's Seeds. Driving through downtown Waterville might not be the best idea. We can swing up through Albion and circle back to the Winslow warehouse area if the farm is a bust. We'll pass over a creek after a few traffic lights. At the intersection after the creek, take a right. That'll put us back on Route 137, which crosses the Kennebec River south of the city. Nothing but trees and open country down there."

"Sounds better than what we're seeing here," said Alex, turning his head to look into the backseat.

"Stay alert, buddy. Keep an eye out behind us."

Ryan nodded eagerly, turning his body in the rear passenger seat to make it easier to see through the back windows of the SUV. Alex's son cradled the same HK416 rifle he had fired at Eli Russell's militia during the attack on their home in Limerick. Ryan was rarely seen without the rifle, a constant reminder of how things would be vastly different for their children. Barely nineteen years old, his son's trajectory in life had shifted in the blink of an eye. The traditional path carved from a middle-class life of comfort and ease erased by a cabal of petty Chinese party officials and bitter military generals. The thought of it surfaced Alex's anger.

He hoped the U.S. had retaliated with more than words and saber rattling. In a dark place within him, Alex wanted to hear that the U.S. had bombed them out of existence. He knew it meant thousands, possibly millions of innocent deaths, but he couldn't envision any other option, and staring across a deserted parking lot at just one of thousands of abandoned business malls dotting the American landscape—he didn't care.

Alex drove the SUV through two empty intersections, crossing over a wide, rushing creek. Signs for Route 137 urged him right at a split in the road just past the creek, depositing them on a two-lane, tree-lined road that stretched as far as he could see.

"This is better," said Alex.

"Yep. Not much down this way. Just keep following

the signs for one-thirty-seven. All we're gonna see is a gas station or two. Maybe a variety store."

"The less we see, the better," said Alex.

His hopes for an uneventful trip were dashed a few minutes later when he spotted a police cruiser sitting in the middle of the road in front of the entrance to the bridge. The road widened as they approached the guardrails lining the side of the bridge. The police car barely covered half of the width of the road. As they closed the distance to the cruiser, Ryan leaned through the gap between the front seats, peering ahead with binoculars.

"Winslow Police Department," said Ryan. "I don't see a car at the other side of the bridge."

Alex considered his options. He didn't feel like dealing with the police, or any authority figures right now—or ever.

"Don't even think about it, Captain. This is probably just a formality. Checking to see who's cruising on over from Waterville," said Ken.

Alex slowed the SUV to give them time to prepare for the encounter.

"Ryan, shove both rifles under the tarp in the cargo compartment and flip the seat up. Keep them low. Stuff your pistol in the cup holder on the driver's side door and cover it with your hat. Make sure the hat completely covers the pistol and won't jar loose if you open the door."

"Got it," said Ryan, going to work in the backseat.

"Why the cup holder? Shouldn't he stuff it in the backpack?"

"If they force us out of the vehicle, the pistol will still be somewhat accessible."

Alex squirmed in the driver's seat and drew a compact semiautomatic pistol from the concealed holster behind his right hip. He tucked it into one of the center console compartments at the bottom of the dashboard and closed the compartment.

"Why isn't yours going into the door?" said Ken.

"Because I need immediate access," said Alex. "If this gets ugly, stay as low as possible."

"How will I know if it gets ugly?" asked Ken, already shrinking in his seat.

"Watch my dad's right hand. If it starts to move toward the pistol—things are about to get really ugly," added Ryan.

"Jesus. Maybe we should turn around and try a bridge farther south," Ken suggested.

"In my experience, all bridges are bad news. Actually, this doesn't look so bad. I have a good feeling about this," said Alex.

"He doesn't say that very often," said Ryan, winking at Alex through the rearview mirror.

"That's reassuring," Ken stated flatly.

"If they ask us to exit the vehicle, we kindly decline and tell them we'll stay on this side of the Kennebec. Stick to the story. Windows down," Alex said, lowering his window.

He stopped the SUV several feet in front of the cruiser and killed the engine, keeping the key inserted in the ignition. Two officers stepped out of the police car and approached them, splitting apart in front of the SUV. Neither kept their hands close to their service pistols, which gave Alex the impression that Ken's assessment was correct. This would more than likely be a quick check to make sure Alex's group wasn't bringing trouble to the other side of the river.

The officer on the driver's side of the SUV walked up to Alex's window, while the second officer took a wider approach to the passenger side. The officer on his side didn't wear a nametag, and his uniform looked worn and dirty. He glanced at the officer's face, noticing that he looked gaunt, his eyes slightly sunken and red. He looked more exhausted than anything. Probably malnourished like the rest of America.

Alex wondered how he looked to the officer. Too well fed? Would that color the way they were treated? Another quick look confirmed that the patches on the officer's cold-weather jacket matched up with Winslow Police Department. That had to be a good sign. If the officers were fake, he doubted the imposters would have slipped into the Winslow police station to retrieve seasonally issued gear. Was he being paranoid? No. Alex wasn't taking any chances. Eli Russell's men had killed two soldiers at a security checkpoint wearing stolen uniforms.

"Morning, officer," said Alex, fully intent on letting the officer lead the discussion beyond the opening pleasantries.

"Morning, Mr...?"

"Fletcher. Alex Fletcher. We're out by Great Pond."

Shit. Did he really just tell them that?

"Whereabouts on the pond?" asked the officer, putting one of his hands on the car door and leaning over to examine the interior.

"Jamaica Point," said Ken. "Not right on the point."

"It's nice over there. One of our officers has a camp over on Long Pond. What brings you over this way?"

Before Alex could respond, Ken answered, "I'm taking these city slickers up to Benton to fish the Sebasticook.

The Belgrade Lakes area was tapped out last fall. Figured we might get lucky with the trout."

"You're not from the area?" asked the officer, addressing Alex.

"Scarborough, Maine. Our house was swamped by the tsunami. A good friend of mine owns a camp next to Mr. Woods," said Alex, nodding his head at Ken. "We stayed with him for the winter."

"With Mr. Woods?"

"No. With my friend. Mr. Woods—Ken—offered to take us up to the Sebasticook. Said it's some of the best fly-fishing in the area."

"There's some good spots on this side of the Kennebec," said the officer.

The second police officer approached the window to the cargo compartment and cupped his hands to get a better view inside. Alex felt his face flush. The fishing poles and tackle boxes sat on top of the tarp hiding their rifles. He hoped it wasn't obvious that something was hidden underneath. Beside the fishing gear, they had loaded a water cooler and a few pairs of fly-fishing waders.

Ken leaned over the center console. "Nothing beats the Sebasticook. Especially up between Benton and Clinton."

"Well, there's no disputing that," said the officer. "Just be careful up there. The folks that pulled through the winter on this side of the river might not take kindly to your presence. Make sure you use public access to the river and avoid private property. It's been a long winter."

"Sounds like things got pretty bad in Waterville. We swung south to avoid driving through the downtown area," said Alex.

"Smart move. I'd say your chances of successfully navigating through the downtown are about fifty-fifty in one of these," he said, patting the window well. "Anyone lucky enough to end up with a running car has kept the fact pretty quiet. They have a tendency to disappear right out from under you. Be careful where you drive. Things have been civil over here, but a functioning vehicle might be too big of a temptation for some."

"Thanks, officer," said Alex, noticing that the second officer had finished his inspection of the cargo area.

"You have a good day, folks," said the officer next to his window, backing away to give Alex room to drive.

Alex turned the ignition and made sure the second officer remained clear of the SUV while he pulled forward. In the back of his mind, he envisioned the officers drawing their weapons and firing point blank into the vehicle. *Fuck!* Every situation turned into a worst-case scenario in his mind. Alex knew it was a survival mechanism—an extreme mechanism honed over the two disasters. He wondered if it would ever go away. The Jakarta pandemic had left him in a heightened state of paranoia. The event had catapulted him into the big leagues—a pathological state of distrust.

In keeping with the thought, Alex turned to Ryan once they had cleared the police cruiser and driven onto the bridge.

"Break out the rifles. Sounds like this could turn into the Wild West pretty quick," said Alex, opening the compartment holding his pistol.

"Good job back there, Ken. You saved me from fumble-mouthing my way into a strip search," said Alex.

"Well, I wasn't exactly lying. If we can spare the time, I'll show you what these rivers can give up. Trout should be swimming. They love the cold water. That'll last another month, maybe two at most. As the water starts to warm, the trout will hide in the cold-water streams. You can still find them, but the rivers will teem with easier catch. Perch and bluegills. I'm telling ya, if you find the right spot, you can fish the rivers from ice-in to ice-out. Your son will love it. Ever been?" asked Ken, turning in his seat.

"No," said Ryan, scooting up on the rear passenger bench to hear what Ken had to say.

"Nothing like casting on the water with a cooler full of ice-cold beers."

"I thought this was about fishing," said Alex, laughing.

"It's about both. The beers give you something to do when the fish aren't biting," said Ken.

"Sounds like a win-win scenario," said Alex.

"Never had a bad day fishing."

"Sounds like fun to me," said Ryan. "Though we're missing the beers."

"I might have smuggled a few out of my secret stash for the occasion," said Ken.

"You're kidding, right?" said Alex.

"I never joke about beer or fishing," said Ken. "We'd have to let them sit in the water for a while."

"We'll see about the fishing," said Alex. "It all depends on what we find at Johnny's Seeds."

Chapter 21

Albion, Maine

"The farm should be coming up on the right," said Ken.

Ryan focused his binoculars on the road ahead. His dad expected to find some form of barricade on the road, to keep people from approaching the farm. A few homes peeked through the trees on the left side, but the road looked clear.

"I'm not seeing a barricade," said Ryan.

"Keep looking," said his dad. "If they're in business, I don't think they'll be too keen on letting anyone get too close."

"Maybe they're out of business," said Ryan.

"If anything, they'll plant the fields," said Ken. "I expect to find some folks out here. Figured it was better than driving up to the seed warehouse. That's the obvious place to start. Most folks don't know about the research farm."

"I'm willing to bet that has something to do with its location," Alex replied.

"It's a little hard to find," said Ken. "Even for Maine."

"Hard to find in Maine is a few steps away from fucking invisible," said Alex.

Ryan chuckled, staring through the binoculars. His dad could be pretty funny, even under the worst circumstances. He'd noticed this with some of the

Marines around the house. Jokes and well-timed comical observations seemed to be the norm, often at the expense of fellow Marines. Some of the humor was pretty brutal, but they all shrugged it off like it was normal. It reminded him of the way his high school cross-country team acted on the bus to meets—except about ten times worse. He figured you had to go through some serious shit as a crew to get to the point where your friends could make a joke about screwing your girlfriend or sister. Running several miles a day around a quiet Maine town didn't qualify. If anyone on his team ever said something that disrespectful about Emily or Chloe, he would have pounded some sense into them.

The telephone line running parallel to the road crossed over the street in front of one of the houses, disappearing into the trees on the other side.

"Dad, I think we're coming up on—there it is," he said, spotting a large white sign with black letters reading Johnny's Selected Seeds. "There's nothing blocking the entry."

"I'm surprised," said Alex, slowing for the turnoff.

As the SUV eased into the gravel driveway, the reason became apparent. A tan-colored Humvee sat in the middle of the car parking lot, next to an olive drab, canvas-backed utility truck with military insignia. The vehicles blocked their approach to a white, one-story building, which Ryan assumed was the research lab. Several plastic-covered greenhouses appeared in the empty fields beyond the building, no doubt protecting thousands of healthy seedlings.

Alex slammed on the brakes when the turret housing an M240 machine gun swiveled in their direction. Two soldiers dressed in Army ACUs started walking toward them with their M-4 rifles slung across their body armor. Neither had his rifle pointed at the SUV, but Ryan had seen his dad quickly transition to a firing position from "sling ready." Within a fraction of the second, these soldiers could riddle the SUV with .223-caliber projectiles. One of the soldiers lowered the barrel of his rifle when the SUV started to back into the road. Ryan shoved his rifle under the front passenger seat, sliding his jacket off to cover the buttstock protruding into his foot well. His dad's rifle was still in the cargo compartment.

"Shit. I think we should take our business elsewhere. Keep your rifle really low, Ryan," said his dad, putting the SUV into reverse.

"I don't think that's a good idea, Captain," said Ken.

"Fuck. This could get ugly. They'll confiscate our weapons on sight, and we'll be lucky if they don't take the vehicle," Alex said, putting the SUV in park. "Plus, the circumstances leading to a shortened stint as Captain Fletcher might bite me in the ass here."

"Let's not make any assumptions. And maybe I should do all of the talking," said Ken.

"Good idea. Ryan, can you—" His dad scanned the backseat. "What did you do with the rifle?"

"It's under Mr. Woods' seat," said Ryan.

"I'm covering the barrel with my foot," said Ken.

"Works for me," said Alex as the two soldiers approached the driver's side window. "Looks like we have a sergeant and a specialist."

"This is a restricted area, sir," said the sergeant, while the other soldier walked along the driver's side of the vehicle.

"Sorry. We had no idea. Our seedlings died in the freak snowstorm a few days ago, and we thought

Johnny's might be able to sell us some seeds to replace the ones we lost," said Ken. "Looks like they're open for business."

"They're open, but not for public business," said the sergeant.

The younger soldier circled around the back of the SUV, peering inside the cargo compartment.

"Is there any way we can talk with someone working here? I've been a customer of theirs for nearly forty years," pleaded Ken.

"Sorry, gentlemen. Johnny's is part of the Maine Independence Initiative. They've allocated every batch of seeds to farms participating in the Initiative recovery effort," said the sergeant.

Ryan fidgeted when the specialist peered inside his window, eyes settling on the black backpack next to him. The backpack contained several magazines for the automatic rifle stuffed under the seat. Ryan forced a smile and nodded at the serious-looking soldier.

"You guys going fishing?" asked the specialist.

"We were hoping to drive up to the Sebasticook from here," said Alex, turning his head to address the soldier at Ryan's window.

"Better get your fishing done while you can," said the sergeant. "I've heard them talking about plans to fish the rivers on an industrial scale. Won't be much left to catch if they put that plan into action."

"Who's 'they'?" asked Alex. "The state government?"

Ryan detected an angry tone, which wouldn't help their situation. He hoped Ken intervened before his dad's tone became overtly hostile.

"Technically the Maine Independence Initiative," said the sergeant. "It's being led by the governor's office."

"Independence from what?" asked Alex in an increasingly exasperated tone.

Ken's hand slowly reached out to touch his shoulder.

"We've been cut off from any communications for most of the winter," explained Ken.

"The state has declared independence from the RRZ. The governor issued a formal declaration several days ago," said the sergeant.

"Secession from the United States?"

"I didn't hear the specifics of the declaration, but I'm pretty sure it was aimed specifically at the RRZ, not the U.S. government," said the sergeant.

"There's no difference at this point," Alex said, rubbing his face with his hands before continuing. "What is your chain of command now?"

"It hasn't changed. We take orders from the governor," said the sergeant.

"Dad, maybe we should get going. Fishing might take up most of the day," said Ryan, hoping his dad didn't take the discussion where he thought it might go.

"Hold on, Ryan," said his dad. "But your unit was given specific Category Five Response tasking, right? That put you under federal control from the beginning."

He sounded genuinely curious asking the question, the confrontational tone gone.

"I've never heard of this Category Five response," said the sergeant. "We got our orders from the governor."

"Your commanding officer never mentioned the battalion's assignment under the National Recovery Plan? Which battalion are you with?"

"3rd Battalion, 172nd Infantry Regiment. National Guard," answered the sergeant. "The battalion CO was on vacation out west when the EMP hit."

"What about the XO?"

"The XO is presumed dead based on confirmed reports."

Alex shook his head slowly, muttering under his breath for a moment.

"Did anyone issue new equipment to the battalion after the EMP? Weapons, vehicles, communications gear?"

"Not that I'm aware of."

"Thank you, Sergeant. Sorry to have bothered you."

"No problem. Ex-military?"

"Marine Corps. Many years ago."

"Thought you might have served. We're recruiting ex-military folks for a new battalion. Governor Dague authorized the formation of a second battalion based out of Augusta."

"I'm getting a little old for that kind of work, but I appreciate the offer."

"If you change your mind, we'll have a recruiting station set up in Waterville," said the sergeant.

"Well, good luck," Alex said, backing the rest of the way into the road. "Sergeant?" he yelled through Ken's window.

"Yeah?"

"What caused the governor to make the declaration now? She resisted the RRZ from the very start."

The soldier stared at the car quizzically.

Shit. Dad blew it.

"I don't understand," said the sergeant, snaking his right hand toward the rifle's pistol grip.

"We left the Portland area to stay with friends near Waterville because we heard rumors on the HAM radio about disagreements between the state and the RRZ. We didn't want to get caught in the middle of it. Sounds like something happened?"

The soldier's hand stopped moving. "Everything was stable until the RRZ sent a convoy of Marines to take the marine terminal in Searsport," said the sergeant. "No offense to your Marines. They were probably just following orders."

"They took over the terminal?"

"Not really. They reached a joint security arrangement with my battalion. Governor Dague wasn't happy. She's not waiting for the rest of the RRZ's security forces to show up and secure the rest of the state."

"Do you know how many soldiers and Marines the RRZ has in southern Maine?"

"Negative. We let the officers and the governor's people worry about that," joked the sergeant. "Right?"

The specialist nodded. "We just do what we're told. Keeps us fed and out of trouble."

"They have a battalion of Marines and a full brigade of soldiers from the 10th Mountain Division. They're driving around in the latest generation Strykers and JLTVs, not to mention Black Hawk helicopters and Little Birds," Alex told them. "I'm extremely worried about the governor's declaration. If she escalates this, trouble will find all of us. Take care, gentlemen."

The SUV accelerated down the middle of the two-lane road before the soldiers could respond. Ryan watched the soldiers walk toward the road, half expecting them to step into the road and fire at them. He reached into the foot well and yanked on the rifle butt to loosen it from its hiding place under Ken's seat.

"Careful with that thing. I don't want you blowing my foot off," said Ken. "And what was that about, Captain?

You trying to get us detained?"

Alex stared straight ahead.

"Earth to the captain," said Ken.

"Dad," added Ryan.

Alex swung his head toward Ryan, a distant, worried look on his face. "Sorry, I was thinking," he muttered, adding words Ryan couldn't hear before turning back to the road.

Ken looked back at Ryan, raising an eyebrow. Ryan shrugged his shoulders and mouthed, "It's okay," which seemed to ease Mr. Woods' concerns, because he faced forward. A few moments of silence passed before his dad spoke.

"Two things. 3rd Battalion, 172nd Infantry Regiment never received their Category Five Response plan load out, which means battalion leadership never saw the orders placing them under federal control."

"All of the other Guard units would have opened their federal orders," said Ryan. "They would have figured it out eventually."

"Without specific orders putting them under federal control, they'd have to follow the governor's orders. They're the only battalion-sized combat unit stationed in Maine, so I wonder if the other units up here just fell in line with 3rd Battalion."

"What does it matter?" Ken asked.

"It matters because the governor has control of an entire battalion of soldiers, which has probably emboldened her to make some dangerous decisions. Squaring off against the RRZ is at the top of the list. And now she's trying to create another battalion? Nothing good will come from that."

"It'll probably end up looking like a civil defense

group. More symbolic than anything," said Ken.

"I hope so," said Alex, glancing at Ryan in the rearview mirror.

He stared at Ryan and briefly shook his head. The topic was closed, and Ryan knew why. Elements of 3rd Battalion, 172nd Regiment never accessed their Cat Five load out. Somewhere near Brewer, Maine, a battalion-sized cache of weapons and equipment was waiting to be discovered.

"Mr. Woods, were you just making that up about the trout fishing?" Ryan asked.

"I never lie about fishing or beer, son," replied Ken, causing them to laugh.

"What do you think, Dad?"

"About the beer or the fishing?"

"The fishing," Ryan said, thinking more about the beer.

"Why don't we find a nice quiet spot on the other side of the Kennebec. One of those smaller streams I was telling you about this morning. Even if we don't catch anything, we'll take care of those beers," said Ken.

"Works for me," said Alex.

"What about the police on the bridge?" Ryan questioned.

"We'll tell them we got sent back by the National Guard."

Ryan felt uneasy about his dad's sudden shift in focus. He hadn't said a word about the fact that they hadn't acquired any additional seeds to expand the gardens. The seeds had been critical to their plan for staying on the lake with the Walkers and Thorntons. He'd overheard his parents arguing about the dangers of making the trip. His dad had been hell-bent on the idea that they needed more seeds to survive, gaining his mom's reluctant approval. Now the seeds were forgotten, pushed aside by the news of the governor's declaration and the revelation that a battalion-sized supply cache sat untouched—less than an hour away.

No way. His dad couldn't possibly be thinking about—

Ryan looked at the rearview mirror and saw his dad watching him. They stared at each other, communicating without speaking for several moments, before his dad winked.

Shit. He was thinking about it.

Chapter 22

Belgrade, Maine

The muffled sound of a vehicle engine carried across the backyard, drawing Kate's attention away from the task of filling the buckets. She walked to the shore and hopped off the dock onto the matted grass. A quick glimpse of the silver BMW confirmed that Alex had returned. The buckets could wait. She headed for the deck, expecting to catch him inside, but he appeared at the side of the house before she reached the stairs.

"Need some help?" he asked, a serious look indicating she should answer "yes."

"I don't need any help, but I'll gladly take some," she said, eliciting no grin or change to his solemn façade.

She grabbed his hand and they strolled slowly across the backyard.

"What happened? No seeds?" she said.

"No seeds," he said, squeezing her hand. "But that's the least of our problems. I'll check on the boat tomorrow—see if I can find a few clearly abandoned boats we can provision for anyone else that wants to leave."

She stopped them. "Alex, you're scaring me. What's—"

"Let's keep walking. I don't want to alarm my parents or the kids," said Alex.

"I'll start walking when you start telling me what's wrong," said Kate.

"The governor of Maine essentially seceded from the United States," he said, pulling her hand.

Kate let herself move forward, wondering how much of his statement was melodrama.

"I'm sure it's just a symbolic protest," she said. "It's not like the state can untangle itself from the RRZ."

"It's trying. Johnny's Seeds no longer sells seeds to the public. They joined the Maine Independence Initiative, which means everything they produce goes to the state—outside of the RRZ."

"Sounds a little odd, but overall it should benefit the state," she said.

"Johnny's Seeds was guarded by soldiers from 3rd Battalion, 172nd Infantry Regiment, a National Guard unit under state control. I'm wondering if Johnny's participation was voluntary," said Alex.

"I thought the RRZ controlled all of the National Guard units?" said Kate, starting to understand why her husband looked despondent.

"So did I, until about two hours ago."

"Where have you guys been for two hours?"

"Fishing and drinking," Alex said.

"I thought I smelled stale beer," Kate said, shaking her head. "Where's Ryan?"

"Over at the Thorntons'," he said, rolling his eyes. "Chloe."

"That's another issue," she said.

Ryan and Chloe's relationship had intensified during the fall, to the point where Alex and Kate decided they needed to revisit the topic of sex, focusing on the consequences of an unexpected pregnancy in their new surroundings. They had no confirmation of sexual contact, but the two of them frequently disappeared—last seen holding hands on one of the docks or walking into the forest next to their house. The absolute last thing they needed right now was a pregnancy.

"Don't remind me. I was hoping it might have cooled off over the winter, but apparently that wasn't the case," said Alex. "It's going to make leaving here extremely complicated."

"We don't have to leave," said Kate.

"The governor is trying to form another battalion. They're recruiting all over northern and central Maine. This isn't going to be a Salvation Army battalion," he said, continuing before she could respond.

"Medina and her RRZ cronies will come down hard on Governor Dague. I wouldn't count out a military response—at the very least they'll seize key facilities and assets. They've already moved Marines up to Searsport."

"When did that happen?"

"Recently. Supposedly, that's what prompted the governor to sign her own death warrant," said Alex.

"Don't talk like that," Kate said, shaking her head. "They're not going to kill her."

"No, but she's skating on thin ice pulling something like this while the National Recovery Plan is still active. The Insurrection Act could be turned around and used against her, especially if an entire National Guard battalion has sided against the federal government. I wouldn't be surprised to wake up one morning and discover that an additional brigade of 10th Mountain Division soldiers arrived during the night," said Alex.

"More soldiers might not be a bad thing," she offered.

"Not if the people up here are perceived as

sympathetic with the Maine Independence Initiative. The soldiers wouldn't be here to usher in a new era of hope and recovery."

"No need to get shitty," Kate said, jumping onto the dock, which swayed underneath her.

"Sorry," Alex said, joining her.

He nestled against her back and put his arms around her waist, pulling her tightly against him, pressing his forehead against the back of her head.

"I love you," he said.

"I love you more," said Kate, taking a deep breath and relaxing in his embrace.

They stayed that way for a few minutes, breathing in synch.

"Is there any way we can stay?" she asked.

Alex hesitated to answer. "I don't see how. We don't have enough seeds to support this many people, even if everything goes right with the harvest. The lakes have been depleted of most fish. I don't think the Maine Department of Inland Fisheries and Wildlife will be stocking the lakes this spring."

"If the state organizes food production, might we be able to fall back on that?" she asked hesitantly.

"It's wishful thinking at best. I don't see how they plan on distributing the food in any consistent, wide-reaching way. Most people don't have cars, and I can't imagine the state has the gasoline or diesel reserves needed to drive kale and potatoes from town to town on a weekly basis. They'll have to limit food-distribution efforts to organized hubs—which will quickly draw large refugee populations. It's a recipe for disaster," said Alex.

"It's something," Kate said. "We have no idea what we'll find once we set sail. What if the situation is just as wrecked in the Caribbean?"

"We have the desalinator and fishing gear. We'll be fine, even if the eastern Caribbean turns out to be a bust. South America should be relatively unaffected by whatever hit the United States. We'll head to French Guiana or the northern coast of Brazil for a major resupply. Argentina will be our ultimate goal."

"Just like that?" Kate asked.

"Barring any unforeseen weather problems, we could be in Fortaleza within sixty days, which is pushing up against our stored food supplies. We'd need to leave within a week or two to stretch the food to South America," he said.

"We've never sailed out of Casco Bay. I think you're oversimplifying things," Kate said, grabbing her bucket and leaving him behind.

"Kate! Think about what we've done so far. We can do this," said Alex, jogging to catch up.

She stopped, staring at the placid lake to find the glimpse of serenity she needed to avoid starting an argument. Not only was he simplifying a forty-seven-hundred-mile open-ocean voyage, he was ignoring the most obvious fact.

"Your parents can't do it. They won't do it. Your dad has made that abundantly clear. How are you going to reconcile that, Alex?"

"They'll come around."

"No, they won't, and if your parents stay, so will Ethan and Kevin. Now we're only removing four people from your Maine starvation scenario."

"Nice," he said, frowning at her. "I'm not making this up. In roughly two months, we're eating off the land for the rest of the year."

"So, somehow we're better off throwing ourselves at the mercy of a foreign government as what, boat people? We have no idea what the political climate will be toward Americans. What are we going to pay them with? Will they even let us off our boat? Will their Coast Guard confiscate our weapons? I think you're romanticizing the other side of the journey, Alex. We won't be received as tourists. Think immigration issues. Think holding cells. Think about the confiscation of everything we own, followed by a dusty bus ride to the nearest shithole border crossing. That's the risk at the other end," she said, stopping at the dock.

"We could try a transatlantic crossing," he suggested.

"I'm going to pretend I didn't hear that," Kate stated before jumping onto the floating dock.

"In thirty days or so, you could be sipping espresso in a French café," said Alex, making the leap.

The dock shifted when he landed, causing Kate to raise her arms for balance.

"Tempting, but sailing through the North Atlantic sounds a lot worse than heading south," she said.

"Half the time, and I doubt our friends across the pond will deport us," said Alex. "We can bring our passports."

"Funny," she said, lowering her bucket into the water.

"I just got this urge to push you in," said Alex.

"I can't even begin to describe how much trouble you'd be in," Kate said, smiling.

"More trouble than I'm already in?"

"You're not in any trouble," she said, lifting the bucket out and setting it next to Alex's.

She wrapped her arms around him and kissed his scruffy neck. Alex smelled about as ripe as he looked,

141

which had become the new norm in their life. She looked forward to the point when they could comfortably swim in the lake. Sponge bathing with a pot of stove-heated water served their utilitarian hygiene needs well, but did little beyond removing the surface layer of dirt and sweat. She yearned for a long, hot bath. Something she imagined would feel like a religious experience at this point. There was no sense in thinking about it right now.

"I guess there's no harm in prepping the boat," she said.

He kissed the top of her head. "I just need to make sure it's still a viable option. Examine the water hoses, inspect the engine, maybe run it for a few minutes if the area is clear," he said.

"You'll have to bring the batteries out to start the engine," Kate reminded him.

"I left one on the boat to operate the bilge pump. I'll bring another in case it's dead," said Alex.

"Or stolen."

"The whole boat could be stolen," said Alex, rocking her gently.

"Then what?"

"Plan B."

"Do I want to hear about Plan B?"

"I don't really have a Plan B—yet."

Kate didn't completely believe Alex. He typically had Plans B through F worked out ahead of time. He was holding something back. Something he had seen. She'd have to shake the truth out of her son. Ryan couldn't keep a secret, especially from his mother.

Chapter 23

Belfast, Maine

Brisk, salty air poured through Alex's window. Tinged with seaweed and other familiar tidal smells, the onshore breeze reminded him of past sailing seasons. He'd head down to the South Portland waterfront with Ryan after the first warm stretch of April weather and start to tinker with the boat. It always marked the beginning of a long, but rewarding period of repairs and restoration. Sanding and varnishing worn teak, repainting the hull, rigging the sails, and sometimes an unexpected engine or electrical project.

All well worth the hassle when the boat cut through the harbor for the first time, a cold beer nestled into one of the cup holders on the steering pedestal. He looked forward to the possibility of sailing out of here, even if the occasion wouldn't be celebrated with a can of local microbrew.

Sailing represented a form of freedom to Alex. A self-determination marked by endless possibilities outside of the United States. Staying holed up at the lake felt like a prison sentence, with few prospects in sight. He didn't want to leave his close friends behind, but he didn't want to eat them either—which could be a distinct possibility in December of next year if they couldn't grow enough food. He stifled a laugh.

"What?" asked Charlie.

"Nothing," Alex replied, watching the harbor appear between the buildings on Miller Street.

He'd chosen to bypass Belfast's Main Street, noting an unusual amount of pedestrian activity on the streets near the town center. All eyes were drawn to his SUV, which left him with an uneasy feeling. He didn't need to take the most direct path to the waterfront. He'd left the *Katelyn Ann* in the center of the mooring field, beyond the farthest marina. He nearly laughed out loud again.

"What?" insisted Charlie from the front passenger seat.

"Really, it's nothing," Alex said, craning his head forward for a better view of the harbor.

The number of boats had decreased dramatically. *Shit.*

"Alex, don't make me beg. I need the humor," said Charlie.

"You really don't want to know," said Alex.

The view opened as the tree-lined streets gave way to a grassy, open promenade overlooking the harbor. The boats had almost disappeared. Charlie started to say something, but stopped.

"This isn't right, is it?" said Charlie.

"No. The harbor was crowded with boats in the fall," said Alex, slowing the SUV.

"Did some of them sink due to the weather? I assume there's a good reason you pull your boat out of the water in the winter," said Charlie.

"Not likely. Not that many," said Alex.

"Maybe we can find another boat," said Ryan.

Alex glanced at his son in the rearview mirror, catching the top of his face and his olive green hat in the reflection.

"We'll soon find out," said Alex, easing the SUV down the hill.

When the SUV cleared the first in a series of dilapidated red buildings flanking the entrance to the marina, Alex noticed activity on the floating dock that extended from the parking lot. A quarter of the boat slips were occupied by a variety of motor- and sail-powered vessels. The *Katelyn Ann* was tied up to the outermost position at the end of the dock.

"That's our boat, Dad!" said Ryan.

"Yeah. That's her all right," he muttered, biting his lower lip.

He didn't like what he saw. Men climbed on and off the boats, including the *Katelyn Ann*, while others milled around on the dock. The assembly of people looked organized. Alex drove the car into the parking lot, turning every head in sight. He parked perpendicular to the waterfront, at the back of the lot. Two men dressed in warm civilian clothes broke off from a small group of armed men seated at an ancient picnic table next to the dock entrance. One of them carried a hunting rifle slung over his shoulder. The other gripped a black handheld radio.

"Keep the guns out of sight," Alex instructed. "Ryan, I want you on the passenger side of the car, with quick access to your rifle. Keep an eye out behind us. We don't know what kind of operation they might be running here. Charlie, you're with me."

"ROE?" asked Ryan.

"Standard. Weapons *hold*. If we come under attack, switch to weapons tight," said Alex.

He'd simplified the Rules of Engagement (ROE) for everyone at the lake. His experience in the Marines taught him the simpler the better for ROE involving the use of lethal force. The situations developed quickly, often requiring quick decision-making. Fewer parameters led to swift, appropriate use of force.

HOLD meant fire in self-defense or under direct orders only, regardless of the situation. This was their default ROE and the most appropriate stance in nearly every encounter. TIGHT meant fire at targets recognized as hostile. This represented a nebulous middle ground, but it kept innocents out of the line of fire. Positively identifying hostile targets wasn't easy in a civilian-on-civilian engagement, but it didn't require a War College degree. Anyone pointing a weapon in your direction during a firefight was probably hostile. FREE turned the guns on anyone not recognized as friendly. This ROE setting was reserved for the worst-case scenarios, like an assault on their house, where all known friendlies were "inside the line," and anyone moving in your direction was up to no good.

"What about us?" asked Charlie.

"Keep your hands away from your pistol," said Alex. "Unless they start shooting at you, of course."

"Of course," said Charlie, opening his door.

"I should probably start the conversation," said Alex.

"And finish it," added Charlie, patting him on the shoulder. "I'm just here for moral support."

"Smart ass," said Alex. "Seriously. I don't want any trouble."

"They have your boat," stated Charlie. "As much as I want you to stay in Maine, I'll help you get your boat back."

"Let's just test the waters here. I have an idea if we run into trouble," said Alex.

They met the two men halfway across the gravel lot. As soon as Alex stepped out of the car, the man with the rifle adjusted his grip on the sling, bringing his hand higher along the nylon strap. Easier to swing it off the shoulder. He didn't unsling the rifle, which showed some restraint—and common sense. At less than fifty feet, Charlie and Alex, carrying pistols in exposed drop holsters along their upper right thighs, had the upper hand on a bolt-action hunting rifle.

The man with the radio nodded at them. "Can we help you?"

Alex chose his words carefully, hoping to start off on the right foot—an elusive approach for him lately.

"That's my boat," said Alex, miserably failing the diplomatic approach.

"Which boat?" asked the man, glancing back toward the dock.

"The sailboat at the far end of the dock. *Katelyn Ann.* I brought her here last fall from Portland Harbor," said Alex.

The man adjusted his gray watch cap and grimaced.

"Shit. I don't…well, there's no easy way to say this, but that boat now belongs to the state of Maine. Sorry. Every boat out here is needed for fishing. The bigger ones go to Rockland, where they can head out into deeper water."

Alex stared past him at his boat, watching two men lift heavy marine batteries into the *Katelyn Ann's* cockpit. The second man tightened his grip on the rifle sling.

"Maine Independence Initiative?" Alex asked.

"Yeah. We're repurposing the boats and assembling crews up and down the coast. This is going to put a lot of Mainers back to work," he said.

147

"On my boat," said Alex, shaking his head.

"I think feeding hungry people is more important than cruising around in a sailboat," said the bearded man holding the rifle.

"I wasn't planning on sailing around Penobscot Bay sipping mai tais. I brought the boat here for a reason," Alex stated. "So I could leave."

"And go where?" asked the leader, shrugging his shoulders.

"Anywhere but here. The last place I want to be caught is between several thousand heavily armed federal soldiers and the Maine Independence Initiative, or whatever you call yourselves."

"We're the militia part of this," said the guy with the rifle.

"Splendid," said Alex. "So, is there any way I can convince you to let me keep my boat? I can't imagine you get too many owners showing up. One boat isn't going to make or break the governor's fishing initiative."

"No," said the leader. "If we bend the rules for you, we have to bend them for everyone."

"I'm sure the people won't come out of the woodwork," said Alex.

"Rules are rules," he said.

"Spoken like a true pawn in someone else's game," Alex said wryly.

"Hey, you're lucky we don't exercise our authority to confiscate your vehicle," said the man with the gun.

"Well, I'll take that as a sign of the good things to come from the Maine Independence Militia. Enjoy your day, gentlemen. Enjoy my boat," said Alex. "Ready to head back?" he asked the others.

"Yep," said Charlie.

When they got back to the car, Alex used a pair of binoculars to scan the area around the dock. He counted six men, including the two they had just confronted. The man with the radio spoke rapidly into his handheld, glancing frequently in their direction. They needed to get moving. Nothing good would come of this encounter. Alex handed the binoculars to Charlie and shifted the SUV into gear.

"You're being awfully quiet," he said to Charlie.

"I'm just in shock that you didn't make more of a fuss about your boat," said Charlie.

"There was no point in arguing with those jackasses," said Alex. "Plus, I have a better idea."

"The Marines in Searsport?" asked Ryan.

"If they're willing to lend a hand," said Alex.

"I have a feeling they'll be up for a little ass kicking," said Charlie.

Chapter 24

Searsport, Maine

The entrance to the Searsport Marine Terminal looked secure enough to repel a platoon-sized attack. Alex recognized the distinct shape of 1st Battalion's Matvees behind the razor-wire-topped fence. Alex wondered if the Marines had any influence on the tight arrangement. Eli Russell's attack on Sanford Airport had redefined the RRZ's assessment of the security threat in Maine.

A sentry from the portable blast-resistant guard post approached the SUV. The Marine standing in the nearest Matvee turret hunched forward, nestling into the M240 machine gun aimed at his SUV's front windshield. He hated being on the receiving end of "the gun," his fate in the hands of a nervous eighteen-year-old.

"Are you sure this is a good idea?" asked Charlie, placing his hands on the dashboard.

"Not really, but it's worth a try," replied Alex. "You good back there?"

Ryan shifted in his seat. "Good to go, Dad. Everything is tucked away."

The sentry, an Army specialist dressed in full combat gear, reached Alex's open window.

"Sorry, sir. No unauthorized vehicles are allowed inside the terminal. I'm going to need you to back into the parking space behind you and head back out the way you came," said the soldier, peering into the front and back seats.

"My name is Alex Fletcher, and I need to speak with the senior Marine on site. They'll want to talk to me. Sorry to dump this on you, Specialist. Do you mind if I park and wait?"

The soldier thought about his request for a few seconds, which was a good sign. If he had no intention of passing along the information, he would have shut Alex down immediately.

"Why don't you back into one of the spaces there," suggested the soldier, pointing to a small parking lot on the other side of the access road. "I'll pass your information on to the Marine garrison."

"Thank you. I know you guys usually have your hands tied with these things, so I really appreciate your help with this."

The soldier nodded and backed away, waiting for Alex to reposition the SUV. Once he had pulled them into the closest parking space, Alex shut off the engine.

"I don't think you should have given them your name," said Charlie. "You might be on their watch list."

"I doubt it. The RRZ and state governor are at odds right now. The state controls these soldiers," said Alex.

"Just saying, Captain Fletcher," said Charlie. "You never know what kind of deals are being made."

The reinforced section of chain-link fence on the left side of the guard shack jolted to life, squeaking along on its track. A few seconds later, the familiar squat shape of a tan Matvee appeared on the outbound side of the worn road inside the compound.

"Let's step out of the car for easier identification," said Alex.

They stopped behind the SUV as the armored vehicle cleared the gate. The Matvee pulled even with the group and screeched to a halt, the passenger-side door springing open. Staff Sergeant Taylor jumped onto the pavement, shaking his head.

"Never thought I'd see you again, sir," said Taylor, reaching out to shake Alex's hand.

"They must have been desperate putting you in charge up here," said Alex, slapping him on the arm.

"Shit. We got a captain up here watching over us, but I had to see this for myself," said Taylor, stepping in front of Charlie. "Looks like you healed up nicely, Mr. Thornton."

"I take a licking, keep on ticking," said Charlie, shaking his hand.

"I see my automatic rifleman seems to have recovered as well," said Taylor, patting Ryan's shoulder.

"His fighting days are over," said Alex guardedly.

"I hope so. I hope all of our fighting days are over," said Taylor, turning to Alex. "So, what brings the infamous Captain Fletcher out for a visit?"

"Just wanted to say hi," said Alex.

"Uh-huh."

"Anyone we know in the Matvee?" asked Alex.

"Negative. The usual suspects are back in Sanford. I got bamboozled into rolling out with Grady's convoy," said the staff sergeant.

"Think they'd be up for a ten-minute ride to Belfast?" said Alex. "The Maine Independence Initiative has seized my sailboat for 'the good of the state.' I'd really like to convince them, peacefully, to return my property."

"And you think the arrival of a machine-gun-equipped, blast-resistant, armored vehicle will expedite your peaceful settlement?"

"It couldn't hurt," said Alex. "If you're allowed to go on field trips without a permission slip, that is."

"Mr. Thornton and your son stay here," said Taylor.

"I'm going to need them to help me with the boat," said Alex.

"All right, but they stay in the Matvee," said Taylor, shaking his head. "I'm gonna get my ass handed to me for this."

Twelve minutes later, the Matvee burst into the marina parking lot, skidding across the gravel toward the dock entrance. The men clambered to get away from the rickety, weathered picnic table, which collapsed on one end in the rush. Alex hopped out of the rear passenger door, catching up to Taylor as they came around the hood of the vehicle. A short, stocky corporal named Rickson already stood on the driver's side of the Matvee, his rifle in the patrol ready position—aiming at the ground in front of the group of confused men. Alex glanced at the roof of the vehicle, noting that the turret gunner had the M240 pointed at a forty-five-degree angle over the militiamen's heads. Taylor walked up to the broken picnic table, leaving Alex behind.

"I believe you have a boat that belongs to this gentleman," said Taylor, pointing back toward Alex.

The leader of the group stepped forward, keeping the table between them. "Sorry. That boat left about ten minutes ago," he said with a worried grin.

Alex turned his head toward the dock. Shit. In all of the excitement rolling up on the marina, he hadn't noticed that his boat was missing.

"They moved the boat. It was at the end of the dock less than thirty minutes ago," said Alex.

153

"We got a report that you were headed over the bridge, toward Searsport. You didn't come from that way, so I figured you were up to some bullshit. Boat's on the way to Rockland," said the leader.

Alex walked up to the picnic table, noticing the man's handheld radio in the gravel next to the crumpled end of the table. Without warning, he lifted his right foot and smashed the plastic radio with the heel of his boot. He slammed his combat boot down several times, until the frame splintered and the radio broke apart into several smaller pieces. The group's leader stared at the shattered radio with his mouth ajar.

"I should have beat you over the head with it," said Alex, broadcasting the truth.

He hadn't smashed the radio for effect to intimidate the group. Alex had replaced the man's head with the handheld, taking his aggressions out on the inanimate object. He'd thought the long winter had dampened his anger, but it came back with little provocation.

One obstacle after another. One asshole after another.

He was tired of it. Very little stood between Alex pulling his pistol and firing at the ragtag collection of shitheads assembled in front of him. His son was the only thing holding him back. Ryan had seen enough brutal, pointless violence to last a lifetime. The last thing he needed to witness was his own father joining the insanity. Instead, he kicked the broken radio at the group, causing one of the men to unsling his rifle. The sharp metallic sound of the M240 bolt sliding back and forth snapped through the air.

"Not a good idea, slick," said Taylor. "We don't recognize your Maine Independence Militia. As far as I'm concerned, you're just a bunch of fuck-stick locals stealing boats. I want all of your weapons on the ground. Right now. Just let them slide off your shoulders."

The leader of the group didn't react until the sound of the first few rifles hitting the hard rock surface jarred him out of his daze.

"Keep your weapons," he said. "The RRZ doesn't have any authority in the state anymore. We've declared independence from these assholes."

Taylor raised his rifle and pointed it at the leader. Corporal Rickson followed his lead and assumed a tactical stance, aiming his rifle at the group.

"Since we don't recognize each other's authority, let's go with firepower. I win," said Taylor. "I want every weapon on the ground. This is for your own safety, and I'm not fucking around."

"You're gonna regret this," said one of the men from the back of the group, dropping his rifle.

The rest of the weapons slid to the rocks, amidst audible, but indecipherable grumbling.

"What else is new," said Taylor, glancing quickly at Alex. "You need anything else from these yahoos?"

"Just my sailboat," said Alex.

"It's gone," said the leader. "Headed to Rockland."

"Does the Coast Guard know what you're up to?" said Alex.

"I have no idea," said the man.

"Maybe they need to be notified that you're stealing boats, starting with mine. They have a base in Rockland, and the last time I checked, they hadn't committed treason against the United States," said Alex.

"Treason? You're kidding me, right? These stormtroopers are the ones that declared war on the United States and violated the constitution. Not us. The states aren't obligated to obey the RRZ," said the leader.

"Actually, they are. Congress passed the 2015 Defense Authorization Bill, which modified the Insurrection Act and made all of this a happy reality," said Alex. "Maine's senators, and most of its representatives, smiled and supported it. You should watch C-SPAN once in a while."

"None of that matters now. The government doesn't exist," said a spindly looking guy in a hunting camouflage-patterned jacket.

"Trust me, it hasn't gone away," said Taylor. "Keep pulling shit like this, and you'll find out exactly what I mean."

"There's more of us than you," persisted the man.

Alex didn't see this going anywhere productive. If they stayed and argued, he'd be sure to draw his pistol and make the situation worse.

"Fuck it. Keep the sailboat. You're gonna need it when they shut down Searsport and nothing useful rolls into town," said Alex. "Ready to get out of here, Staff Sergeant?"

"Ready to roll, sir," said Taylor, keeping his rifle pointed at the leader's chest.

"Once we get you out of Searsport, we won't need the RRZ!" yelled the leader.

"Really? Who do you think directs these ships to the terminal? Governor Dague?" said Alex, shaking his head. "Better play nice, gentlemen. Rumor has it that Portland Harbor will be open for business soon. Want to take a wild guess on how many ships will pull into Searsport once that happens?"

"We'll see about that," said the man.

"By the way, I hope they replaced the impeller on the

sailboat. I removed it last fall—in case someone stole the boat," said Alex, checking his watch. "Fifteen minutes out? I bet that engine's running pretty hot right now. Probably ready to shut down on them, if they haven't blown a few seals already. Have a nice day, gentlemen."

"Did you really remove that thing you mentioned?" said Taylor once they got behind the Matvee.

"Yeah. It supplies seawater to the cooling system. If they're lucky, the diesel will shut down before any major damage occurs. Either way, the engine will require some TLC before it runs again," said Alex. "Sorry I dragged you guys out here."

"Are you kidding me? This is the most exciting thing we've done since you left," said Taylor.

"Somehow I highly doubt that," said Alex. "Seriously. I appreciate the assist."

"Now what?" asked Taylor.

"Plan B, or C if you ask my wife," said Alex.

"How is Mrs. Fletcher doing these days?"

"She's doing well, but she's not gonna be happy about Plan B."

"Sounds like my kind of plan," said Taylor.

Chapter 25

Colonel Sean Grady sat at his makeshift desk in the battalion TOC, staring out of the hangar bay door at the same scene. Little changed except the sky. Helicopters flew in and out all day. Vehicles drove back and forth across the tarmac. Soldiers milled around the tents on the other side of the runway. It had all gone stale quicker than he imagined in the fall, which in many ways was a good thing. Stale kept his Marines alive, which was why he didn't look forward to the RRZ's imminent move.

Relocating the RRZ north to Portland was guaranteed to stir up a hornet's nest, and the timing couldn't be worse. The state governor's declaration of independence from the RRZ had stoked the long-dormant embers of government distrust. Dormant wasn't the right term. Frozen. The winter had been too damn cold and messy for people to worry about anything but keeping warm and staying fed—neither of which the population did well. When the winter's survivors emerged from hibernation, Governor Dague didn't waste a moment directing their anger at the federal government—particularly the RRZ.

Taking this circus north was going to cause a shit storm of protest throughout the state. Medina was planning a rapid, unannounced redeployment, leaving roughly one hundred and forty thousand Mainers on the wrong side of the fence. She was figuratively pulling the rug right out from under them. On top of that, the RRZ would abandon a few hundred thousand refugees barely scraping by in the FEMA camps along the New Hampshire border.

"Not really abandoning them," Medina had insisted at their last commander's meeting. They were welcome to relocate farther north and continue to be supported by the RRZ. Of course, the refugees would have to move the camps without help. Medina couldn't spare the time or manpower to help them, since she wanted to arrive en masse at the Portland Jetport. RRZ officials didn't want to give Governor Dague enough time to muster an armed protest or send elements of her National Guard battalion to complicate the move.

Dague was playing a dangerous, unpredictable game with her constituents. The RRZ structure was far from ideal, but it represented a real conduit between the federal government and recovery efforts. Materials, supplies, fuel, information—everything needed to jump start the nation flowed through Washington, D.C., and its proxies as defined by the National Recovery Plan. Under RRZ protocols, state governments functioned in a strictly advisory role unless the RRZ Authority decided to expand that function.

Dague had resisted the RRZ's implementation from the beginning, essentially killing any chance of a mutually beneficial relationship. To Medina's credit, RRZ leadership tried to integrate the governor's staff into the decision-making structure, but her attempts were repeatedly rebuffed. Dague wasn't interested in "helping" the RRZ. On a number of occasions, Maine's governor very publicly stated, "Maine is better off without the RRZ." She couldn't have been more wrong.

Grady's ROTAC phone buzzed, vibrating the table. He lifted it from a coffee-stained map and checked the digital display, which read "Centurion." The garrison in Searsport. Things had been quiet up there since he left Captain Williams and twenty-four Marines to ensure the facility's continued support of the RRZ.

Dague had played along with the establishment of the garrison, only to spin the nature of the agreement in her favor. According to Dague, the Searsport garrison was the first overt step in the RRZ's "quiet war" against Maine. She declared independence from the RRZ in the same speech. The state would have been better off if Grady had arrested her at the terminal and displaced the National Guard unit. He pressed connect on the phone.

"This is Patriot," he said.

"Sean, this is Alex Fletcher."

"Alex!" he said, drawing a few looks from the Marines. "I thought you might have moved on to warmer weather. Good to hear your voice."

"Well, it's hard to leave good friends. We decided to stay at the lake and make a go of it," said Alex.

"I'm glad to hear that," said Grady. "We could use a friend or two up north."

"That's what I've come to understand. I borrowed Staff Sergeant Taylor to help me with a Maine Independence Initiative problem," said Alex.

"Shit. Please tell me it didn't go sideways," said Grady.

"The biggest fallout will be some hurt egos," said Alex.

"Shattered egos can lead to big problems, Alex."

"We didn't push it too far. The state confiscated my sailboat, which I was about to use to get out of here."

"You're leaving?" said Grady.

"That's only part of it. Food is getting a little scarce up here. I added eight mouths to the equation by staying, which burned through our supplies faster than I anticipated. I don't think we can plant enough food for seventeen people, and the way things are shaking out up here, it doesn't look like we'll be able to take food from King Dague's land. They're co-opting everything up here. I figured I'd make it a little easier for everyone by leaving."

"I have a feeling they're way better off with you around. We all are," said Grady, pausing. "So, what can I do for you?"

"I was hoping to make a little trade," said Alex.

"I can run some supplies up your way, Alex. I know you don't want to ask, but I'd be more than happy to help out," said Grady.

"And I would have given you the information I have regardless, though I'll take you up on your offer. I might not have to if my suspicions are correct," said Alex.

"Information. Sounds interesting. What does the infamous Captain Fletcher know that we don't?"

"Let me ask you this. What does the RRZ know about 3rd Battalion, 172nd Infantry Regiment?" said Alex.

"I know the battalion aligned itself with the state," said Grady, testing the extent of Alex's knowledge.

"Because the commanding officer and executive officer are MIA?"

"Sounds like you've done a little digging," said Grady.

"So you already know?"

"I met the new battalion commander in Searsport," said Grady. "I got the impression he didn't understand the full national picture."

"Interesting," said Alex.

"Why do you say that?"

"Did you notice their equipment?"

"Yeah, the Adaptive Combat Rifle mystery has been solved. I'm just glad their Cat Five load out didn't include heavy vehicle-mounted weapons," said Grady.

"I don't think they received their Category Five load out," said Alex.

"No. I saw new rifles," said Grady.

"They've had those for a few years. I saw the ACRs in a news segment on one of the local channels," said Alex. "Sean, they didn't get a Category Five load out. I talked to a few soldiers from the battalion. They'd never heard the words 'Cat Five.' One of them was a sergeant. Every Marine in your battalion knows about the Category Five equipment."

Grady thought about this for a moment. Jesus. If Alex was right, Governor Dague might be sitting on enough vehicles and weapons to equip another battalion. At the very least, she could upgrade her current National Guard battalion, which could embolden her.

"This isn't good," said Grady. "The last thing Governor Dague needs is a shiny new battalion to play with."

"Are you sure the RRZ doesn't already know this? The biometric security system on each of the CONEX boxes delivered to Sanford Airport was registered to your fingerprints. I find it hard to believe that they can't monitor access," said Alex.

Hard to believe, indeed.

"The boxes sent to Sanford were processed after the event. My biometric information and the override code that I gave you were uploaded immediately prior to the boxes being shipped from a central facility somewhere in the Midwest. The Category Five gear at Fort Devens was accessed by the codes in my secure Cat Five pod. Only I had the combination to the pod. We're talking several reinforced warehouses filled with vehicles, weapons, ammunition, supplies—everything needed for thirty days of sustained operations. The warehouses were located in a secure, stand-alone facility within Fort Devens."

"How could Dague not know about this? National Guard units across the state accessed load outs, all of them reporting for duty to the RRZ authority," said Alex.

Alex was too perceptive for an impromptu conversation.

"3rd Battalion, 172nd Infantry is Maine's only battalion-sized, combat-deployable unit. The vast majority of National Guard units in the state are service and support groups like the transportation detachment and the engineering company assigned to Sanford Airport. Aside from new communications equipment, computers and repair items, they had all of the gear they needed to accomplish their assigned RRZ tasks. To Dague and her staff, nothing would have looked out of place with the other National Guard units. Hell, even I didn't put it together. I figured they picked up new rifles, and that was the extent of it. Why would they need new vehicles and heavy gear when a brigade from the 10th Mountain Division was doing most of the security work in the state? Bad assumption."

"I bet she knows that 3rd Battalion doesn't belong to her," said Alex.

"Oh, I guarantee she does. I imagine it became very clear when every unit in Maine gave her the one-finger salute—except for 3rd Battalion. Once she figured out that the CO and XO were MIA, I'm sure she took every necessary step to insulate 3rd Battalion from the rest of the units. The new commanding officer probably has no idea that she played him."

"She sounds like a clever one," said Alex.

"Very clever—and very dangerous. I don't think she understands the stakes. Medina has been extremely patient with her," said Grady.

"Well, if you happen to secure 3rd Battalion's load out, I could use any rations you find," said Alex.

Grady laughed. "Sounds like an even trade to me. I could do one better and establish a Forward Operating Base at your position on the lake. You're close to Waterville, and it looks like you have easy access to the interstate and roads heading into western Maine. The RRZ wants to establish a remote presence north of Portland."

"Why? Are you guys headed north?" Alex asked.

Alex's question caught him off guard, though it was a logical deduction based on Grady's suggestion to put an FOB near Waterville—in retrospect.

"None of the Marines beyond the officers on my headquarters staff know we're moving. Play along and say something like 'just kidding.'"

"I'm out of earshot," said Alex. "When is this happening?"

"I don't have the date, but I do know that when it happens, it'll go fast. Medina wants us out of here within two days of making the general announcement. She doesn't want to give Governor Dague enough time to coordinate a response."

Alex remained silent. Grady knew the wheels inside Fletcher's head were spinning, trying to calculate the overall impact of the move on his situation.

"This is a bad idea," said Alex. "She'll have trouble coming at her from two sides."

"That was our assessment of the situation. The refugees will move north, pushing against the residents of southern Maine.

"You'll have your hands full trying to police the relocation of FEMA camps in York County."

"The refugees will be on their own, aside from supplies provided by the RRZ," said Grady. "Medina even plans to stop patrolling and administering the camps, to free soldiers for other northern garrisons."

"Like the one you want to put near my house?" said Alex.

"That one would be much smaller," said Grady.

"I think I'll take a pass on the FOB, Sean," said Alex. "I can't afford to paint a bull's-eye on my family again."

"Understood," said Grady. "Just trying to help my old company commander."

"Old is the operative term. I appreciate the offer, but we should be fine with whatever rations you can spare from the load out—if that's still on the table. I'd like to keep my life as uncomplicated as possible for now," said Alex.

Grady was relieved to hear that Alex wasn't interested in the FOB.

"There's only one catch in getting you the supplies, Alex," said Grady. "And it's a big one."

"Always a catch."

"It's not my doing. I would gladly deliver what you need, but I can't guarantee that I'll be able to get my hands on the supplies. Medina won't assign my battalion to secure the load out. She'll task Colonel Martin's 4th

165

Brigade Combat Team with that. They'll put every helicopter at their disposal into an air assault on the facility and call it good. I won't be involved in any way. The only way I can guarantee you the supplies is with an FOB," said Grady.

"I can't do that, Sean. Even if I were to consider the idea, which I'm not, I can't take the risk of Medina pulling the FOB away when shit gets crazy up here, and it *will* get crazy if she doesn't figure out a way to work with the state government."

"There's one other possibility, but it falls well outside of the uncomplicated zone," said Grady.

"I'm listening," said Alex.

"I don't think Kate will like this option," said Grady.

"You're killing me, Sean. What are we talking about?"

"All right. Let's say I got my hands on the codes to open the warehouses, and I passed them on to you…"

"Are you fucking kidding me?" said Alex. "I'm not exactly working with SEAL Team Six here."

"Your crew can hold its own," said Grady, remembering Staff Sergeant Taylor's after-action report detailing the attack on Alex's house in Limerick. "More than hold its own."

"I don't know. We're looking at too many unknown variables," said Alex.

"I'm just throwing it out there for you. The warehouses are probably in an obscure, out-of-the-way location for security reasons. Beyond the stares and glares you'd get for driving a vehicle, you might be looking at an easy mission. Once you get inside the facility, it's just a matter of locating the right warehouse. Everything is stacked for quick access. You load up as much food as possible and lock up on the way out. Nobody will notice a few missing pallets of B-rats or MREs."

"You make it sound so easy," said Alex. "Like nobody else has thought of this."

"You can recon the area and decide if it's a go."

"I don't have enough gas to be driving back and forth between reconnaissance trips."

"Staff Sergeant Taylor can top you off and give you extra cans of gas," said Grady. "He'll give you a ROTAC, too. Sanitized, of course."

"How many sanitized radios does the battalion have at this point?" said Alex.

"As many as we can get away with creating," said Grady, hoping Alex didn't press him on why.

"I see," Alex replied. "I'll take the fuel and the radio, but I need to run this by Kate and the others."

Grady sensed a shift in Alex's tone. He'd gone flat, possibly putting together the pieces that didn't fit.

"Sounds like a plan, Alex," said Grady. "I'll work on acquiring the codes and location."

"I can't wait," said Alex. "And, Sean?"

Here it comes. No way this got past him.

"Yeah?" said Grady.

"Can you do me a favor and let Harrison Campbell know what's about to happen?" Alex asked. "He knows where to find me if he's interested in getting ahead of the storm."

Or heading straight into it.

"I'll send someone to give him a heads-up. You sure you want more mouths to feed?" asked Grady.

"If Harrison Campbell decides to join us, our situation would drastically improve," said Alex. "I'll be in touch shortly."

"Sounds good, Alex. Stay safe," said Grady, disconnecting the call.

He leaned back in his folding chair, staring at the RRZ Authority compound on the other side of the airport. Alex's call had been sheer providence. Medina's recent actions didn't add up, and Grady suspected there was more to the impending RRZ relocation than the military commanders had been told. He selected a preset call sign on his "sanitized" ROTAC and pressed send. Colonel Richard Martin, 4th Brigade Combat Team's commanding officer, answered immediately.

"What's up, Sean?"

"I'm pretty sure I've found an untraceable way to verify our problem," said Grady.

"A reliable way?"

"As reliable as it gets. A good friend," said Grady.

"He may not be your friend when this is over."

"He'll understand," said Grady. "Either way, he should be insulated from the fallout."

"If this is what we think—nobody will be insulated."

"Let's hope he finds what he's looking for," said Grady.

Chapter 26

Belgrade, Maine

Alex slumped into the couch facing the floor-to-ceiling windows overlooking the deck and the lake. He looked weary, but not from physical work. Mentally exasperated might be a more accurate description. Within the span of three days, he'd seen one plan after another crumble beneath them.

Kate sensed a big decision hinging on this conversation, which jaded her perception of his state of mind. Conflicted?

The boat wasn't an option, which meant they were staying. But Alex seemed unsettled. She could see it on his face. He was about to propose something that wouldn't sit well with any of them, especially her. She glanced at Alex's father, imperceptibly raising an eyebrow. He returned the gesture with a similarly subtle tightening of his lips. Amy Fletcher caught their exchange and shook her head.

"What's going on?" demanded Alex's mom. "Why all the secret looks?"

"Nana's on a tear this morning," said Ryan, setting a glass of water on the coffee table and sitting next to Kate.

"Never mind, young man," said Amy Fletcher. "Your father looks like he's seen a ghost, and your mom is twitching her eyes at your grandpa. Something's up."

Kate was glad Amy jumped in. Alex might have sat there for ten minutes, grimacing and winding up for what he had to say. Alex's mother leaned forward in the leather armchair next to the flagstone fireplace and raised her palms. "Well?"

"Well what, Mom?" Alex said testily. "Is it possible for you to settle down a little?"

"No, it's not. I'm hungry and cranky. Lunch is simmering, and I'd like to eat."

Alex rolled his eyes, and Kate almost laughed. Alex and his mom had been at each other since they reduced the food rations. Neither one of them had responded well to the cutback, which had provided plenty of comical moments in the house. Kate and Tim had shared hundreds of "looks" over the past month, as the two of them bickered about every possible mundane facet of living.

"All right, you two," said Tim. "What are we looking at, Alex?"

Alex weighed his thoughts and started, "There might be an easy way to solve our food problem."

"Nothing easy is worth having," said Tim.

"I think it's 'nothing worth having comes easy,'" Amy corrected.

"I was just saying," said Tim, shaking his head.

"Well, you have to get it right if you're going to say it," said Amy.

"I'm living with the Bickertons," muttered Alex, causing Ryan to laugh.

"Anyway. What is this supposedly easy way to solve the food issue?" said Kate. "Before the three of you kill each other—over food."

"It involves a trip to the Bangor area," said Alex, grimacing.

"That sounds risky," said Kate.

"We'd be on the interstate for most of the trip," Alex explained, "which is probably the safest way to travel."

"Most of the trip," stated Tim.

"Most of it. The rest will be spent on local roads, presumably well outside of Bangor city limits, searching for a storage facility."

Ryan shifted uncomfortably on the couch next to Kate, avoiding eye contact. Alex was omitting way more than he was including in his description of the trip.

"Just a storage facility?" Kate asked.

"Doesn't sound too bad. How far away from the interstate?" said Tim.

"I don't know yet, Dad—and it's not any old storage facility. Something a little different," said Alex, meeting Kate's eyes. "And a lot bigger."

"What are we talking about?" she asked.

"A battalion-sized Category Five load-out depot. Probably twenty to thirty warehouses of gear and supplies. Untouched. There's enough food in a depot like that to feed five to six hundred soldiers for thirty days," said Alex.

Tim Fletcher whistled. Kate had to admit, it sounded like a tempting prospect. With the SUV, Jeep, and trailer, they could load up enough food to last another winter. Possibly more. They might even consider two trips. Two years of food security. It sounded too good to be true.

"Untouched?" said Kate. "How is that possible?"

"A crazy set of circumstances," said Alex. "One of the soldiers we ran into yesterday said something odd. It led me to believe that the battalion based out of Bangor hadn't been issued their category five equipment," said Alex, explaining the rest of his conversation with Lieutenant Colonel Grady.

Kate processed the story, analyzing the variables and identifying potential risks or flaws in their logic. Overall, it seemed like a relatively low-risk venture, as long as Alex approached the facility with caution. Still, a few aspects of the mission didn't add up.

"Why doesn't Grady send someone to check it out?" asked Kate.

"This is the only way it stays a secret long enough for us to take what we need," said Alex.

"Doesn't he have a few vehicles without tracking devices?" she said.

"Yeah, but, I don't know, honey. This has to be easier than trying to sneak an armored vehicle two hundred miles through Maine. We'll do this carefully. If anything seems out of place, we bolt," said Alex.

"Assuming it's not too late," said Kate.

"I can't imagine we'll run into a problem. If the facility is being used, we'll know before we get too close. My biggest concern is attracting the wrong kind of attention from locals," said Alex.

"Nothing we can't handle," Ryan said.

Kate shared a quick look with Alex.

"Nothing we want to handle," said Alex. "The name of the game is avoidance, Mr. Ryan."

"I was just saying," said his son.

"Well, you won't have to worry about that," said Kate.

Before Ryan could respond, Alex shook his head and pointed at their son. "Ryan's coming," said Alex. "We need two people per vehicle."

"Take your new neighbor friend," Kate suggested, "or your dad."

"Hey, why did I get listed behind the neighbor?" Tim groused.

"I'm going, Mom," said Ryan. "Dad and I are a team. It's already decided."

Kate shook her head. "I don't want the two of you out there."

"Why not?" Ryan persisted.

Kate didn't want to answer.

"She doesn't want to lose both of you," said Amy. "I know where she's coming from."

"We'll be fine, Mom. Seriously, it's a one-hour drive each way. I'll keep Dad out of trouble."

"I need Ryan, Kate. He's far more observant than either Charlie or Ed, and we won't take any unnecessary chances. I promise."

"You were about to say that he's better in a gunfight," said Kate.

"Firefight," Ryan corrected.

"Same thing," she said, glaring at her son.

"I'm a lot more careful with him around," said Alex. "Plus I feel safer."

"You better not let anything happen to my boy."

Tim chuckled. "I have a feeling Ryan is the one keeping tabs on his dad."

Kate appreciated their attempts to lighten the conversation, but she wasn't in the mood for the distraction. Her analytical mind wasn't finished with the scenario. "We have enough gas for this?" she asked.

"Staff Sergeant Taylor filled up the SUV and gave us twenty additional gallons. Waterville to Bangor is fifty-five miles. Depending on the exact location of the storage site, we could be looking at a one hundred to one hundred and twenty mile round trip," Alex told her. "We'll be in good shape, even if the mission is a bust. Taylor sends his best, by the way."

"How did he get stuck in Searsport?"

"Luck of the draw," said Alex. "Plus he's one of the best staff NCOs in the battalion."

"Why can't they make the trip? Never mind. Tracking devices. Big brother again."

Big brother. Huh. She started to form a thought; then Amy stood up from her seat.

"What else?" asked Amy. "I'm starving."

"What are you cooking up?" Tim asked.

"Everyone's favorite. Savory stroganoff and barbeque beans with natural bacon flavor."

"Yeah, everyone's favorite," Alex repeated flatly.

Kate stifled a laugh. "I sure as hell hope you find something other than freeze-dried food in one of those warehouses."

"Careful what you wish for," said Alex. "We're looking at B-rations and MREs. After about twenty days of those, you'll be begging for savory stroganoff."

They all laughed, except for Kate. Something bugged her about the whole deal, though it did seem to be pretty straightforward. Not a lot of "moving parts," as Alex would say.

"When will you leave?" she asked.

"As soon as Grady sends me the location and the codes to access the facility."

"I don't like the fact that he's doing this on the sly. Something doesn't add up."

"It's funny you say that," said Alex. "I kind of had the same feeling when I was talking to him."

"Maybe you need to trust your instincts."

"My instincts say we have to take the chance," said Alex. "Otherwise, we'll have to think seriously about taking Grady up on his offer to station Marines here. We know that's not a good option."

"If this trip doesn't pan out, we'll have to consider it."

Chapter 27

Belgrade, Maine

Alex and Ryan looked ready for a small war—in stark contrast to Ed's interpretation of their "road trip" north. He'd anticipated the rifles, but not the full military load out. Tactical vests, thigh holsters, dozens of extra magazines, night vision. Not at all what he expected. Certainly not what he had been led to believe, or he wouldn't have been so quick to approve of the trip. He gave the trailer hitch coupler lever a tug to make sure it was secure before stepping away from the Jeep.

"Did I miss the war declaration?" Ed asked wryly, shrugging his shoulders.

"You're still funny," said Alex, smiling as he patted the hand guard of his rifle. "Just a precaution. I really don't expect a problem, but I'm not taking any chances. Not with something this important."

Ed shook his head, breaking a grin. "Charlie's gonna throw a fit. I told him civilian clothes and a stripped-down rifle. This could add an hour to our departure."

"Mr. Walker, is Chloe inside?" Ryan inquired.

"She's out back, but I don't want...I think you might scare her looking like that," said Ed. "Can it wait until we get back?"

Ryan's eyes darted between the house and Ed. "Sure, Mr. Walker. Sorry. I didn't think about that."

He looked genuinely apologetic and extremely disappointed.

"No worries, Ryan. I didn't expect your dad to show up dressed like a Navy SEAL," said Ed, winking.

The front door of his cottage slammed with a sharp crack, announcing Charlie's arrival. Without looking in Charlie's direction, he patted Alex's shoulder.

"Don't antagonize him, please," said Ed, getting the words in before Charlie started his diatribe.

"What the hell? Why do I look like I'm going to church, and the Fletchers are dressed for prolonged combat operations?" said Charlie, jogging up to them.

"We took a vote and decided to suit up the most capable in the group," said Alex.

"What?" Charlie stomped.

"Alex," Ed warned. "Don't."

"Just kidding, my friend. I made a last minute decision to enhance the group's security posture," said Alex, checking his watch. "We have time if you want to bump it up a few notches."

"I *told* you," said Charlie, pointing at Ed. "Be back in a few minutes."

"Before you go, let's take a quick look at the map. I just got the coordinates and access codes from Grady. Looks even easier than I originally thought," said Alex. "Closer at least. Grab your map, Ed."

Alex pulled a folded map out of one of the pouches on his vest and expanded it on the hood of the Jeep. When everyone was situated around the map, he pointed to an area northwest of Bangor International Airport. A pencil mark was visible near the end of a road that appeared to stop at the western boundary of the airport.

"Mark this on your map, Ed," said Alex.

Ed reached into the front seat and grabbed his map, refolding it so the airport was centered in the middle of the compact map area. He laid it on top of Alex's and copied the location with a pen from his pocket. Alex watched him with a pained look.

"What?" said Ed.

"Using a pen on a map—ughh," said Alex.

"Marine Corps no-no? Sorry, I didn't have a chance to run to Staples to buy office supplies," said Ed, finishing his sacred transgression against the map. "Runway Road looks like a dead end."

"It'd be easy to box us in there," said Charlie.

"Yeah. We'll have to make an assessment when we turn off New Boston Road. It's a quarter of a mile from the turnoff to the point where Grady said we should find the first gate leading to the facility on the left side of the road," said Alex, shifting his finger to an area north of the road. "The storage depot is up here somewhere."

"You sure you want to do this during daylight hours?" said Charlie.

"I don't want to be dicking around in the dark—especially on unfamiliar ground. We'll push our arrival as close to sunset as possible, so we don't have to use our lights going in. I presume we'll be coming out of there after dark. Is everyone good with that?"

Nobody had a problem with the plan, which didn't surprise Ed. The drive from the interstate to the storage site looked easy enough. Maybe five to six miles tops, depending on which interstate exit they used. Keeping the lights off on the way in was important. Few things would draw more attention than a pair of headlights, and the last thing they wanted to do was attract any local attention. Alex had no idea how long it might take them to locate

178

the food once they reached the warehouse depot. If people from one of the nearby neighborhoods decided to investigate, they'd have an audience on their hands at the facility. The less distance between the interstate and the storage site, the better.

"Which exit do you anticipate taking?" asked Ed.

"Probably the Cold Brook Road exit. I don't want to jump off the interstate any sooner than necessary. The exit before Cold Brook will require us to snake through a handful of rural roads to find Route 2," said Alex.

"I was just going to say that we should keep this as simple as possible," said Ed.

Alex nodded. "I agree. It's a fairly straight shot to New Boston Road from Cold Brook. Three turns in total. Easy deal if we get separated."

"We don't separate," said Ed, wondering why he would say something like that.

"Not on purpose, but we need to consider every possibility. If we find ourselves separated and unable to communicate via radio, I say we get on the interstate and head south to the Hampden Road exit. Go a little past the exit and pull to the side of the interstate," said Alex.

"What if one of us is forced to take Route 2 past that exit?"

"Then you keep going and head home," Alex replied. "Whoever makes it to the exit waits an hour and returns to base."

"This group doesn't separate," said Ed. "Under any circumstances."

Alex shook his head.

"Now what?" said Ed. "Did I violate another sacred Marine Corps rule?"

Alex grinned. "No. You just reminded that I almost

forgot the most important rule. Never leave a Marine behind, or in this case, never leave a friend behind. We stay together no matter what."

Chapter 28

Hermon, Maine

Interstate 95 had been empty…and not in a two o'clock in the morning, sparse traffic kind of way. They'd seen nothing. Not a single car, stopped or moving, on either side of the four-lane highway for fifty-three miles. It was the loneliest feeling Alex could recall—ever. For the first time since waking up on his sailboat to a bizarre purplish-red glowing sky, he felt pangs of hopelessness.

The rapidly approaching green sign read Exit 180 Cold Brook Rd. Hermon. Hampden. They were less than fifteen minutes from the moment of truth. Alex glanced at his watch. 7:08 PM. They were cutting it close. Sunset was in thirty-four minutes.

"Radio Charlie and let him know this is the exit," said Alex.

Ryan grabbed the radio from the center console while Alex scanned the off-ramp ahead. They had heard reports over the HAM radio that some of the towns along the turnpike had erected barricades to dissuade travelers from exiting. Of course, they'd heard this during the late fall, when they could still power the radio with the deep cycle batteries they had brought from the Limerick compound.

He doubted any of these blockades were still active at this point. There was nobody on the road to stop. Winter had effectively sealed everyone in place—permanently.

For most civilians, where you stood today was most likely where you'd stand a year from now. Maybe longer.

"They're good, Dad," said Ryan.

Alex eased the car onto the ramp, glancing in his rearview mirror to confirm that Ed followed. The turn tightened after the shallow exit drive, bringing them several hundred feet away from the interstate and eventually winding left to reveal distant stop signs flanking the road. They arrived at Cold Brook Road, searching for signs of activity. Like the highway, the town of Hampden, Maine, appeared dormant.

"Looks clear," said Ryan, staring south with binoculars.

"Fucking ghost town," muttered Alex, staring at the empty gas station and variety store across the street. "Make sure they stay really close." He accelerated north onto Cold Brook Road.

When they crossed over the turnpike, Alex glanced out of the driver's side window at the empty highway. Ahead of them, a sprawling complex of oversized gas stations and long, one-story garages appeared, surrounded by dozens of what he assumed were abandoned semitrailers. As they cruised past the once popular truck stop, Alex scanned for signs of recent activity. He noticed a few of the red gas tank covers next to one of the stations sat overturned on the asphalt, a clear indication that the underground tanks had been pumped dry.

Smart. Without electricity, the station wouldn't be able to pump the gas without an independent generator. Depending on when they were last filled before the event, the tanks represented a sizable cache of different fuels—from diesel to premium-unleaded gasoline. Most stations held up to 40,000 gallons of fuel, but an interstate stop like this might hold twice as much, the difference represented by the diesel fuel greedily consumed by semitrailers. He wondered who had arrived to pump the fuel. The state? Someone like Eli Russell?

He kept the cars moving north toward Route 2, passing a tall, dark gray silo set amidst a sea of one-story warehouses, local businesses, and empty parking lots. The area looked untouched by time, which was mostly true. Few people had likely visited this road since winter arrived.

By the time they reached Route 2, the businesses had given way to modest homes set back from the road. In another month or two, thick foliage from the trees and bushes would obscure most of the houses from the two-lane road.

"Mr. Thornton says it's creepy up here," said Ryan.

"He isn't joking," said Alex, keeping conversation to a minimum so his son could concentrate.

Just above the horizon, the sun was a deep red globe surrounded by fiery orange clouds when they turned onto New Boston Road. The north-south orientation of the pine-tree-lined road yielded a deep canopy of shadows. If they had arrived fifteen minutes later, he might have reconsidered their headlights ban. Alex impatiently watched the digital odometer measure the mile and a half to Runway Road. He also counted about twenty driveways before they reached their final turn, surprised to find so many homes on a crumbling road near one of the business ends of the airport.

He slowed at a stop sign next to a red, two-story barn, looking in each direction along Runway Road before turning right. They were on the final stretch. Alex's stomach tightened as the car accelerated past several widely spaced mobile homes situated parallel to the road. The road deteriorated once they passed the last trailer home, bits of asphalt rattling around the SUV's wheel wells. Tall pine trees flanked the road, followed on the right side by a string of worn electrical poles. Someone had decided to run electricity beyond the last cluster of houses on Runway Road.

Using the same trick his son had used at Johnny's Seeds, he watched for the point where the electrical lines crossed the road, figuring it would lead them to the storage site turnoff. Less than a minute later, despite the growing darkness, he spotted the lines.

"I bet that's it," he said, slowing the SUV.

The overhead lines approached, and he knew they were in the right place. The trees opened on the left side of the road, revealing a wide asphalt reinforced turnoff leading into the forest. The turnoff was clearly designed to accommodate large, multi-axle vehicles coming in or out of the hidden storage. Alex turned the SUV and pointed at the sturdy road penetrating the forest, activating his high beams. Roughly a hundred feet down the road, a chain-link cantilever gate shined in the darkness.

"This is it," he said, shutting off the lights.

He glanced over his shoulder, seeing that Ed had brought the Jeep to a stop at the edge of the turnoff, hopefully keeping an eye on the road they had just travelled.

"I'm going to reposition Ed and Charlie. They'll watch the entrance while we recon the site."

"Got it," said Ryan, reaching between the front seats and lifting his rifle out of the rear passenger foot well. "Mind if I check out the gate?"

"That's fine. Bring the NVGs and scan as far forward as possible, but don't go past the gate," said Alex. "And watch yourself. We have no idea what we're going to find here."

"Yep," said Ryan, getting out of the car.

Alex turned the car off and opened the door, standing outside for several moments, listening. Beyond the low rumble of the Jeep's engine, all he detected was the light rustle of the pines in the breeze. He signaled for Ed to stop the Jeep's engine. Moments later, the sound of the pine boughs intensified, no longer masked by the Jeep's idling engine. He closed his eyes and listened. Absolutely nothing.

Ryan appeared on the other side of the SUV's hood, strapping a pair of NVGs over a backward-facing, olive green ball cap. He looked calm, but serious. The past nine months had prematurely stripped away the child, leaving an undeveloped adult behind. The transition had been too quick. Ryan filled the void by embracing the warrior culture, the only thing he knew since the event. The result had been chilling, more for Alex than Kate, because he recognized the façade Ryan wore, day in and day out.

He'd seen it on the faces of the young Marines in Iraq, who had been completely unprepared for what they'd seen on the road to Baghdad. A disaffected mask of calm confidence and bravado. It wasn't a bad thing. They'd all worn the mask at one point or another. None of them had been prepared for the horrors they'd experienced, just like his son couldn't have known that he'd wake up in Boston one morning to a changed world. Ryan had responded better than Alex expected; he would have been a good Marine officer. He wore the mask better than most.

"Careful, and use your radio headset," said Alex.

Ryan nodded enthusiastically, removing a wired earpiece from one of the pouches on his vest. Alex did the same, testing his radio. When they were on the same channel, Ryan walked down the access road, his rifle in the patrol carry position. Alex jogged over to the Jeep.

"Where's Ryan going?" Ed asked, glancing nervously around at the trees.

"There's a gate about a hundred feet down the road," said Alex. "He's going to check it out."

"Is that a good idea?"

"He's not going any farther than the gate," said Alex.

He glanced across the front seat at Charlie, who was watching the road behind them with binoculars.

"How does it look back there?" Alex asked him.

"Looks clear. We didn't see a soul on the way in," said Charlie. "It's almost like they evacuated this part of the state."

"Looks can be deceiving. I'm sure there are plenty of folks around," said Alex. "The sooner we get out of here, the better."

"I'm almost wondering if we can't make two trips."

"The thought crossed my mind," said Alex. "We have enough gas, though it would pretty much exhaust our supply. Let's see how the first trip goes before we start making plans for a second."

"I just want to get the hell out of here," said Ed. "Can we move this along?"

"Not a bad idea. I was thinking you should park facing the way we came, so you could keep an eye on the road while we make our way down to the site," said Alex. "Just in case we attracted any unwanted attention on the drive in."

"Are you planning on driving the rest of the way in?" asked Charlie, eyes still peering through the binoculars.

"I think we should be fine driving down. There's nothing out here. We'll talk on our primary channel," said Alex, tapping the handheld radio clipped to his vest. "You still have the piece of paper with the gate codes?"

"No, Alex. The paper flew out of my hands while we were speeding up the turnpike. I didn't want to say anything," said Charlie.

Ed chuckled.

"Sorry. Old habit, I guess," said Alex, pausing for a second. "Not that I couldn't picture you losing the codes."

"Nice," mumbled Charlie.

"Don't worry, Alex. We got this covered," said Ed. "I'm keeping a close eye on Scarface here."

"Scarface? Where did that come from?" said Charlie.

"Oh boy," mumbled Alex.

"I distinctly remember you yelling, 'Say hello to my little friend,' when Eli Russell's crew was rushing the cottage," said Ed.

Charlie shook his head. "I don't think I said that."

"My wife heard you say it," said Ed. "Pretty much everyone heard you say it."

"I highly doubt I'd say something like that," insisted Charlie. "I haven't seen that movie in years."

"Just like the good ole days," said Alex. "I miss this."

"How about I put him in your car for the drive back?" said Ed.

"Hey!" Charlie protested. "I have feelings too."

Ed laughed. "We'll be waiting for your call."

Chapter 29

Bangor, Maine

Alex walked ahead of the creeping SUV, approaching the gate with a small notepad in his left hand. His other hand swept a powerful LED flashlight beam back and forth, searching for anything out of place. Several feet in front of the gate, he stopped in front of a black box mounted to the side of a thick metal pole. After checking for obvious booby traps, he lifted the latches on the box and opened the weather-sealed cover, revealing an illuminated keypad. Holding the notebook next to the keypad, he pressed the fifteen-digit code—followed by the # sign. The gate rumbled on its track, retracting into the forest on the right side of the road.

He wasn't sure if this was a good sign or a bad one. Anything connected to the grid's power distribution system would be vulnerable to the massive energy surge created by the electromagnetic pulse, so Alex assumed the gate was connected to an independent battery pack, something sizable and long lasting. Unfortunately, he wasn't familiar enough with the Category Five storage facilities to be sure. For all he knew, on-demand generators at the storage site powered the gates. He didn't care either way, as long as the site was still abandoned.

"The first gate is open. We're heading through. Any

new developments out front?" Alex asked, stepping through the gate opening.

"Negative," said Charlie. "It's dark and quiet."

"Perfect. Let's hope it stays that way," said Alex, waving Ryan forward. "I don't know how far this road goes into the forest. Hopefully not too far. It's even darker in here."

"We're ready if you need us," said Charlie.

"Sounds good. Fingers crossed, guys," said Alex.

"And toes," Charlie added.

Alex crossed behind the SUV and jumped in the front passenger seat, sticking his rifle through the open window. Ryan kept his head forward, watching the road in front of them through the NVGs.

"Anything?" asked Alex.

"Has to be a turn up there somewhere. I've got a wall of trees across the road in the distance," said Ryan.

"That's kind of what I figured," said Alex. "Last thing they need is someone staring down the road at a bunch of warehouses."

"Just like our property in Limerick," said Ryan.

"Yeah," said Alex, remembering the nearly perfect sanctuary they were forced to leave. He adjusted his rifle, pushing the vertical fore grip against the side mirror and bracing the adjustable stock in his shoulder. "Take it slow. Fifteen miles per hour. Call out anything you see."

The SUV eased forward, its tires crackling over frequent pinecones and small branches. Every sound hit Alex's ears like a gunshot, causing him to reconsider his plan to approach the storage site perimeter by vehicle. He dismissed the thoughts as paranoia, the crunching sounds reinforcing his assessment that the road hadn't been used in months.

Alex peered into the thickening darkness ahead of the vehicle, unable to distinguish the road from the forest less than a hundred feet away.

"Definitely a left turn coming up," said Ryan.

"Got it," said Alex. "Do you need any IR illumination?"

"No. Looks like a gradual turn. Maybe two hundred feet away," said Ryan.

Alex activated his radio. "Coming up on a left turn. I'm guessing about a thousand feet from the gate. I'll throw a chemlight onto the road to mark the turn, just in case I need you to approach without lights."

"Roger," said Charlie. "Standing by."

Alex removed a chemlight from one of the pouches on his vest and waited for the turn. He spotted the turn in the last vestiges of dark blue light and cracked the green chemlight, holding it outside of the SUV so it wouldn't obscure Ryan's windshield view. When he felt the vehicle turn, Alex dropped the glow stick, leaving the marker behind.

"Can you see the chemlight?" Alex asked.

"Affirmative. Green chemlight on the road," Charlie replied. "Looks like a straight shot all the way to the turn. We could see your brake lights the whole way."

"Yeah. No surprises so far," said Alex, staring ahead as the SUV straightened out of the turn.

"I have a tall fence line coming up in maybe five hundred feet. I'm pretty sure there's a gate, but it's still a little hazy. No lights at all coming from beyond the gate," said Ryan.

"Good. Take us about a hundred feet out from the fence. I'll recon the site on foot, from the forest," said Alex, switching over to his headset.

"We have another gate coming up," said Alex. "The site looks dark."

"Copy," said Charlie.

Alex asked Ryan, "Still nothing past the fence?"

"Totally dark," said Ryan. "And definitely a second gate. I can see a keypad box on the left side."

Alex could detect the empty space between the opaque pines flanking the road, but little beyond that. The early night sky was unwilling to lend any illumination to the scene beyond the windshield. The SUV slowed, coming to a halt in the murkiness.

"We're about a hundred feet out," said Ryan.

"Shut her down for now," said Alex. "And I'll need the NVGs."

Ryan stopped the engine, pulling the keys out of the ignition. Alex opened the door and checked his gear while Ryan unstrapped the night-vision goggles.

"I'll stick pretty close to the road until I get closer to the gate," said Alex. "I want you in the woods—listening."

"We could use another pair of NVGs," said Ryan.

"We'll make sure to grab a few once we get inside," said Alex. "Among other things."

"I thought we had a strict shopping list?"

"If we find something we need in the same warehouse, we're taking it," said Alex.

"What about a Humvee?" Ryan asked, handing over the NVGs.

"I'm pretty sure they can GPS track high-end items like that, though we might consider borrowing one to transport more food."

Alex tightened the NVGs over his black watch cap and adjusted the straps until the goggles aligned with his eyes when flipped down.

"Stay out of sight, and stay on your radio," he instructed.

"Be careful, Dad."

Alex walked in front of the SUV and watched his son melt into the pine trees next to him.

"Charlie, I'm approaching the gate on foot. Get ready to move out," said Alex.

"We're ready. Still quiet up here," said Charlie.

"Roger. I'll be in touch shortly."

Alex walked briskly along the right shoulder of the road, studying the scene beyond the fence. The single-lane road formed a boulevard between two rows of warehouses. From this distance, he could see warehouses lining each side of the road. The green image faded after he counted six similarly sized structures on each side. As he closed the gap to the fence, another series of warehouses materialized in the green murk. He also noticed a twenty-foot clearing between the fence and the forest on the left side of the road. Although he couldn't see it, Alex assumed the same clear space existed on the right side of the road, forming a twenty-foot buffer around the perimeter of the fence.

The buffer made sense from a security standpoint. It prevented intruders from reaching the fence unobserved, and it sometimes signaled the presence of an electrified fence. He couldn't imagine any way in which the facility could power an electric fence without an outside electricity source, but he'd keep it in mind on the approach.

Alex pushed through the stiff pine boughs next to the road and broke into the untamed forest, immediately regretting the decision. Branches scraped his legs and

192

arms, snagging his rifle and knocking his night-vision goggles askew. This wasn't going to work. Whoever built the facility must have planted additional pines in the forest surrounding the site. He'd never seen a more tightly packed pine forest. It was nearly impassible, and any advantage he might gain from trying to observe the facility from a concealed position would be eliminated by the noise he'd make breaking through the branches. He backed out of the trees and kneeled next to the road.

"Everything all right up there?" Ryan called.

"Affirmative," said Alex. "The forest is too thick for a quiet approach. I'll wake up half of the state moving ten feet."

"I was about to call you about that," said Ryan.

"I'll approach along the road. Seems quiet enough. I'm seeing several warehouses past the fence."

Charlie responded, "Sounds like we're in business."

"Give me a few minutes to make sure we're alone," said Alex, focusing on the fence.

He passed the keypad on the other side of the road and crouched at the edge of the gap, listening for the telltale hum of an electric fence. Nothing. The fence looked fairly standard for a security perimeter. Chain link, eight to ten feet tall, topped with razor wire. Staring down the long length of the fence to the right of the gate, the tall, matted grass separating the trees from the fence looked undisturbed. If the fence had been electrified at one point, he would expect to see a few lumps, big or small, on the ground outside of the fence.

Turning his attention to the facility, he saw the entry road split left after the front gate, connecting to an additional boulevard of structures. He counted nine warehouse fronts on each side of the center thoroughfare.

Eighteen on each road, assuming the number was the same on the unobserved row. Thirty-six in total. He sure as shit hoped the food was in one of the first warehouses, or they were in for a long night.

"I'm looking at the entire facility. We have two interior roads lined with nine massive warehouses on each side. Night vision isn't registering any light sources inside the complex," said Alex.

"We could be here all night searching thirty-six warehouses," said Ed.

"We'll have to split up and search," said Alex. "I'm going to open the perimeter gate. Ed, bring the Jeep and trailer down. I think we're good to go."

"Copy that. We're on our way. Is it all right to use lights?" said Charlie.

"Wait until you reach the turn," said Alex. "See you in a few minutes. Ryan, bring up the BMW."

Alex crossed the street and flipped his night-vision goggles up. Using a small flashlight to read his notebook, he entered the same code on the keypad. The fence gate sprang to life, retracting along its metal track. He tensed, half expecting klaxon alarms to sound and bright lights to flood the perimeter. Instead, the small city of two-story-high, corrugated warehouses stood dark and silent against the thin clanging of the gate. The SUV pulled next to him.

"Go ahead and hit the lights," said Alex.

A moment later, the center boulevard was awash in the SUV's high beams, exposing a sterile concourse flanked by gray buildings. The vast sea of faded asphalt looked pristine. Untouched. He could barely believe places like this existed, waiting for a "Category Five" disaster. The whole concept still seemed wild, almost unfathomable—until last August.

"Holy shit," mumbled Ryan. "We should just move everyone here. Tell Colonel Grady we'll keep an eye on it for him."

"I'd be lying if I told you the thought didn't just cross my mind," said Alex, gawking at the buildings.

It could work, if Governor Dague didn't stumble upon the codes to open the former 3rd Battalion commanding officer's secure pod.

What are the chances of that, if she hasn't already figured it out?

Even if she searched the commanding officer's house and found the document-sized safe, only the battalion's commanding officer knew the code. He might have been required to transfer the pod and sealed codes to the unit's executive officer prior to leaving the state on vacation. Alex had no idea what type of protocol was in play here, and it didn't matter. Even the slightest risk of discovery wasn't worth taking. They would stick to the plan. He hopped on the SUV's driver's side running board and gripped the roof rack.

"Pull between the first pair of warehouses," said Alex. "Time to go shopping."

Alex jumped to the pavement when Ryan stopped the vehicle between two towering storage bay doors. Beams of light struck the face of the warehouse next to the SUV, grabbing Alex's attention. Two headlights appeared on the access road. Probably the Jeep. Alex didn't like *probably*.

"Charlie, did you just make the turn?" Alex signaled for Ryan to stay in the SUV.

"That's us," said Charlie. "Did you think someone got through us?"

"Just being cautious."

"Or a little paranoid. We're in the clear, man...holy smokes that's a big place," said Charlie.

"You're only seeing half of it," said Alex. "Pull up behind us until we figure out the best way to proceed. We're going to take a look in one of the warehouses. Get a feel for the general layout."

"Can't wait to go shopping," said Charlie. "Looks like thirty Costcos put together."

"This is better than Costco," said Alex. "More like Cabela's, for Special Forces."

"I hope so. We need some more night vision."

"See you in a minute," said Alex, turning to Ryan. "I want you wearing your helmet."

"Dad, I don't need the helmet out here," Ryan protested.

"Just do me a favor and wear it. I'd wear one too if we had extras," said Alex. "Never know what's out there."

"All right," said Ryan, killing the engine and reaching behind the seat for the ballistic helmet.

Alex and Ryan jogged to the warehouse on the passenger side of the SUV and approached the smaller entrance to the right of the massive rolling steel door. A covered keypad greeted them where the doorknob should be. Alex pulled the crumpled notepad out of one of his cargo pockets and flipped on the flashlight, punching a new fifteen-digit code into the keypad. He paused before hitting the # key.

"Stay at the door and watch our six when I go inside," said Alex, pressing the final key.

The door clicked, opening inward several inches. Alex pushed the door gently, illuminating a sliver of the pitch-black warehouse with his flashlight. A short buzz sounded inside the building, causing Alex to douse the flashlight and raise his rifle. He aimed through the dark two-foot crack, waiting for more input. A hollow, jolting sound echoed from the interior, immediately followed by the steady, industrial hum of a generator. Bright lights replaced the darkness beyond the partially closed door, clunking as they activated row by row, back to front.

"I keep waiting for the other shoe to drop," said Alex.

"What does that even mean?" asked Ryan.

"I have no idea," said Alex, pushing the door open.

He couldn't see it at first. Alex took several steps into the well-lit warehouse, his mind simply refusing to acknowledge the obvious. He squinted like it was an optical illusion until it finally registered.

There's nothing here. Oh, fuck!

"Turn the car around. I want it facing the gate," said Alex.

Ryan aimed his rifle in the direction of the other warehouses on the road. "What's going on?"

"It's empty. I'm checking the one on the other side. If it's empty, we're getting the fuck out of here."

Alex sprinted past the SUV, ignoring Charlie, who was yelling something from the approaching Jeep. He punched the code into the keypad and kicked the door after it opened, directing his flashlight inside. A bare concrete floor and rows of empty industrial-sized shelves stared back at him.

Motherfucker.

Grady had used them. He was back on the asphalt before the warehouse's generator started, running toward Ed's Jeep.

"Get in the SUV now!" he said. "We have to leave."

"What are you talking about!" yelled Ed, pounding the hood of the Jeep.

"The warehouses are empty, and Grady fucking knew it. He just needed us to confirm it," said Alex, mumbling the rest. "I knew there was something wrong with this. Fuck."

"I don't see why we're leaving the—" started Ed.

"If they can see that we opened the gates or the warehouses, we need to get as far away from here as possible. Right now! In one vehicle! We don't have time to fuck with the trailer. Let's go!" he said, pushing Charlie toward the SUV.

Ryan completed a three-point turn between the buildings, stopping in front of them.

"Ed, you drive!" yelled Alex. "Charlie behind the driver. Ryan behind me."

"Why am I driving?" asked Ed.

"You want to shoot instead?" said Alex.

"Come on! I think you're overreacting here," said Ed, pulling the front door open for Ryan.

"If I'm overreacting, we can come back and get the Jeep. Right now, we're getting the fuck out of here—together. Trust me on this," said Alex, walking behind the SUV.

He freed his rifle from the sling ready position and smashed its buttstock into the taillight housing, hitting the plastic cover repeatedly until he was certain that the bulbs were shattered. Pieces of red and white plastic trickled onto the pavement at his feet.

"What the fuck are you doing?" yelled Ed.

"Smashing the brake lights!"

He aimed the buttstock at the aerodynamic fin above the lift gate's window. He hit the thick plastic fin, which resisted the rifle strike. His next blow skimmed off the fin and spider cracked the window below it.

"Press the brake pad!" yelled Alex.

Light from the fin's imbedded taillight enveloped him in a red aura. He hit the plastic piece three times, until the light failed, turning the buttstock's attention to the entire rear window. A few solid blows broke through the safety glass, covering the road in hundreds of small, opaque pieces.

"Let's go!" he said to Ed, who stood next to the open driver's door, mumbling obscenities.

Ed climbed in and slammed the door. Alex slid into the passenger seat and buckled his seat belt, verifying that all of the doors had been shut.

"Your job is to get us to the interstate," he said, patting Ed on the shoulder. "Windows down and rifles out. I have a bad feeling about this ride."

When they reached the perimeter fence, Alex held his breath, exhaling when the gate started moving along the track. He wouldn't have been the least bit surprised if the gate had remained in place, locking them inside. As Ed edged the SUV up to the painfully slow gate, Alex swiped the ROTAC from the center console.

Chapter 30

Main Operating Base "Sanford"
Regional Recovery Zone 1

Lieutenant Colonel Grady sat in the troop compartment of a UH-60M Black Hawk helicopter at the far western edge of the main tarmac, alternating glances between his ROTAC and the RRZ authority compound framed by the compartment door window. Staff Sergeant Jackson sat directly across from him in the main troop compartment, which held six more combat-loaded Marines.

His Black Hawk sat at the end of a staggered line of six helicopters waiting mission approval to fly north. Orders that would originate from Grady when Fletcher called with final verification that the storage facility was empty. Of course, Alex might not call at all. If the warehouses were empty, as they suspected, Alex would immediately know that he'd been conned into visiting the storage complex. He might smash the ROTAC and speed off, knowing damn well that Grady needed the information.

Anything was possible with Alex, which was why the commanding officer of a Marine infantry battalion was watching his phone like a giddy teenage boy after a text to his high school crush.

Come on, Alex.

A voice materialized in his headset. "Colonel, we'll

have to shut down and top off if we don't launch in five minutes," said the pilot. "I can go cold now to save fuel. In *ready launch* I can have us in the air within two minutes."

"Negative. Should be any minute now," said Grady.

Damn. Maybe he'd played the schedule too tightly. He'd received a text message from Alex when they were a mile from the interstate exit, which put the verification phone call a minimum of ten minutes out. He figured Alex would be careful approaching the site, so he added another ten to fifteen minutes to the timeline. They'd started the helicopters when the text message arrived, waiting ten minutes before loading the Marines. Ten minutes would give all of the RRZ folks enough time to hear the helicopters and ask their questions about the unscheduled flight operation.

Tower controllers, pilots, and ground personnel in the hangars had been briefed to say it was scheduled engine maintenance; thirty minutes to run live diagnostics. The Marines entered the tarmac from a gate on the western fence line, using the closest hangar to mask their approach to the helicopters. With the port-side troop compartment doors closed, RRZ security officers or observers within the walled compound couldn't see inside the helicopters. If they could, they would undoubtedly raise further questions.

Grady peered through his window at the row of dark, open hangars facing the RRZ compound. Armored vehicles lingered in the shadows, waiting for the order to speed across a recently cleared section of eastern tarmac toward the main RRZ compound gate. Additional vehicles hid behind the cluster of tents between the primary runway and auxiliary taxiway. In undisclosed locations, snipers sighted-in on the visible security officers, ready to take them out if they fired on the approaching soldiers. When the order was passed, a reinforced company of infantry soldiers would descend on the compound, with the ultimate goal of detaining Medina and her staff. All of this hinged on a phone call from Alex Fletcher, which was ten minutes overdue.

Almost on cue, his ROTAC vibrated, dragging his eyes from the menacing hangars.

"Grady," he answered, knowing he was about to take an earful.

"That's all you can manage?" Alex snapped.

"Alex, I don't have time to explain what's going on. I just need to know if the warehouses were empty," said Grady. "We can sort out the rest later."

"The rest?" said Alex, and the line went quiet.

"Alex?" said Grady.

"The first two were empty. We didn't stick around to check the rest," said Alex.

Grady turned to the second lieutenant seated next to him and nodded emphatically. The young officer passed the confirmation order over the mission's primary VHF frequency, instantly telling designated units that Operation Quick Switch had entered the final execution phase.

"Where are you now?" said Grady.

"Driving as fast as fucking possible to get out of here," said Alex. "Who has the equipment? I get the impression it's not Governor Dague's people."

The helicopter jolted as the landing gear left the tarmac. Through the window next to Grady, the murky tarmac drifted away, dark silhouettes racing across the airfield toward the RRZ compound, and flashes erupted from the main gate. The Black Hawk tilted forward and gained speed, quickly leaving behind the scene below.

"Hello?" Alex prompted.

"We just launched an assault on the RRZ compound. I'm in a Black Hawk headed to Augusta to secure Governor Dague," said Grady. "It's a little hectic over here."

"Sorry if this is a bad time for you, Sean, but I'm a little worried about making *hard contact* on my way out of here. What am I looking at?"

"Paramilitary types. Government sponsored, so most likely professional security contractors," said Grady.

"Most likely? Wait a minute, you don't fucking *know*?"

"We've received reports of similar groups being used in other trouble spots. We think they arrived a month or so ago," said Grady.

"How did they get here?" said Alex.

"We're not one hundred percent sure. RRZ compound security was augmented about a month ago with personnel and vehicles from a C-17 Globemaster. 4th Brigade's Prophet system picked up encrypted UHF signals from the west at the same time. The signals changed position rapidly, heading north. We think additional aircraft delivered the rest of the group. Possibly by parachute," said Grady.

"How many?"

"Four to five hundred would be consistent with reports from other military commanders," said Grady.

"Five hundred? That's a small army, Sean."

Grady heard him talking in the background of the phone call.

"Sean, if we're caught, our families will be in serious danger. I can't believe you did this to us!"

"Alex, it was the only way to get eyes on the warehouse without tipping off the RRZ," Grady explained. "Medina was on the cusp of launching something big against the state, and she didn't trust the military."

"Yeah, well, I kind of understand where she's coming from," said Alex.

"I wouldn't leave your ass totally hanging in the breeze, Alex. Two of my sanitized Matvees will arrive in your neighborhood within five minutes. I have a squad of Marines watching over your families. Two of my helicopters will continue to your position to provide support. They've been armed with hellfire missiles in case you run into any armored vehicles," said Grady. "I'm sorry it had to go down like this, but I knew you wouldn't agree to check out the site if I leveled with you."

"I can't eat an apology, Sean. If we pull through this intact, I better be looking at enough MREs to build a floating dock across the lake."

"I'll personally deliver them, Alex. Get your ass south on the turnpike and run like the devil. Two Black Hawks will contact you when they hit Waterville in roughly thirty minutes."

"Shit. We have company," said Alex, followed by frantic yelling on the line.

"Alex? You there? Alex!"

The call disconnected. Thirty minutes might be too long. Grady pressed the transmit button on his headset.

"Contact Hellfire zero-five and zero-six. Tell them to proceed north at maximum speed. Troops in contact," said Grady.

Chapter 31

Main Operating Base "Sanford"
Regional Recovery Zone 1

Bethany Medina stood in front of a row of glowing computer monitors, speaking rapidly into her ROTAC.

"I just received a call from Homeland telling me that 3rd Battalion, 172nd Infantry Regiment's Category Five storage site has been accessed."

"With the codes?" asked Jerold Berkoff.

She wanted to call him 'Jerkoff' so bad she had to pause.

"Yes, Berkoff. I didn't say *breached*. I said *accessed*."

No wonder none of this was working. The RRZ had thrown one incompetent idiot after another in her lap.

"I don't have any personnel at the site, ma'am," said Berkoff. "I don't know what to tell you."

"How about telling me 'I'll get someone out there right away to check it out,'" said Medina. "I need to know who's out there."

"Copy that. I have a team close to the site," said Berkoff. "What are my rules of engagement?"

"I want to know who sent them—how they got the codes. Detain and interrogate using any and all means at your disposal. Time is critical," said Medina. "And, Berkoff?"

"Yeah?"

"Put all of your teams on ready alert. We may have to execute the plan tonight."

"Do you want me to pre-stage any of the teams closer to their targets?" he asked.

Medina considered the question carefully. Putting unfamiliar military-grade vehicles on the streets, even for a short time, might draw the wrong kind of attention from Dague's expansive network of observers. On the flip side, the storage-site intrusion represented a significant, immediate problem. She had to assume that the perpetrators knew exactly what they were looking for—a battalion-sized weapons and equipment load out. When they found the warehouses empty, all bets were off, especially if Colonel Martin or Lieutenant Colonel Grady were behind this.

That was the worst-case scenario. She'd have to move fast to remove Dague and the state government before the military could formulate a response to the missing cache of gear. The best-case scenario involved Governor Dague somehow uncovering the codes and finding the warehouses empty. She'd probably blame the RRZ and somehow overreact, giving Medina a good reason to take action with the Counter-Insurrection Battalion.

The muted crackle of sporadic gunfire reached her ears, drawing her attention to the communication center's door.

"Ma'am, do you want me to pre-stage any of the teams?" Berkoff repeated.

The gunfire grew more consistent.

"Negative. Just send the team to investigate," she said, ending the call.

Voices and rustling chairs filled the hallway as staccato

bursts of heavy-caliber machine-gun fire sounded. She started to wonder if the airport was under militia attack again, but dismissed the thought before it wasted any mental space. She didn't believe in coincidences. Less than five minutes ago, someone had accessed a hidden top-secret weapons cache site in northern Maine. A site she had emptied a month ago. No. This wasn't a coincidence.

Medina opened the door and poked her head into the hallway. Ian McEyre, her chief of staff, ran down the hallway toward her, dodging panicked staff members. Past him, at the end of the hallway, Eric Bines, the RRZ compound's security chief, spoke with three heavily armed men wearing black body armor.

"We're under attack by our own soldiers!" yelled Ian. "Six helicopters just took off, headed north."

A window shattered in one of the nearby offices, followed by screaming.

"Gather the staff in the communications center. Hurry!" Medina said, passing Ian.

In the aftermath of the militia attack last fall, the room housing the RRZ's encrypted communications equipment had been reinforced with Kevlar shielding and sandbags. Located in the center of the building, it doubled as the headquarters building's "safe room."

"Eric!" she yelled, picking up her pace.

Her security chief patted one of the heavily armed men on the arm, sending them through the stairwell door behind him.

"Eric! Tell your men to stand down!" she said. "There's no point."

Eric Bines spoke into his handheld radio before rushing to meet her. The gun battle outside intensified, the sounds spilling through the broken window in the office next to them.

"Ma'am, I'm under strict Homeland orders to defend this installation against any and all attacks," said Bines.

"This is different, Eric. If the military turned on us, it's over," Medina stated. "There's nothing we can do but wait for D.C. to fix this."

Bullets passed through the wall ten feet away, filling the hallway with drywall dust. Medina crouched next to Bines, who aimed at the stairwell door with his MP-9 submachine gun. His radio crackled with frantic reports.

"I have to go," he said, through the door.

Medina shook her head, unwilling to process the man's death wish. If he wanted to die a pointless death, that was his problem. She had a duty to protect her people, and that was exactly what she intended to do. Ian emerged from one of the rooms, hustling two men toward the communications center several doors away.

"Ian, I need you to enter my security override code into the automated keycard system and reboot the external doors," said Medina.

"That'll lock out the security team," Ian reminded her.

"Just do it. Right now. They'll get us all killed if they use the building as their Alamo."

Ian sprinted down the hallway, pushing several people out of his way to reach the communications room, which housed their surveillance and security equipment. A group of administrative personnel burst out of the stairwell door, yelling and pushing their way into the hallway. Medina backed against the outer wall and waited for them to pass.

"Is the first floor clear?" she yelled to the last of the group.

One of the women stopped long enough to nod. "I saw a few security officers guarding each door, but that's it."

"Get inside the comms center," said Medina, staring at her ROTAC. She took a deep breath and selected Colonel Martin's call sign. "Colonel Martin"—she heard heavy gunfire in the background—"I tried to order Mr. Bines to surrender, but I'm afraid he's hell-bent on defending the compound to the last man. I've disabled the key card readers at all external doors, so they can't retreat into the building. I'd like to keep my staff alive."

"They're putting up one hell of a fight," said Martin. "Get all of your people into the safe room and wait for my call. I expect this to be over in five minutes."

"Most of the staff is already there. I'm told we have security officers guarding the ground-floor doors, from the inside."

"All right. We'll do everything we can to keep the gunfire away from your safe room. Make sure your people are lying down. The Kevlar only goes up to shoulder height," said Martin.

"Colonel Martin?"

"Yes, ma'am?"

"I didn't do enough to work with Governor Dague from the beginning," Medina admitted. "I knew better."

"This isn't your fault. The blame for this lies about seven thousand miles west of here, in the People's Republic of China. Don't ever forget that. You were dealt a tough hand, and you played the cards the best you could. Not every RRZ made this much progress," Martin assured her. "Launching a paramilitary coup against the state government would have erased that legacy and catapulted the state into bloody civil war. It's already happened in three recovery areas. You've done well."

"Funny. That's not the picture Homeland painted," Medina countered.

"Of course not. I listen to the same rosy reports, but I also get the real story from the military commanders on the ground in the areas that have collapsed," said Martin, the sound of gunfire on his end of the call escalating.

Automatic fire erupted near the building, sounding closer than before. Through the stairwell door, Medina heard yells and more gunshots.

"They're falling back to your building," said Martin. "You better get to the safe room and lock it. Do not let any of the security team inside."

Medina ran for the communications center door, a full-scale battle echoing through the hallway. She reached the room at a dead sprint, frantically grabbing for the door handle.

"Barricade the door!" she screamed, slamming it shut and scanning her microchipped badge over the electronic reader installed in the wall.

She punched a quick code in the keypad, and the card reader glowed red. She had locked the door from the inside. Only Ian McEyre or Eric Bines possessed badges that could override her lockout. If Bines survived the battle outside and made it back to the communications center, only a stack of furniture would keep him out.

While members of her staff moved desks in front of the door, she watched the surveillance screens, focusing on the camera views aimed at the entrances. The green night-vision images showed several security officers huddled around each door, firing at unseen targets, while one of them repeatedly swiped his badge over the card reader. One by one they started to fall as bullets visibly splintered the siding around the door and struck the ground near the crouched men.

She recognized Bines on one of the screens. Helmetless, he crouched behind a failing wall of body armor and rifles, holding his phone. Medina's ROTAC chirped. She checked the orange digital display and shook her head. Bines had sealed his fate when he refused to accept the reality of their situation. Seconds later, his unprotected head snapped back, a dark green stain hitting the door behind him. The rest of the team tried to run for the northwest corner of the building, only to be stopped halfway, their deaths marked by a sudden crescendo of gunfire heard through the communication center walls.

A group of soldiers quickly surrounded the main entrance door, peeling away moments later. The camera feed disappeared, followed by an explosion that shook the safe room. Screams punctuated the approaching sound of gunfire inside the building.

"Get on the ground!" she yelled as bullet holes peppered the top of the wall next to the door.

She saw the card reader blink red several times, followed by frantic banging on the door.

"Governor, open the door! They've breached the building!" said a muffled voice beyond the reinforced entry.

"You need to surrender!" she yelled back. "They'll kill all of you if you don't surrender!"

"Open the door! They're here!"

A long burst of automatic fire exploded in the hallway, penetrating the door.

Medina crouched next to the computer displays, finding the security camera feed above the entrance. Two men in black body armor fired in different directions while a third pulled a critically wounded officer across the hallway, leaving a thick blood trail. More automatic fire thundered in the hallway, splintering the door and ripping into the security team. The rate of fire increased for several seconds, suddenly ceasing. She held her breath as 10th Mountain Division soldiers crowded the door.

"Governor Medina?" she heard.

None of the men on the display aimed rifles at the door.

"I'm here!" she yelled, approaching the door.

"My name is Captain Royer. We have instructions to secure the communications center. I need you to open the door so we can get this sorted out. Nobody will get hurt. You have my promise. Colonel Martin is on his way up."

"What's going to happen to us?" she yelled.

"Nothing, ma'am," said the Army officer.

"Nothing, as in we just go back to our jobs?" she said, knowing that wasn't what the captain had in mind.

"We'll search for weapons first. After that, I presume you'll be temporarily detained with your staff. I need you to open the door now, ma'am," said Captain Royer.

"I need to speak with Colonel Martin," she said, watching the screen.

The officer pressed a transmitter button on his vest and spoke. A moment later her ROTAC chirped. She answered it with a question.

"Colonel, what's going to happen to us?"

"That's up to you, ma'am. Lieutenant Colonel Grady is on his way to Augusta. We're bringing Governor Dague here until the threat from the Counter Insurgency Battalion has been defused," said Martin.

"I'll do everything I can to help with that," said Medina. "Unfortunately, getting the CIB deployed wasn't a simple phone call. It attracted a lot of attention."

"We won't give Homeland or the White House any reason to escalate the situation, as long as you and Dague can function in a hybrid leadership role," said Martin.

"I don't understand," said Medina.

"The RRZ concept is here to stay, and nobody is more qualified to run the RRZ than your staff. Governor Dague agrees that she's not equipped to do your job," said Martin.

"Then why has she put up so much resistance?"

"The New England RRZ governance structure had several permutations, based on the type of Category Five catastrophe we faced. None of the permutations included a tsunami wiping out the seaports from Connecticut to Portland, so Homeland decided to follow the New England RRZ protocol created for a nuclear strike against Boston," said Martin. "It placed the entire RRZ infrastructure burden on Maine, which caused an unusual amount of friction."

"That's an understatement," Medina said. "I think D.C. underestimated the independent spirit of the Maine population."

"That too," said Martin. "So, the job's still yours if you want it."

"What about Governor Dague?"

"That's for you and the state governor to figure out. Dague will arrive here in less than an hour."

"That doesn't give me a lot of time," said Medina.

"No, but it sounds like you've already given a lot of thought to how you could have better approached the situation last fall."

"I used to sit in the annual training meetings, shaking my head at some of the protocol recommendations," said Medina. "Like I said, I knew better."

"Well, for what it's worth, I think they picked the right person for the job. Especially for one of the nation's critical RRZ's."

"Do you want to know a secret?" Medina asked, swiping her badge on the card reader.

"Always," said Martin.

Medina punched her code, waiting for the reader's lights to turn green before opening the door to face Colonel Martin.

"I was never trained for this job," she said. "The real governor and his chief of staff never showed up at Andrews Air Force Base."

"I'm beginning to suspect that might have been a blessing in disguise," said Martin, extending his hand. "I assume you'll stick around?"

She shook his hand. "Looks like you're stuck with me."

Chapter 32

Bangor, Maine

Alex jammed the ROTAC into the center console, pounding the dashboard with his other hand. He muttered a few choice words about Grady.

"What's going on?" asked Ed, slowing for the second gate.

The chain-link fence hummed on its track, taking an eternity to open.

"There's a military coup underway in Sanford," said Alex, hitting the side of his door impatiently.

"Jesus," hissed Ed, edging the SUV closer to the gate.

"Who cleaned out the warehouses?" Charlie asked. "If it was the military, we shouldn't have anything to worry about."

"It wasn't the military," said Ed. "Was it?"

"No," Alex answered. "Medina called in some kind of paramilitary group to deal with the state government. They've been in possession of this stuff for nearly a month."

The gate had barely cleared Ed's side of the SUV when he gunned the engine, propelling them toward Runway Road.

Charlie asked, "Does he think they're out here?"

"He didn't say, but I'm guessing they'll have a group

nearby. The sooner we get to the turnpike, the better," said Alex, watching the road ahead of them through night-vision goggles. "Can you see the road?"

"Barely," grunted Ed. "Shouldn't I be the one wearing the NVGs?"

"Normally, yes," admitted Alex. "But I'm going to need them to spot any unwelcome roadside companions. You should be able to see it better once we get out of these trees."

"I hope so. I'm just driving in a straight line right now."

"You're right on track," said Alex, taking hold of the wheel. "I'll guide us onto Runway Road."

Ed accelerated after the turn, comfortable with the twilight scene unfolding at forty miles per hour. Alex kept his limited field of view through the NVGs focused forward, scanning the distance for anything that didn't belong on the road, especially vehicles. A brisk wind churned through the windows, chafing his face and chilling the cabin. They rode in darkness and silence two-thirds of the way to New Boston Road.

"Anything?" asked Ryan.

"Looks good so far," said Alex. "How are you doing, Ed?"

"I can see the road well enough to keep us out of a ditch. I'll need help with the turns."

"I see the barn coming up on the left. That's our turn onto New Boston. Can you see it?"

"Kind of. It's silhouetted against the horizon."

Alex lifted the NVGs to check the ambient light guiding Ed's journey. He was concerned about his friend's ultimate ability to navigate the roads if they came under attack. Alex's attention would be more focused on coordinating a defense than guiding Ed to the interstate. One wrong turn or missed intersection could put them deeper into unfamiliar territory. His eyes took a few moments to adjust before he could make an assessment.

The deep orange glow of scattered clouds had all but vanished, replaced by a thick cerulean blue ribbon above the trees. He could see the two-story barn against the deep blue horizon, but only because he knew what he was looking for. Ed would need his help if they ran into trouble. Alex lowered the goggles, spotting something in the distance on the other side of the intersection.

"Faster, Ed. I'm seeing something farther down Runway Road," said Alex.

"Past the intersection?"

"Yeah. We need to beat them to the turn," said Alex, feeling the SUV respond to the accelerator.

"Faster. I'll let you know when to slow for the turn," said Alex.

"I'm pushing fifty-five," said Ed.

Alex squinted at the green image. The horizon light washed out the distance view, affecting the long-range clarity of the picture. Something was in the middle of the road, growing larger. Had to be a vehicle. It looked like they'd beat it to the intersection.

"Start to slow down," said Alex. "Can you see the barn?"

"I got it," said Ed, decelerating the SUV.

"Take the turn as fast as you can."

"Right," mumbled Ed.

Alex wondered if the other vehicle would slow. He couldn't tell what it was doing at this distance, without magnified optics. The night-vision image sharpened, unveiling a substantial vehicle with a figure leaning out of the passenger side window. A bright green laser appeared, extending from the passenger to the hood of their SUV. Without hesitating, he grabbed the steering wheel and jerked it left.

Ed tightened his grip on the wheel and countered Alex's move, keeping them from crashing off the road. Instead of careening wildly into a telephone pole or mailbox, the SUV instantly shifted lanes as red-hot tracers passed down the left side of the vehicle. Ignoring the screams and chaos in the SUV's cabin, Alex raised his rifle and fired an extended burst through the windshield at the oncoming vehicle.

The bullets created a tight pattern of holes in the safety glass, surrounded by compounded spider cracks that partially obscured his view of the approaching intersection. The green laser went wild, indicating his bullets had the desired effect. With the barn rapidly approaching, he shifted his rifle into the passenger side window, triggering the infrared laser attached to the HK416's hand guard.

"Contact, right side!" he yelled, feeling the SUV speed into the turn instead of slowing.

As the car turned, the threat crystallized. A staggered column of two pickup trucks was less than fifty feet from the intersection, one with bullet holes peppered across its windshield. Now he understood why Ed had gunned the engine. The trucks would barely miss slamming into them. Alex aligned the green laser with the windshield of the lead vehicle and pressed the trigger, firing a short burst. Ryan unleashed a fully automatic barrage of bullets.

The lead vehicle swerved left in a cascade of sparks as their bullets struck the metal chassis and windshield. The pickup truck slammed into a utility pole ten feet from the intersection, abruptly stopping and ejecting two passengers through the bullet-riddled windshield. The second truck barreled forward, gunfire exploding behind its windshield. Sharp cracks followed by hollow metallic pops broke through the sound of the SUV's screeching tires, and their vehicle fishtailed onto New Boston Road.

The SUV straightened and accelerated, Ed desperately trying to put some distance between their car and the team sent to kill them. Alex reloaded and twisted in his seat, seeing that Ryan and Charlie had already braced their rifles against the rear seats' headrests, aiming through the shattered rear window. Ryan reloaded while Charlie fired single shots through his night-vision scope at the pursuing truck.

A blinding light caused Alex to squeeze his eyes shut, followed by a staccato rhythm of snaps and metal thunks. He flipped up his NVGs to see two brilliant headlights bearing down on them.

"Damn it!" yelled Charlie, firing wildly at the truck.

A few ricochets zipped through the SUV cabin; one striking the windshield in front of Ed.

"What the fuck is happening back there?" asked Ed, slinking as low as possible in his seat.

"It's under control," said Ryan, firing a long burst at the truck and knocking out the passenger-side headlight.

The pickup swerved briefly, but resumed the chase, accelerating toward them at ramming speed.

"Doesn't sound like it!" yelled Ed.

Another fusillade of bullets struck the SUV, ripping through the cabin. Alex's headrest crumpled when a round snapped one of the posts holding it in position. Another projectile hit the top corner of Ed's seat, passing through the fabric and smashing the digital dashboard display. Ryan and Charlie ducked below the tops of their seats, riding out the barrage. Anticipating a possible problem, they had secured a single layer of sandbags, reinforced by sheet metal, behind the back row of seats. The barrier prevented bullets from penetrating the backs of the seats, but did nothing about the bullets flying through the top half of the SUV's interior.

Before either of them rose to fire, the pickup truck slammed into the back of the SUV, pushing them forward. Alex was unexpectedly thrown against the seatbelt, momentarily stunned by the blow. Ed gunned the engine, breaking them free of the metal battering ram. Another salvo of bullets hit the SUV, striking from a high angle and drilling through the rear cargo compartment roof.

"Son of a bitch!" Charlie cried out.

Alex turned his head to see a bloody hand illuminated in the pickup's single high beam.

Enough of this shit.

He unbuckled his seatbelt and turned in his seat, leaning against the passenger-side dashboard. Keeping the rifle barrel clear of his son's head, he aimed through the mini-reflex sight mounted to his ACOG scope and switched to semiautomatic.

"All guns fire in three, two—"

"Wait! I'm not ready!" said Ed.

"Fire!" screamed Alex, pressing the trigger.

He fired repeatedly above the glaring headlight, hoping to hit the windshield. Ryan's muzzle blast filled the rear compartment, illuminating their cabin as he emptied a thirty-round magazine at the truck. Alex kept firing until his rifle clicked empty. By the time Charlie started to fire again, the pickup truck had disappeared.

"Where is it?" yelled Charlie.

"Veered off the road," said Alex.

"I think it rolled to a stop," said Ryan. "It was too dark to tell for sure."

"But you think it stopped?" asked Alex.

"I'm pretty sure. It definitely slowed down."

"Jesus Christ!" said Ed, rising a few inches in his seat.

"Jesus Christ is right. He's the only reason none of us took one to the head," said Charlie.

"I think you deflected one with your hand," answered Alex.

"Yeah, it's a little fucked up," said Charlie, holding his bloodied hand between the front headrests. "Look at this thing."

Ed turned his head, hitting the mangled hand with his right cheek.

"Careful!" howled Charlie. "What the fuck is wrong with you?"

"Well, don't stick your fucking hand in my face. What did you expect?"

"I didn't expect you to ram my hand with your head," countered Charlie.

"All right! Cut it out!" yelled Alex. "Reload your rifles."

He lowered the night-vision goggles and scanned the darkness around the vehicle. Nothing ahead or behind them. New Boston Road was a straight shot to Route 2. No crossroads, just houses. They needed to get to Route 2 before any more paramilitaries responded. The absence of crossroads on New Boston Road could work against them.

"Ryan, can you wrap Charlie's hand so he can still use it?"

"Got it," said Ryan, digging around for the medical kit.

"I don't think that was the last of the shooting for tonight," said Alex, checking the road again.

"Faster?" Ed asked.

"Faster," said Alex, pulling a roadmap out of the glove box.

He wanted to check on alternate routes to the turnpike in case they ran into another hostile team.

Chapter 33

Dexter, Maine

Jerold Berkoff pinched the bridge of his nose and tried the call again. His ROTAC display flashed "attempting to connect." He'd give it ten seconds before reaching out to Medina. The team dispatched to check on the storage site had been located in an empty house less than five minutes away. They should have reported by now, unless something bigger was in play. Medina had certainly hinted at the possibility.

Putting all of his units on "ready alert" meant one of two things: Either the state government had discovered the facility or the military units attached to the RRZ were sniffing around where they didn't belong. Both scenarios threatened to kill the element of surprise he needed, which was critical to his battalion's success. He had too many groups going in too many directions to fight against an alerted enemy. Pre-staging key assault units made more sense given the circumstances.

"Damnit," he hissed, seeing no change to the ROTAC display. "McKenzie?" he said, causing a stir in the brightly lit trailer.

A bearded man wearing tan cargo pants, a MultiCam combat shirt, and a black and white checkered shemagh spun his stool to face Berkoff.

"Sir?" asked the contractor.

Berkoff considered issuing the order without Medina's permission, but killed the thought. He wanted this operation to go as smoothly as possible, and pissing off an RRZ administrator wouldn't contribute to that plan. As much as he enjoyed commanding a Counter Insurgency Battalion, Berkoff wanted a more stable position, preferably in a comfortable position within one of the RRZs. If he overstepped his authority here, regardless of the outcome, he could cross New England North off his list, along with the rest of the RRZs on the East Coast. Medina struck him as a petty, spiteful bitch.

"Nothing. I was just getting ahead of myself," he said, dialing Medina's code instead.

The governor took longer than he expected to answer, especially given the circumstances.

"Anything?" she asked in greeting.

"Not yet, ma'am," he said. "The team sent to investigate hasn't reported."

"How far out are they?"

"They should have arrived a few minutes ago," said Berkoff.

"A few minutes ago? All right," she said, pausing for a moment. "Order your team to pull back and stay out of sight. Homeland just confirmed that our mystery guest never opened any of the warehouses. They entered the codes to get through the two gates and apparently departed. We're thinking this might have been someone involved in building the site. Maybe someone with an override code, but not the warehouse codes. The two code sequences are separate. Homeland is checking the construction contract information. Probably two companies involved. One to build the fence, and the other to build the warehouses."

"The keycard system looked the same. Whoever installed one likely installed the other," said Berkoff.

"They're trying to get to the bottom of this."

Jesus. It didn't take a rocket scientist to figure this out. The same crew installed all of the security devices.

"Why wouldn't they open the warehouses?" he pressed.

"I don't know, Berkoff," said Medina. "I'm getting my information from Homeland, and they're telling me the warehouses weren't breached. Pull your team back so they don't tip our hand in this."

What? Tip what hand?

Medina wasn't making a lot of sense. If they were dealing with a curious local builder, what would it matter if his team appeared? It would probably keep them from coming back. If Medina was wrong about her assumption and this was one of Dague's military units, they needed to know right away. She wasn't thinking this through.

"Ma'am, I think we should at least figure out who we're dealing with here," he said.

"Not without more information from Homeland," she said. "I don't want your team spotted. Call them back immediately."

"I can't reach them, ma'am," said Berkoff.

"What do you mean?" said Medina. "Can't or won't?"

"I've been trying to reach them for the past few minutes. They should have reported by now. I'm about to send another team out to check on them."

"I don't think it would be a good idea to saturate the area with your people. It'll draw attention to the site. If locals find the storage facility, they might report it to the Maine Independence Initiative."

Now she wasn't making any sense at all. His ROTAC buzzed, indicating a second call. He checked the display. Finally! Berkoff was about to tell Medina that the team had made contact, when he reconsidered. He let the call go unanswered, knowing the team would immediately call the communications center.

"Berkoff?"

"Sorry, ma'am. I was just thinking of a way to handle this without drawing attention," he said, stalling for time.

"Homeland thinks this was a false alarm, and I agree. Cancel my order to put the battalion in ready alert status."

McKenzie swiped one of the ROTAC handhelds off the desk in front of a row of open laptops, putting the phone to his ear.

"Don't you think we should…maybe we should wait…until we know more?" he said, distracted by McKenzie.

"I'd rather the battalion was not primed for an attack that won't happen for a few days," she said.

Berkoff barely heard what she said, covering the mouthpiece with his other hand as McKenzie swiveled to face him.

"Caretaker Three-Two reports heavy contact with a single vehicle leaving Site Zulu. Two KIA and two WIA. No survivors in Caretaker Three-One," said McKenzie.

Berkoff put an index finger to his lips and answered Medina. "I agree, ma'am. I'll keep trying to reach the team. If I don't hear from them in ten minutes, I'll call back for further orders."

"Very well. I'll let you know if Homeland uncovers anything else."

Berkoff lowered the ROTAC to the desk in front of him and looked up at the waiting faces.

McKenzie tilted his head, giving him a "what the fuck?" look.

"Where is Three-Two right now?" Berkoff asked.

"In a field off New Boston Road, about a mile from Runway," McKenzie answered. "Their targets are out of sight. Last seen heading south on New Boston, toward Route 2."

"Shit. Six KIA?"

McKenzie nodded.

"What hit them?"

"Three to four hostiles in a late model SUV running without lights. Automatic weapons, IR lasers, night-vision goggles, helmets," McKenzie rattled off. "They knew what they were doing. Military for sure, possibly Special Forces. Don't they have a company of Rangers down in Sanford?"

"Yeah," muttered Berkoff, thinking through his options.

Medina was full of shit. She was either compromised or utterly clueless. Why else would she completely reverse her decision at such a critical moment? He'd have to take matters into his own hands until he figured out what was going on with Medina.

"Move all sections into echelon alpha pre-stage positions, and send a team to recover Three-Two. I want to be able to move on our primary targets within two hours," said Berkoff.

"That's a tight time frame," said McKenzie. "Are you sure you don't want to wait for the RRZ to get more clarification?"

"Let's get the ball rolling. Something doesn't add up here, and I'm not going to take the fall if Medina is full of shit. Ultimately, we answer to Homeland," he said, picking up the ROTAC and scrolling through his contacts list. "And McKenzie?"

"Sir?"

"I want that hostile SUV taken out," said Berkoff. "I don't care what it takes."

***

Bethany Medina handed the ROTAC to Colonel Martin and shook her head.

"He didn't buy it?" asked Martin.

"I don't think so. He changed his tune too quickly," she said. "My guess is he'll follow my original order to move all units to their final pre-staging positions."

"Primary targets?"

"Major elements of 3rd Battalion, 172nd Infantry Regiment, along with all critical state government administration sites."

"Time frame?"

"Two to three hours if he goes for a fully coordinated, simultaneous attack. Less if he learns the truth about what happened here. He's probably on the phone to Homeland right now, so I'd expect sooner than later."

"Shit," said Martin. "Looks like we're going to war."

"With Homeland?"

"Just Berkoff," said Martin. "If we do this right."

"We?"

"I need you to stall Homeland when they call," said Martin.

"For how long?"

"Long enough for us to put Berkoff out of commission. After that, it won't matter what Homeland knows."

"I think you're underestimating what Homeland—" She paused before continuing, "—what the federal government will do when they learn the truth about what happened here."

"I've already spoken with 10th Mountain Division's commanding general about that very issue. He's prepared to deploy the division's ready brigade to Maine in support of our mission. Unless Homeland has a Counter Insurgency Division up their sleeve, I'm not worried."

She shook her head. "You've thought this through."

"The decision was a long time in the making, ma'am, and I'm not the only military leader that feels the same way. If we work together, we'll get through this with minimal disruption of the RRZ."

"What do you need from me?" asked Medina.

"Stall Homeland and identify Berkoff's pre-staging areas. We have a rapid response battalion ready to head north. Depending on the distance, we might be able to hit Berkoff's units in their pre-staging areas, or en route to their targets."

"I can't do that to him," she said. "He's here because of me."

"Negative, ma'am," said Martin. "He's here because Homeland sent him based on your assessment of the internal security situation within the RRZ. It was Homeland's choice to send a paramilitary group instead of providing you with the resources to negotiate a settlement with Governor Dague. You're doing exactly what needs to be done to keep the RRZ running smoothly. If Berkoff won't stand down, we have to take him out."

"We're not giving him a *chance* to stand down," said Medina.

"If I thought for a second he would load his battalion on the next flight of C-17s that arrived at Bangor International, I would try to talk to him. I don't see that happening. Do you?"

The colonel was right. Like Eric Bines, the RRZ Authority compound's security chief, Berkoff would follow Homeland's orders to unseat the state government, even if it meant "disappearing" and waiting for another opportunity. Martin needed to engage and destroy Berkoff's force now, or risk a protracted, low-intensity conflict against a well-armed and adequately trained group of contract soldiers. The result could undermine the progress everyone had worked hard to achieve.

"Berkoff's digital overlays are on the laptop in my office," she said, effectively signing Berkoff's death warrant.

Chapter 34

Plymouth, Maine

Icy wind whistled through the holes in the windshield, bathing Alex in a stream of subfreezing air. The SUV jolted, and a particle of safety glass from one of the spider cracks rattled against his night-vision goggles. He leaned as far over the center console as possible, resting his head against Ed's arm. It was the only way he could see through the windshield from his seat. The bullet holes created by his rifle were concentrated in an area the size of a volleyball, but the cracks obscured most of the passenger-side view.

He'd briefly considered knocking the entire windshield out, but just as quickly realized a missing windshield would cause more problems than it might solve. He'd have a clear view of the road, at the cost of dealing with a sixty-mile-per-hour wind, along with hundreds of loose fragments. He could deal with this arrangement for another thirty minutes.

A grouping of signs appeared in the distance.

"We're coming up on an exit," said Alex.

A dim red light bathed his peripheral vision for several seconds before vanishing. He didn't bother trying to see through the windshield while Ryan examined the map. The light reflected off the glass, obscuring his view.

"This should be exit 161," said Ryan. "Puts us on Route 7."

"I think we should get off this highway," said Ed. "Do you have to lean on my arm that much?"

"It's the only way I can see," said Alex. "Ryan, how far until Newport?"

"Four miles, maybe a little more."

"I want to get past Newport before we get off the interstate. It's not a big town, but it's big enough to hold trouble. After that, we'll look for a way to get onto Route 2. Take the back way home," said Alex. "Still looking clear behind us?"

"You'll know if it isn't," said Charlie.

"We'll have helicopter support in less than ten minutes," said Alex, squinting through the goggles.

Something didn't look right, but it was impossible to tell from this distance.

"Slow down a little," Alex instructed Ed.

An overpass materialized in the green image, followed by a clearer picture of the southbound lane. Alex studied the scene for anything out of place. He'd experienced the same feeling of dread approaching the previous two exits.

"Everything okay?" asked Ed, slowing the SUV further.

Alex gave it a few more seconds before making a final determination. He didn't see anything out of place.

"Yeah," Alex said. "The exits make me nervous."

"You think? That's why I want to get off the highway. Anything could come barreling down one of those on-ramps. We're too exposed out here," said Ed.

"I know, but I feel safer here than on some constricted back road," said Alex.

"I don't feel safe on either," said Ed.

"I said safer," added Alex. "We won't be *safe* until we've made contact with those helos."

They drove under the concrete overpass, their silver SUV a shadowy phantom in the weak light of a late third-quarter moon. Ed brought the vehicle's speed back to sixty miles per hour, which was as fast as his friend would drive without lights. Alex didn't blame Ed. Without night vision, the gray strip ahead of them barely extended the length of a semi-trailer. Alex had to announce the slightest curves, which was another reason he couldn't take his eyes off the road for a second.

"Shallow left curve starting in about ten seconds," said Alex.

"Got it," said Ed, easing his foot off the accelerator.

The SUV stayed in the middle of the two-lane interstate for most of the curve, drifting slowly right.

"You're drifting to the right. Just barely," said Alex, immediately feeling Ed's arm muscles tighten.

The vehicle eased back into the middle of the road, settling into a straight section of highway a few seconds later.

"You're good. It's a straight shot from—" Alex saw more signs ahead. "Ryan, is there another exit right after 161?"

His view through the windshield disappeared as Ryan checked the map.

"Shit. Sorry, Dad. Exit 159. Doesn't seem to lead to any major roads," said Ryan, dousing the light.

Alex could see part of the overpass. How had Ryan missed this? It must have been separated by a centimeter on the map. Before he could continue to mentally chastise his son, a row of vehicles appeared on the road.

"Stop the car!" said Alex, lowering his window. "Windows down. We have—fuck!—Humvees blocking the highway. Turn us around!"

The SUV screeched to a halt on the asphalt, the acrid smell of burnt rubber filling the car as Ed executed the quickest three-point turn he'd ever witnessed. Alex unfastened his seatbelt and leaned out of the window, searching the tree-lined median for a way to cross into the northbound lanes. When the SUV gained momentum, he spotted a sizable gap in the trees.

"Follow my laser," he said, triggering the visible red laser pointer attached to his rifle.

He aimed the light, which appeared green in his goggles, toward the middle of the gap. The car tugged right, slowing as it hit the roughly paved shoulder.

"You got it?" said Alex.

"I got it, but I can't see what I'm driving into!" yelled Ed.

"It's a slight dip. You might want to put us into four-wheel—"

The SUV's nose dropped, the front tires crunching into the hard ground spanning the median.

"—drive," Alex continued, relieved when the SUV lurched forward again.

"They're shooting at us!" screamed Charlie as bright flashes streaked past the back of the SUV.

"Gun it, Ed!" said Alex, watching tracer flashes ricochet through the trees to their right and skip off the highway behind them.

The SUV careened into the northbound lanes, skidding to a momentary stop before accelerating away from the overpass. Alex turned in his seat to see dozens of tracers punch through the thick pines and sail harmlessly behind them. He didn't see any vehicles blocking the northbound side near the overpass, so they were temporarily in the clear.

"Hit the lights and drive as fast as this thing will go," said Alex.

"Are you sure the lights are a good idea?" asked Ed, jamming the accelerator.

"It's more important to gain some distance. We need to get to the last exit before they can put those guns to use against us. If we can get off the highway, we should be able to hide on the back roads until our air support arrives," said Alex, checking his watch. "Which means we need to stay alive another seven minutes."

Alex slid into his seat as the SUV picked up speed and the wind outside of the window became unbearable. Ed activated the headlights, switching to high beams and illuminating the empty highway. The lights didn't matter at this point. Not on the highway. Alex flipped his NVGs out of the way.

"How we looking back there?" he asked, looking over his shoulder.

"Clear so far," said Charlie, his face buried in his riflescope. "If they get behind us, we're screwed."

"We'll be off the highway before they get into effective range," said Alex.

"I'm worried about the place between effective and maximum range," said Charlie. "You know, the place where you can still hit shit."

"Ed, be ready to jump the median again," said Alex. "Just in case."

"Shit," muttered Ed.

A few seconds passed before Charlie yelled, "They're coming! Three Humvees."

Alex stuck his head out of the passenger window and scanned ahead for signs of the upcoming exit. Beyond the headlights' aura, he saw what might be a white U-turn sign coming up on the left.

"How far back are they?"

"Hell if I know," Charlie replied. "You left the range finder behind."

Alex muttered a curse. "I'm looking for a ballpark figure, Charlie."

"Looks farther back from where we broke through."

Ed looked at him and shook his head with an annoyed look. Alex met Ed's glance and raised his eyebrows, silently mouthing, "Charlie." Alex did the math. A quick dashboard check told him Ed had pushed the SUV to ninety-three miles per hour. They had at least twenty miles per hour on the Humvees, maybe more depending on the weight of the armor kit installed on the government vehicles. They had a speed and distance advantage on the interstate, but Charlie was right. If they hit a long, flat stretch, the turret-mounted M240s could reach out and touch them in a very bad way. He remembered they had a long, shallow curve coming up, which gave him an idea.

"Forget the U-turn. We should fall out of their line of sight when we hit that long curve," said Alex. "Charlie, let me know when we break their line of sight. We'll look for an opening in the trees. If we can cross over without them seeing, it'll buy us more time."

"We're going too fast to spot openings," Ed pointed out.

"We'll slow down once they can't see us," said Alex. "Kill the lights before we turn, and I'll do the laser trick. Good to go?"

"I guess."

Alex patted Ed's shoulder. "I feel like we have the band back together."

"I preferred retirement," said Ed, pushing the SUV to one hundred miles per hour.

Alex braved the wind for a few seconds, feeling it tug on his night-vision straps. They couldn't afford to lose the NVGs, especially if they needed to maneuver on the back roads. He steadied them with his right hand and stared ahead, watching the U-turn sign fly down the left side of the SUV, followed by a paved break through the median.

"I lost them!" said Charlie. "They can't see us."

Alex scoured the farthest reaches of the SUV's headlights, looking for a sign of a break in the trees. He spotted what looked like a gap, but it snapped past them a few seconds later. They were moving too fast.

"Count to ten and slow us to sixty!" he yelled over the rushing air.

The signs for the exit appeared as distant green dots by the time Ed reached seven. Still too far—and they were out of the curve.

"Kill the lights and slow down. We need to get across now!" said Alex, craning his head farther to find an opening.

As the SUV slowed, he found what they needed. Alex flipped his NVGs into place.

"Slow down! There's something coming up!" he yelled, pulling his rifle through the window and kneeling on the seat.

The SUV decelerated, and he triggered the laser, guiding Ed to the gap in the median.

"I see it," said Ed.

Alex braced himself for the drop off, but Ed eased them off the road at a shallow angle, slicing through the gap. They emerged from the trees heading north in the southbound lanes, less than fifty feet in front of two oncoming vehicles.

Instinctively, he dropped into his seat as the two dark cars buzzed past them. Ed never saw the cars appear, which probably saved their lives.

"What the fuck was that?" yelled Charlie moments before the sound of screeching tires filled the cabin.

Alex twisted in his seat in time to see one of the cars skid sideways down the middle of the highway. Before he could respond to Charlie's question, the truck's right-side tires dug into the asphalt and flipped the vehicle. He watched it tumble down the interstate, throwing off sparks until it vanished on the far side of the road. The second car had disappeared altogether, as far as Alex could tell. He felt instantly nauseous.

"Woo-hoo, fuckers!" screamed Charlie. "You see that shit?"

The SUV's sudden acceleration pinned him to the seat. He took a moment to fasten his seatbelt before getting his head back in the fight.

"Holy shit," whispered Alex.

"What the hell just happened?" asked Ed.

"You don't want to know," said Alex, still not sure himself.

"We just played chicken and won! That's what happened!" said Charlie, slapping Ed on the shoulder.

"Watch your sectors," said Alex. "We're a long way from safe."

"What's up with you, man?" said Charlie. "We just cheated death!"

"I know," he muttered, his hands trembling.

Ed croaked, "Now what?"

Alex leaned his head out of the window, scanning ahead.

"I see the overpass for the exit. We'll drive up the on-ramp. No lights," he said.

"Let me know when," said Ed.

"Yeah," said Alex, still dazed by their run-in with death.

If they had emerged a second later, they'd be dead from a head-on collision. A second earlier, and they'd be in a running gunfight—with the same result. Less than thirty seconds later, they hit the on-ramp.

"Stop us at the top," said Alex. "Facing north."

"Left turn or right turn?" said Ed.

"Left," replied Alex. "Anything, Charlie?"

"Nothing. They must have missed the commotion."

"The other car disappeared. I figured it burst through the trees. No way they missed that," said Alex.

"There were two cars?" asked Ed.

"Yeah, we cut right through the middle of them," said Alex.

"Jesus. I'm glad I didn't see any of it."

"Hold on, Alex. I have something happening back there," said Charlie. "One vehicle just cut through the median. Heading south. That's odd."

"They're probably backtracking. They have no idea which direction we took," Alex said. "That still leaves two on the other side."

"I say we head north on Route 7 and disappear until the helicopters show up," said Ed.

"Sounds good to me," said Alex.

"Alex," said Charlie, "the southbound Humvee just stopped."

Tracers flashed past Alex's window, causing Ed to jerk the wheel left. The SUV swerved off the road and scraped a jagged wall of ledge running along the ramp. Alex heard and felt one of the tires blow out, the car leaning to the left. Ed pulled them off the rocks and gunned the engine, speeding the damaged SUV toward the top of the ramp. Streaks of light flew overhead, visible through the moon roof.

"They don't have a shot!" said Charlie. "The ramp curves around the rock wall you hit. They can't hit us right now."

Ed stopped the vehicle.

"What are you doing?" Alex roared.

"They'll be able to hit us at the top of the ramp," said Ed. "It curves back."

"We can't stay here," said Alex. "Get us onto Route 7."

Ed shook his head. "I don't think that's a good idea."

"Ed, we can't stay here. They'll drive right up on us. Please get us moving," demanded Alex.

The SUV pitched forward, the engine whining as the RPMs climbed.

"Use your lights. They already know we're here," said Alex.

The vehicle gained speed as they approached the top of the winding ramp. Alex watched the interstate through his window, trying to anticipate his enemy's next move. They had fired from the outer limit of their effective range, which meant focusing gunfire at the top of the ramp would not be the best option. If Alex were in command of the group, he'd keep one gun stationary, focused on the ramp, and send the other vehicle up the highway. The nose of a Humvee appeared on the highway.

"Get us through, Ed," said Alex.

The SUV raced toward Route 7, chased by an erratic stream of tracers. The bright green flashes struck the rock wall and ricocheted in every direction, bouncing off the road behind them. By the time the gunners adjusted their fire to compensate for the SUV's speed, the vehicle flew past a stop sign, taking a hard left turn. A second set of tracers seared through the SUV's rear compartment, puncturing the thin metal chassis.

Several red-hot tracer fragments bounced through the cabin, hissing and crackling as they dug into the leather seats and fabric lining of the roof. One of the tracers imbedded in Alex's headrest, igniting the material. Alex ignored the fire, calmly urging Ed to move them out of the kill zone at the top of the ramp. Each tracer represented five 7.62mm steel-jacketed projectiles, which had mercifully passed through both sides of the cargo compartment without deflecting. If the burst had struck the SUV five feet forward along the left side, the result would have been catastrophic. The SUV shot forward, Ed flooring the accelerator to get them to safety.

Seconds later, the rear driver's side wheel exploded, pulling the vehicle to the left. Ed wrestled with the wheel to keep them on the road, slowing the SUV to thirty miles per hour. A low-grade rumble reverberated through the chassis, the rough asphalt road grinding through the flattened tires. With their speed and maneuverability advantage eliminated, they'd have to come up with a different plan to survive the next several minutes. Trying to evade Humvees on shitty back roads with two flat tires wasn't going to work. Alex scanned the roadside, looking for turnoffs or businesses. If they could get off the road unobserved, they might be able to hide long enough for the helicopters to arrive.

A long chain-link fence on the left side of the road led to an open gate. Beyond the gate, a row of large open-bed stake trucks led to a one-story building with six closed garage bays. A sign supported by two posts labeled the facility as a Maine Highway Department Public Works Depot. The jagged tops of a distant tree line rose above the building. He had an idea.

"Follow the laser," said Alex, unbuckling his seatbelt.

He directed the rifle-mounted laser at the entrance, guiding the SUV into a slow turn into the compound. The driver's side tires dug into the packed gravel surface beyond the fence, slowing them considerably.

"Can you see the outline of the building in front of us?"

"Barely."

"Head toward the far right side. I think this is one of those public works places where they store sand and salt for the winter. We'll go all the way to the back and hide near the trees. If they follow us in, we'll head into the forest on foot," said Alex.

"On foot?" Ed echoed.

"It'll buy us plenty of time for Grady's team to get here," said Alex, pointing the laser at a tight opening between the trucks and the public works garage.

"Hey, Alex?"

"Yeah, Charlie?" said Alex, focusing on the laser.

"We should count on them following us," said Charlie. "We're kicking up dust."

Alex turned his head to look behind the SUV. A light

green plume followed them. Shit. There was no way they would miss that.

"Looks like we're on foot, then," said Alex.

"Damn it, Alex," muttered Ed. "We should have kept going."

"It doesn't matter. Let me off just past the garage and head as far back as possible. Get into the woods and keep moving away from the facility," said Alex, stuffing the ROTAC in one of his cargo pockets.

"Where are you going, Dad?" Ryan asked.

"I'll distract them and head west into the forest. It should buy us enough time."

"I'm going with you."

"No," said Alex. "I need you with Charlie and Ed. I'll fire a few bursts at them from behind and hide."

"Dad, we'll be more effective together."

"This isn't up for debate, Ryan. I can't afford the distraction."

"I can fight, Dad," Ryan protested.

"I didn't say you couldn't. I won't be able to do what I need to do with you nearby."

"That's bullshit!"

"I don't really care," said Alex.

Ed stopped the SUV on the far side of the building. A hangar-like structure sat fifty feet beyond the garage. To the left of the structure, a tapered mound of dirt rose to the height of the roof.

"I'll go with you, Alex," said Charlie. "Just like the good ole days. Ryan, you go with Mr. Walker. You need to keep that man alive if you plan on marrying his daughter."

"Oh my God," huffed Ryan, followed by a brief round of laughter.

"Keep going until I call you on the radio," said Alex, patting the handheld attached to his vest. "Let's go, Charlie."

"Dad?" Ryan said through the open car window. "Don't do anything crazy. Mom will be pissed if I don't bring you back. She made me promise."

"Is that so?" He smiled. "Looks like your mother was playing both sides on this one. I made the same promise."

Alex patted his helmet through the window. "No bullshit heroics. Straight into the forest and keep going. This will all be over in ten minutes."

"Ten minutes," repeated Ryan.

Alex pounded the side of the door. "Use your lights to find the way."

The SUV sped away, its headlights transforming the public works pit into daylight in his night-vision goggles.

"What's the plan, boss?" asked Charlie.

Alex scanned the tree line beyond the second building, making a quick calculation.

"I think that pile of dirt has a commanding view of the rest of the compound," said Alex, lasing the dark conical shape. "We'll wait for them to pass and climb high enough to engage when they dismount to investigate the SUV. Then we'll get the hell into the forest and disappear until the helicopters show."

"What if they don't?"

Alex checked his watch. Three minutes.

"They'll be here," said Alex. "Let's hop in the back of one of these trucks."

They sprinted to the back of a large utility pickup parked behind the garage and climbed into the bed. The light from their SUV disappeared, returning the public works compound to a dark green hue. Alex poked his head over the top of the truck bed, checking the avenues of approach.

The Humvees had two options to reach the back of the facility, one on each side of the garage. They would pass through without lights, giving Alex little warning to duck his head below the top of the bed.

"We'll have to stay low and listen. Once they pass by, we'll hop out and start climbing," said Alex.

They didn't have to wait long. The approaching sounds of crackling gravel filled the air, joined by the familiar, low rumble of diesel engines. Alex pressed flat against the gritty metal bed as the Humvees passed slowly down the left side of the pickup. When the sounds started to fade, he took a quick peek to confirm that the Humvees had disappeared behind the mound of dirt. He pressed the transmit button on his handheld.

"Ed, this is Alex. You there?"

"We're about two hundred feet into the forest. It's slow going."

"Humvees just passed our position," said Alex. "Whatever you do, don't stop moving. We'll draw them away."

"Got it," said Ed.

Alex reached into his cargo pocket to check the ROTAC screen. No calls. They were cutting it close. He considered calling Grady to get the Black Hawks' net call sign, but knew it didn't matter. The helicopters would get there when they got there. It was up to them to stay alive long enough to hear the sweet sound of the rotor blades.

"Ready?" he said, patting Charlie's shoulder.

"Fuck yeah."

They climbed out of the bed, pausing behind the truck to check for dismounted paramilitaries. It was clear.

"Let's go," he said, taking off for the back of the dirt pile.

Alex started climbing the mountain of dirt, quickly discovering that it was tightly packed sand. All the better to stop bullets, not that they would stick around long once the rounds started flying. He struggled for several seconds to reach a point near the top of the pile, finding himself with a clear view of the two Humvees. Charlie grunted below him, taking a few moments to reach the same height on the opposite side of the mound.

Alex took a second to analyze the scene. The Humvees were parked parallel to the back fence, next to the SUV. The turrets faced the forest; the gunners were likely scanning the trees beyond the chain-link barrier with telescopic night-vision sights. The doors on the military vehicles opened simultaneously, disgorging heavily armed figures. They needed to act immediately.

"I want you to concentrate on the turret gunners," said Alex.

"They're protected by turret armor," said Charlie.

"Not so much when they're facing us," said Alex, pressing and holding the trigger for a long burst.

Sparks exploded across the leftmost Humvee as dark figures scrambled for cover. One of the men dropped to his knees, reaching for the open door frame next to him. Charlie's rifle barked repeatedly, knocking the man to the ground while Alex unleashed a fusillade against the second vehicle. Bullets ricocheted off the Humvee's armor and windows, causing the men hiding behind the vehicle to duck. One of the contractors kneeling behind the hood of the leftmost Humvee pointed at the dirt pile, yelling to the rest of his team. The man's head snapped backward.

"I think they're on to us!" yelled Charlie.

"Take a few shots at the turret gunners," said Alex, noticing that the turrets had almost completely traversed in their direction. "We're out of here after that!"

A snap passed by Alex's head, followed by a hiss. Their secret was out. Alex triggered his IR laser and pointed it at the rightmost turret. The armored protection kit provided three-hundred-and-sixty-degree coverage, but left the gunner partially exposed toward the front. He fired two quick bursts at the top edge of the forward armor, hoping to place a bullet through the exposed opening.

When the M240 didn't answer his gunfire with a torrent of 7.62mm bullets, he knew he had either hit the gunner or scared him out of the turret. As long as the machine gun remained temporarily quiet, he didn't care what had transpired. Alex emptied the rest of his magazine at the men huddled near the Humvee and took cover behind the mound. Charlie was still firing.

"Slide down the back of the hill!" said Alex, grabbing the back of his vest and pulling. "We need to get out of here right now!"

Bullets snapped past the edge of the mound as they slid down the sand to the bottom of the mound's wide base. Based on the layout of the compound, Alex decided against running across the facility toward the western fence line. He couldn't guarantee a zero sight-line journey. The eastern side, which was closest to the mound, would be obscured from the Humvees by a mobile office trailer and several public works vehicles.

Once on the ground, they ran diagonally toward the fence, keeping the gigantic mound of sand between them and the shooters. Alex watched the entrance beyond the garage, expecting to see the third Humvee barrel into the compound at any second. They reached the fence unobserved, and Alex put his hands together to give Charlie a lift over the fence.

He heaved Charlie's heavily loaded frame as high up the eight-foot fence as possible, turning his attention to the mountain of sand. Tracers flew past the pile, indicating that the 240s were back in the fight. He watched as the trajectory of the tracers changed, shifting right. Shit. The Humvees were on the move. Alex slung his rifle over his back and started climbing the fence.

"Get up and over, man. They're coming," hissed Alex.

He reached the top as Charlie dropped to the other side. Swinging his right leg over, Alex pulled himself over the top and dropped, crashing to the ground next to his friend. A sharp, deep-seated pain shot up his left arm, which was trapped underneath him. He rolled onto his back, crying out when the arm shifted. Charlie kneeled next to him.

"I think I broke my arm," said Alex.

Charlie reached across his body, accidentally grabbing Alex's arm. The contact sent a shockwave of pain through his arm, which Alex muffled with a grunt.

"Sorry, Alex," said Charlie, pausing momentarily. "What do you see on my hand?"

A slick, dark green stain covered the palm of Charlie's hand. "Blood."

"You probably don't want to—"

Alex craned his neck to examine the useless appendage, seeing the forearm bent at an odd angle in the long sleeve of his jacket. Compound fracture. He dropped his head against the forest scrub.

"—look at your arm," finished Charlie.

"Get me up. We need to get clear of the fence," said Alex, extending his good hand to Charlie.

Alex was on his feet running, already a hundred feet into the forest, when he heard the diesel engines. Through the thick tangle of dead bushes and low pine boughs behind him, he watched two dark shapes creep past the fence. He patted Charlie on the shoulder, about to congratulate his friend, when the high-pitched squeal of the Humvees' brakes pierced the night.

"Get behind a thick tree, and get down!" he yelled as one of the Humvee's backed into sight.

A long string of tracers stitched through the trees, passing overhead. Alex nestled into the spongy forest floor, pulling his legs into a fetal position behind him. He groaned from the pain of pressing his arm into the ground, but he needed every square inch of his body blocked by the tree, and he needed his good arm free to operate his rifle. A second stream of tracers stitched through the base of the trees, bullets striking low against the trunk in front of him. The ground between Alex and Charlie exploded from the hail of bullets.

Alex risked a glance toward the fence, seeing that the Humvee had been repositioned to point at the fence. The second Humvee was out of sight, likely depositing mercenaries farther down the fence line. Within minutes, they'd have to contend with a flanking maneuver. He didn't see any way out of this.

"Any ideas?" he yelled to Charlie.

Charlie shook his head as tracers passed between them. "You always come up with the plan!"

"Watch your right flank! The second Humvee kept going!"

Keeping his body hidden from the M240's fusillade,

Charlie turned onto his left side and aimed his rifle toward their right flank. A concentrated burst of gunfire hit Charlie's tree, tracers slicing inches from his prone figure. A metallic crack was followed by a string of curses as Charlie quickly pulled his gun behind the tree.

"Son of a bitch! They broke my rifle!" he said.

"Does it still shoot?"

Charlie leaned around the tree and fired several times at the Humvee.

"Yep!"

"Then it ain't broke!" said Alex, pressing his rifle's vertical hand-guard grip against the tree and firing a wild burst toward the fence.

His gunfire was met by a furious volley of well-placed bullets, one ricocheting off his ACOG scope and grazing his right cheek.

"Fuck!" yelled Alex, pulling his rifle back.

He turned on his back and lifted his neck to examine the forest behind them. Streaks of light sailed through the darkness, striking trees and spinning through the pine boughs. The ground appeared flat. There was no way they could make a run for it without being torn apart by the Humvee's machine gun. Their only choice was to hold in place and hope the helicopters showed up within the next minute or two. He didn't anticipate surviving longer than that. Long beams of light reached out from their right flank, probing the trees and ground around them.

"Stay as low as you can!" said Alex. "They're using IR beams on our right flank."

"Fuck that," said Charlie, shifting his aim to the right.

A quick blast from his rifle was followed by a distant scream. The beams of light disappeared. The problem with IR beams was that they worked both ways if your adversary had night-vision equipment. Bullets hissed over Alex as the flankers fired in the general vicinity of the M204's tracers' general hit pattern. Alex hit his radio transmit button.

"Ed, where are you?"

Static filled his headset for a few seconds.

"We're headed south as fast as we can move," said Ed. "What's going on at the compound? Sounds like they're still there."

"We're pinned down about a hundred feet from the fence. No way we can move. They've got a group flanking us through the trees. We need those helicopters," said Alex.

"We can hear them," said Ed. "That's why we're busting ass to get out of here."

"The helicopters?"

"Yeah! They're close. Can't you hear them?"

Alex dug through his right cargo pocket for the ROTAC phone, seeing a deep orange glow through the open pocket flap. He flipped the NVGs up and read the illuminated display. *Missed call-Hellfire 05. Time 20:05*

"Two minutes ago," he muttered, selecting "Hellfire 05" and pressing SEND.

Chapter 35

Plymouth, Maine

The helicopter banked left, giving Staff Sergeant Dan Hurley a temporary reprieve from the endless treetops. The interstate edged into view through the gunner's station window, snaking south through the pines. They had followed the highway since Augusta, tracing its meandering path for nearly forty-five miles until they spotted two "still warm" vehicles crashed near one of the exits.

The helicopter's FLIR (Forward Looking InfraRed) pod had spotted the heat signatures nearly a mile out, prompting the pilot to call their ground contact. No answer. They hovered above the wrecks long enough to confirm that neither vehicle matched the description they were given by the Marines. The pilots continued north on the highway until one of the Marines reported seeing a stream of tracers fly into the air to the southwest.

"Gunners, I still have no contact with our guy on the ground. Do not engage unless you identify a target that is firing at one of the helicopters. We have multiple friendlies on the ground," he heard through the headset mounted into his helmet.

Two lines of tracers arched over the distant treetops, the scene drifting out of Hurley's view as the helicopter continued its sharp turn. The pilot steadied the utility helicopter on a new bearing, headed southwest. They'd be above the ground battle in less than ten seconds at this speed.

"All stations. I have contact with the ground. Troops in contact. We're going in hot. Port side, stand by to engage targets marked by laser. Friendlies will be marked by a ground flare. Be advised. A second group of friendlies is on foot several hundred feet south of the compound," said the pilot.

"Port-side gun station, solid copy," he said, listening to the Marines confirm the pilot's order.

In his peripheral vision, the Marines crowded the port-side cargo door, readying their weapons. He felt the helicopter shift left, flying a straight course for several seconds before banking hard right and slowing. Barrel flashes and tracers appeared below the dense pine canopy at the helicopter's eleven o'clock. Hurley swung the GAU-2/A 7.62mm Minigun toward the battle, revving its six barrels without feeding the ammunition. The electrically driven, air-cooled gun could fire up to fifty 7.62mm rounds per second at a sustained rate, utterly devastating anything in its sights. He found the flare burning brightly under a barrage of tracers. Now all he needed was a target.

A bright green laser answered his prayers, pointing at the source of the tracers—a Humvee partially obscured by the lead edge of the trees near the compound's eastern fence line. He triggered his gun's IR laser, matching its point of aim with the helicopter's. When the two aligned, Hurley depressed the spade trigger for a full second.

A continuous stream of low-intensity tracers belched from the minigun, ripping through the trees and blanketing the Humvee in sparks. The 7.62mm bullets couldn't penetrate the Humvee's primary armor, but that wasn't his intention. Hurley's mission was to turn the less protected turret into a charnel house, ensuring that nobody in his or her right mind would climb behind the M240 machine mounted inside. To drive home that point, he fired a longer burst at the Humvee, focusing the stream of tracers at the top of the Humvee.

"Targeting hostile foot mobiles one hundred feet south of friendlies," said the copilot, who was operating the FLIR.

The helicopter's target designation laser shifted left, penetrating the trees a hundred feet north of the friendlies. Flashes appeared in the general vicinity of the laser, followed by the hollow ding of bullets striking the helicopter's aluminum hull.

"Copy. Circle the target saturation area," said Hurley.

The laser drew a shaky, oval pattern over the flashes. Hurley waited for the flare to drift a few degrees right of his line of fire to minimize the possibility of skipping rounds into the friendlies. He held the trigger down for three seconds, blanketing the circled area with more than one hundred and fifty projectiles.

"FLIR registers good hits on foot mobiles," said the copilot. "Coming off target. Zero-Six lining up for a pass."

The helicopter's laser disappeared as they broke out of the trees and flew over open ground. He caught a glimpse of trucks and a few structures before trees filled his gunstation window. The helicopter banked left, giving him a view of Hellfire Zero-Six's gun run. Minigun tracer fire showered a different Humvee, causing a secondary explosion on the ground. The Marines hollered, cheering the gunner on. A few shorter bursts from the gun were directed at the forest in front of the first Humvee, presumably striking a second group of foot mobiles.

"We're coming in for a hover above friendly ground unit. Zero-Six will land in front of the garage and disembark Patriot elements. Watch for a third hostile vehicle possibly entering the compound from the north," said the pilot.

The crew acknowledged the pilot as they flew over the compound and approached the flare from a southerly direction.

Chapter 36

Plymouth, Maine

Alex lifted his head a few inches off the ground after he was certain the second helicopter was finished. Dozens of tracers and bullet ricochets from the friendly miniguns had ripped into nearby tree trunks and branches. He wasn't complaining, but he wasn't taking any chances either. His flare continued to burn brightly on the ground between them, whitewashing his view through the NVGs. He pushed the goggles off his face, squinting at Charlie's red, glowing form.

"You okay?" whispered Alex.

"Aside from the 7.62 millimeter haircut?" said Charlie, who remained face planted into the ground. "Yeah, I'm good."

"Check the right flank, in case something survived," said Alex.

"Nothing survived that," said Charlie, rolling onto his side to scan the trees through his riflescope.

"One of the helicopters is going to hover directly above and keep us safe while a squad of Marines secures the area," said Alex.

"Does that mean I can just lay here for a while?"

"Yeah, that's pretty much all I plan to do for now," said Alex.

The deep, rhythmic thumping grew louder, preceded by a growing wind that rustled the pine boughs and swept a fine layer of dirt from the compound through the trees. As the dark shape of Hellfire Zero-Five moved into position above, a maelstrom of pebbles, sticks and dried pine needles pelted them, causing Alex to bury his face in his arms. A quick burst of minigun fire sent a line of red tracers toward an unseen target, presumably the second Humvee.

Small-arms fire erupted in the compound, punctuated by the buzz-saw sound of the minigun above them. Spent casings tumbled through the branches, jingling as they struck the ground next to Alex. Either the third Humvee had showed up, or a few survivors had decided to fire at the offloading helicopter. Alex's ROTAC buzzed as the crackle of gunfire thinned. He didn't recognize the call sign.

"Alex Fletcher," he answered.

"This is Sergeant Keeler. I'm moving my squad toward the fence, due west of your position. We'll clear the vehicle and cut a hole in the fence. Have you out of there in a few minutes."

"Copy, Sergeant. You know where to find us. Any sign of the third Humvee?"

"Negative," said Keeler. "I have a few AT-4s waiting for it to make an appearance."

"I hope you get to use them," replied Alex, switching to his handheld radio. "Ed, this is Alex. Can you hear me?"

"Barely. Are you guys okay?"

"I broke my arm, but that seems to be the extent of it. We're just waiting for a squad of Marines to sweep the area. Where are you now?"

"Somewhere south of the SUV. We stopped moving when the helicopters started firing. Do you want us to head back?"

He could barely hear Ed over the incessant noise and rotor wash of the helicopter above him.

"Did anyone follow you into the woods?" said Alex.

"I don't know. We've been hauling ass since we got over the fence. We can't see a damn thing."

"Just stay where you are. Lay low and listen for any sounds."

"I hear helicopters and gunfire," said Ed. "That's about it."

"Do what you can until we get this sorted out," said Alex. "How's Ryan?"

"I think he's enjoying this way too much," said Ed. "The apple doesn't fall too far from the tree. See you in a few."

"I'm not sure if that's a compliment."

"It is if you're trying to stay alive," said Ed.

Alex laid his head on a thick root protruding from the bottom of the tree trunk and watched the red flare sputter against the ground. All he wanted was a stretcher and a helicopter ride home. He highly doubted either was in his immediate future, unless the paramilitaries had disabled the SUV before chasing them. Over the drone of the helicopter rotors, he heard the sharp metallic snap of bolt cutters breaching the chain-link fence. He closed his eyes and took a deep breath, waiting for the Marines to surround his position.

"They're here," said Charlie.

"Mr. Fletcher?" yelled a voice in front of them.

A figure in full combat kit appeared at the outer fringe of the flare's light, aiming a rifle at Alex.

"Yes. Alex Fletcher and Charlie Thornton. We're on the ground with the flare between us."

"Can you bury the flare for me?" said the Marine. "I need to positively ID one of you."

Alex grabbed the flare with his right hand and jammed it into the soft forest floor, burying it as far as possible to give the Marine a chance to use night vision to identify them from a distance.

"Confirmed! I have Alex Fletcher on the right. Mr. Thornton on the left," said the Marine, rushing forward. "Hasty one-eighty facing east."

As the Marine rifle squad sprinted into positions around them, Alex rose to his knees to greet the squad leader.

"Sergeant Keeler, good to see you again," said Alex.

"The pleasure is all mine, gentlemen," said Keeler. "If you don't mind, Hellfire Zero-Six would like to get airborne ASAP."

Alex struggled to get off his knees.

"Need a hand, partner?" said Charlie, pushing himself off the ground with his good hand.

"I don't know who's helping who here," said Alex.

Sergeant Keeler heaved Alex to his feet by his vest, swiftly grasping Charlie's good hand and swinging him into an upright position.

"We need to move," said Keeler, striding ahead of them.

Alex flipped his NVGs in place and followed the sergeant to the helicopter, pulling Charlie through the darkness. Once inside the Black Hawk, Alex slipped a pair of crew headphones over his NVG harness and spoke with the pilot.

"Thanks for the rescue. We were about a minute from

the end when you guys showed up. Drinks are on me," said Alex, feeling the helicopter lift off the ground.

He dropped into an empty, forward-facing seat between two Marines.

"You're lucky we can't take you up on that offer," said the pilot.

"One of these days," said Alex. "Hey, did Zero-Five mention picking up two additional friendlies? My son and another friend are on foot, south of the facility."

"Zero-Five has located them using infrared. Tell them to proceed due south. They're less than a hundred meters from the interstate," answered the pilot. "Zero-Five will pick them up in the southbound lanes."

"Roger. I'm calling them now," said Alex, pressing the transmit button on his handheld.

"Ed, this is Alex. I need you to continue south another hundred meters, three hundred feet or so. You're almost to the turnpike," said Alex.

He could barely hear Ed's reply.

"Say again, Ed. I didn't catch what you said."

"—not us," said Ed.

"Not us? Did you say not us?"

"Some—else," said Ed. "Been trying—contact."

"Stay put. We'll fix this," said Alex, keying the helicopter headphones.

"Pilot, my guy on the ground is telling me that's not them. I can't hear what he's saying. I think he's whispering. Can you have Zero-Five do another sweep with their FLIR?"

"Stand by," said the pilot.

Alex felt the helicopter bank sharply, increasing speed as it came out of the turn.

Charlie yelled across the troop compartment, "What's going on?"

"I think there's another team tracking Ed and Ryan!" he said, the implication hitting him hard.

Neither Ed nor Ryan had night-vision gear. They didn't have a way to fight in the dark. His earphones crackled.

"Mr. Fletcher, Zero-Five has two sets of infrared signatures. They're less than ten meters apart. One group is headed right for the other. Too close for guns," said the pilot.

Alex shook his head, muttering, "No. No. No."

It wasn't supposed to happen like this. Ed and Ryan were supposed to be out of danger. Where the hell did more of these contractors come from? Why were they between the highway and his son? He needed to come up with something. Without night vision, his son and Ed stood no chance against seasoned military contractors. Night vision. That was it.

"Is this helicopter equipped with infrared countermeasures? A flare dispenser?"

"Affirmative," said the pilot.

"Tell Zero-Five to light up the sky above the heat signatures," said Alex.

Chapter 37

Plymouth, Maine

Ryan lay prone, his rifle canted sideways to keep it as low as possible. A twig snapped, barely audible over the distant thunder of helicopter rotors. The men were close, most likely directly in front of them, but he couldn't be sure. Even with his eyes adjusted to the darkness, the blackness betrayed no movement. He let his peripheral vision do the work, remembering what his dad said about the motion sensitivity of his eyes' photoreceptors. Still nothing.

A muted crunch drew his attention to the left, in front of Mr. Walker. He had to do something. The men searching nearby were bound to catch a glimpse of them soon. Without night vision, the earliest warning would be a hail of bullets tearing through flesh and bone. Ryan had no intention of dying on his stomach while hoping for a miracle.

He'd take the initiative, throwing the mercenaries off balance. It was their only chance of survival. Unfortunately, he couldn't warn Mr. Walker. The men were too close to whisper. Sliding his thumb along the rifle hand guard, he located the pressure switch for the flashlight attachment. The powerful LED light would render their adversaries' NVGs temporarily useless, giving him a second or two to fire, unless they were using generation four night-vision gear. If that was the case, he might get one of them before they shot him in the head. Shit. He couldn't just lay here and wait to be shot. The light was worth a try. He took his right hand off the rifle's pistol grip and planted it into the soft, moist forest floor, tensing his muscles for a solid boost.

His dad's voice came over the earbud planted in his left ear.

"Ed, Ryan, listen closely. You have two targets due south of your position, less than twenty feet away. One of the helicopters is headed in your direction right now, but they can't fire without hitting you. They will fly directly overhead and drop several high-intensity flares. Once the flares ignite, you should be able to see your targets. Don't hesitate. Just start shooting. Click your radio transmit button twice if you copy. Ed first. Then Ryan."

Ryan eased his hand to the remote transmit button on the shoulder of his vest and waited for two breaks in the static before pressing it twice. A hand gently patted him on the shoulder as the sound of helicopter rotors deepened.

This is it.

He found the trigger again, stretching his thumb around the pistol grip to verify that the safety was disabled. He knew the rifle was set to automatic fire, but he had to check. There was no room for error. Especially now. When his stomach started to vibrate from the booming sound of the approaching Black Hawk, he took some of the slack out of the trigger.

Any time now.

A high-pitched engine whine mixed with the rotors as the helicopter thundered overhead, turning night into day. Ryan fired a long burst into the two body-armor-clad figures appearing less than fifteen feet away, sweeping the point of aim of his rifle across their twitching bodies. With Ed's rifle barking rapidly next to him, he switched to short, successive bursts until the two men dropped out of sight, leaving a fine red mist drifting in the flares' dancing illumination.

Ryan twisted onto his side and withdrew a fresh rifle magazine from one of his vest pouches, reloading and listening for movement in front of them. As the earsplitting din of the helicopter faded, he rose behind the tree next to him and fired into each body's legs, not detecting a reaction. The men were dead.

The magnesium flares launched by the helicopter crashed through the canopy, igniting anything they touched on the way down. Ryan crouched as a flare swept through the pine boughs above them, setting fire to the tree before bouncing off a thick branch. The pyrotechnic device landed on one of the dead mercenaries, burning intensely for a few moments before suddenly fizzling. His face went cold when the flare died.

"I think they're about as dead as they can be. Let's go," whispered Mr. Walker, squatting next to him, "before the forest burns down around us."

They took off running, using the yellow-orange flickering light of the flaming trees to guide their way.

"Ed, Ryan, what's your status?" said his dad.

Ryan waited for Mr. Walker to answer. That was the protocol they had established between them. Only one of them answered radio calls to avoid confusion.

"Go ahead, Ryan. I think your dad would rather hear from you," said Mr. Walker.

"Dad, we're fine. Heading south toward the highway. I think they started a forest fire."

"Good to hear your voice, buddy. Move as fast as you can to the highway. We think the third Humvee dropped off the team you encountered. The pilots are eager to get out of here," said Alex. "And thank you for keeping my guy safe, Ed."

"I'm pretty sure it was the other way around," said Mr. Walker, patting Ryan on the back again.

He liked hearing Chloe's dad talk about him like that. Mr. Walker hadn't been a big fan of his for obvious reasons. Ryan stuck to avoiding him and, in turn, evading Chloe. He felt bad about doing that to her, but Mr. Walker's stares and pointed comments made him feel uncomfortable. His mom did a decent enough job explaining why the Walkers might want to put the brakes on their relationship, but it still hurt to be away from her. Maybe things would change between them. He hoped so. He also hoped all of this meant they could stay in Maine.

They reached the edge of the trees, pointlessly scanning the starlit sky for the helicopter. They heard it approach before they saw it, a dark mass descending in front of them. Four shadowy figures hopped to the pavement and ran in their direction, shining lights in their faces. Ryan turned his head and squinted, hearing one of them report "confirmed" into his helmet microphone. The lights disappeared, leaving them flash blind.

"Mr. Fletcher, Mr. Walker. Please follow me," said the Marine, grabbing his hand and pulling him through the powerful rotor wash toward the waiting helicopter.

Just outside the helicopter, one of the Marines took his rifle and cleared it, handing it back and keeping the magazine. Hands grabbed his vest and pulled him inside, where he was directed to empty harness seats and told to hang on. He searched through the darkness for his dad, seeing nothing but night-vision-equipped helmets and balaclava-covered faces.

"Where's my dad?" he yelled.

The last Marine to jump into the helicopter answered, "Your dad and Mr. Thornton are in the other helicopter. They're both injured, so we're assessing whether they need to be transported to a medical facility. My orders are to take you to your house in Belgrade. Your dad has been notified that you're safe."

"Okay," he yelled, turning his head to find Mr. Walker. "Mr. Walker?"

"Right behind you," a voice called out. "And I think you can call me Ed at this point."

Ryan really liked the sound of that.

Chapter 38

Belgrade, Maine

Kate heard the helicopters before the deck's side stairs announced Staff Sergeant Evans' presence, the wood creaking from the added weight of his combat gear. She'd been outside listening since the Marines had passed word of the harrowing rescue. She let go of the deck rail and turned to the house. A diesel engine revved in the distance.

"Ma'am, they're less than a minute out. The helicopters will touch down just south of here on Jamaica Road. One of my vehicles is heading out to meet them," said Evans, standing in front of a two-story wall of wide, angled windows.

The soft glow of candles illuminated the great room behind the wall of windows facing the lake, turning the Marine into a dark silhouette.

"Can your medic treat them here?" she asked, walking toward the house.

"He'll thoroughly clean the wounds and do what he can to keep Mr. Fletcher and Mr. Thornton comfortable. Their injuries are painful, but not life threatening. We're working on a plan to deliver a medical team from Augusta to set your husband's arm and do a real stitch job on Mr. Thornton's hand. They might be preoccupied until the morning, or longer," said Evans.

"All hell breaking loose tonight?" said Kate.

"We'll be fine here," said Evans, opening the sliding door.

"Your colonel doesn't think so, or I wouldn't have a squad of Marines at my house," Kate pointed out.

"It's just a precaution," said Evans. "And a bit of a fig leaf."

"I think you mean olive branch? Offering a fig leaf is what you do to cover up an embarrassment."

"Whatever the saying is," said the Marine. "He really needed their help."

"He should have asked. A few pallets of field rations and MREs isn't adequate compensation for a dead husband and son," Kate remarked, eyeing the stack of olive drab containers stacked in the hallway leading to the front door.

Evans looked down as she stepped through the door.

"I know, ma'am. I'm really sorry," he whispered.

The dry heat from the wood-burning stove warmed her face like a sunny day. The flickering light of several widely spaced candles illuminated the great room and eat-in kitchen. Her daughter, Emily, and the rest of the teenage girls sat on the floor in front of a wide, U-shaped sectional couch, playing cards. Samantha, Linda, and Alex's mother sat on the leather sections behind them, looking to her for word. Tim Fletcher placed a glass on the kitchen counter and turned to face her.

"They're on their way. I can hear the helicopters," said Kate, catapulting the room into a frenzy.

As the extended family rushed toward the front door, Kate looked at Evans.

"Luckily for you, all this group cares about is getting their people back in one piece," said Kate. "You might want to have your medic put something strong in my husband's IV bag. He's the one you need to worry about."

"I'll take that under advisement," Evans said, looking even more contrite than before.

They waited in the wide front yard, keeping their distance from the armored vehicle parked squarely in the middle of the trampled grass. The silent mass of steel stood vigil over the house, anchoring a dozen Marines spread in a three-hundred-and-sixty-degree perimeter throughout the property. An impenetrable row of evenly cut arborvitaes stretched across the front edge of the grass, creating a privacy screen from the dirt road connecting the lot to the rest of the neighborhood. The trees were somewhat pointless, since the house was located at the far northern end of the access road. You'd have to be hopelessly lost, or terminally nosy, to travel to the end of the road.

Staff Sergeant Evans stood at the edge of the compact trees, watching the road through a handheld night-vision scope. She was relieved to have the Marines guarding the house, even if their arrival had been one hell of a surprise. The house exploded in panic when the battery-powered wireless motion detectors installed a hundred feet down the road registered movement. Linda led everyone into the trees north of the backyard while Tim manned one of the protected firing positions they had constructed on the second floor of the house facing the road.

When he reported two military vehicles pulling up to the property, they assumed the worst. The mission to Bangor had failed, leading the paramilitaries to their doorstep. The sudden arrival of two Matvees less than an hour after Alex's departure was hard to interpret any other way. They all breathed a sigh of relief when Tim reported that the "Marines had landed."

The good vibes ended when Staff Sergeant Evans, unable to adequately explain the need for his presence in Belgrade, confessed that their husbands and her son were headed into an uncertain situation. Kate interpreted "uncertain" to mean dangerous, which turned out to be an understatement. A military coup was underway in the state, and her husband was driving into the middle of it. They waited in sheer silence for word from the helicopters sent north toward Bangor.

Evans had understood the gravity of their situation. He had a ten-year-old son and six-year-old daughter waiting with his wife in the Military Dependents Camp at Fort Devens. His family's safety was completely dependent on the commanders calling the shots at the base. He was as helpless as Kate and the rest of them. She felt bad for heaping the blame on Evans. He'd drawn the short straw tonight. If anyone in Alex's group had been killed, the Marines would have witnessed a hostile environment unlike any combat zone they had ever seen. The thought brought a quiver to her lip. She didn't want to think about what could have happened. Kate was just glad they were safe.

"They just made the turn," said Evans.

The group edged forward in the darkness. Evans cracked a green chemlight and tossed it to the ground between the trees and family, casting a faint glow over them. Kate squeezed Emily's hand, and her daughter squeezed back. The sound of heavy tires grinding against the uneven dirt road penetrated the trees, followed by the deep hum of a powerful diesel engine. The Matvee rumbled past the evergreens, squeaking to a halt several feet beyond Evans. The passenger-side doors opened, disgorging two Marines, who rushed to the back of the troop compartment. The rear hatch swung to the right, exposing the road to a dark red light.

Ryan jumped to the ground, turning to help Ed. They reached up to help Alex slide out of the back, onto his feet. Her husband's left arm was wrapped in a compression splint that ended at his wrist. Alex grimaced when he hit the ground, sucking air between his teeth. Ryan pulled the good arm over his shoulder and backed out of Charlie's way.

"I got this!" yelled Charlie. "Jesus Christ, I feel like I've been admitted to a nursing home."

Charlie's feet hit the ground unevenly, his sizable frame wobbling on impact. He stumbled backward, unconsciously extending his bandaged hand to catch the back of the Matvee. When his hand smacked into the armored hatch, Charlie screamed loud enough to wake the entire lake. Ed quickly grabbed him before he crashed to the ground.

"Told you I had it," he grumbled, sparking laughter from everyone.

When the four of them finally stood upright behind the Matvee, one of the Marines inside the vehicle started clapping. They all joined in a round of applause and whistles for the returning crew, before the families rushed forward to swarm them.

Emily ran ahead of Kate, throwing her arms around Alex's uninjured side. He winced before kissing the top of her head and squeezing her tight with his good arm.

Kate hugged Ryan tightly, ignoring the rifle magazines and combat gear fastened to his body armor. She wept silently, tears streaming down her face. Kate could barely wrap her arms around her son, but she kept him locked in place until he protested. She didn't want to let her son go. The relief she felt holding his living, breathing form caused her to feel weak, almost fragile. She couldn't go through this again. Not with either of them.

"You're not going anywhere, ever again," she said, sniffling.

"I'm fine, Mom," Ryan said, trying to squirm out of her bear hug. "It wasn't a big deal. Dad had it under control."

"It sounded like a big deal," she said, easing up on him.

"Everything was more or less fine. This is just from falling off a fence," said Alex, nodding at his splinted arm.

"Save it. I got the full story from Staff Sergeant Evans," said Kate.

"Yeah, he fell off the fence dodging machine-gun bullets!" yelled Charlie. "You should have seen it! And they say *I'm* the klutz. Whheeeee, he went sailing!"

"I thought we agreed to play down certain aspects of our trip," said Alex, letting go of Emily to hold Kate.

"Fuck that, man. We just survived against all odds. I thought we were gone for sure until those helicopters showed up!"

"Maybe I didn't get the full story," she said. "Ryan, I expect a full report from you, since I'm obviously not going to get it from your—"

"He's gone to find Chloe," said Alex, nibbling her bottom lip.

She tilted her head for a more passionate kiss. Despite the fact that he smelled like a combination of gun propellant, musty pine needles, and blood, she couldn't get enough. He responded to her not-so-subtle advance and returned the deeper kiss. She broke it off, conscious that their daughter was holding on to them.

"Later," she whispered in his ear, opening their family cluster to bring Emily closer.

"Dad, do you think things will go back to normal now?" asked Emily.

"I think it'll get better, sweetie," said Alex, meeting her eyes with doubt.

A distant boom punctuated the night, causing Alex to look toward Staff Sergeant Evans. The Marine cracked a second green chemlight, holding it in front of him. Three successive explosions followed the first.

"Welcome back, gentlemen. If you don't mind, I'd like to get everyone inside," said Evans, motioning for them to follow him across the yard.

When the families were clear of the road, the Matvee turned around and raced away.

"How long will they be here?" Kate asked.

"I don't know," said Alex, pausing as several muted detonations echoed across the lake. "Probably depends on how long that lasts."

"I hope they stay," said Emily, speaking for all of them.

Chapter 39

Belgrade, Maine

Alex's arm throbbed inside the plaster short-arm cast lying across his lap. He stared at the lake through the spacious windows, still slightly dazed from four days of taking pain medications. Dark, hazy thoughts dominated his mental horizon. While grateful to be alive, sharing stolen time with his family, he couldn't stop focusing on the long-term cost of the trip. His arm would be useless for most, if not all of the summer. Charlie's hand was out of commission for more than a month.

The combination of injuries represented a significant setback to their gardening project, which was barely a feasible endeavor with all hands participating. Alex knew logically that it wasn't the end of the world. They'd be fine. Grady had promised him food and supplies, which he had no reason to doubt. Emotionally, his outlook dimmed at the thought of sitting around idle, reliant on outside assistance. He'd planned so carefully over the past five years to specifically avoid this situation.

Maybe he was just angry at having the rug ripped out from under him after spending so much time believing that he was ready for anything. Who was he kidding? Ninety-nine percent of the population had it far worse than the Fletchers, even now. Alex had to remember that.

He hadn't failed on any level. If anything, he'd succeeded in the face of insurmountable odds, with a little help along the way. A lot of help, but that was how it worked. No man was an island. No family was an island. However that saying went. Words to live and die by.

"What are you thinking about?" asked Kate, appearing next to the couch with a steaming mug of coffee.

"Just staring out into space. Feeling sorry for myself," he said. "Is that for me?"

"It wasn't, but anything to lift your spirits," she said, walking around the leather sectional to put the mug on the glass coffee table in front of him. "Ken is going to help us plot the garden beds. He knows a few others in the neighborhood that might be able to help."

"More mouths to feed," he mumbled, reaching for the coffee mug.

"Alex," she started.

"Sorry. We need all the help we can get, not to mention that the neighbors are here to stay. I'm still dusting the cobwebs off that record. It's just hard going from our compound in Limerick to coexisting in a community of strangers."

"We'll make it work somehow."

Alex wasn't sure how, but as long as the military subsidized their food, they'd figure it out eventually.

"Alex!" yelled his dad, the front door slamming behind him.

"On the couch," he called, shaking his head and winking at Kate.

"I know where you are. It's where you always are," said Tim, rushing into the room.

"I might have broken an arm, Dad," said Alex.

"Didn't realize you walked on your hands," said Tim, shifting the rifle sling on his shoulder. "Someone's here to see you."

The house started to vibrate almost imperceptibly.

"Who?" asked Alex, pushing off the couch to stand up.

"Lieutenant Colonel Grady," said Tim. "We've got a Matvee and four of those big-ass armored trucks idling in front of Charlie's house."

"Grady came up?" said Alex, kissing Kate on the cheek as he hurried around the couch. "This should be interesting. Three MTVRs? That's a lot of carrying capacity."

"I don't know what the hell they're called. Back in my day they were called five-tons, and they had a canvas cover over the back. Barely protected us from the rain, let alone an RPG."

Alex patted his dad on the shoulder. "Times were tougher back then, Dad."

"Why does that sound like you're patronizing me?" Tim followed him down the slate-tiled hallway to the front door.

"I have no idea," said Alex, smiling at his dad.

Sean Grady stood at the far end of the front yard, talking with Ryan. The two of them nodded and grinned like they'd known each other for years. The Marine shook his son's hand, holding onto his shoulder. A classic man-hug. Ryan took off down the compacted dirt road, disappearing behind the row of pines.

"Are you supposed to be wearing your helmet?" asked Alex.

The fury he'd promised to rain on Grady never materialized, along with the best intentions to endlessly lecture the officer that once served as a platoon commander under him. Sean's smile, the familiar scar, the way he genuinely embraced Ryan—he let the anger go. Just like that, it was gone, leaving Alex feeling lighter.

"Alex, I want to—"

"Apology accepted," Alex cut in. "You don't need to mention it again."

"Alex, I don't expect—"

"Seriously, Sean. I think this is my new mantra. Let it go."

"Is your son feeling all right?" Grady asked Alex's dad.

"That's the first logical thing he's said since the fall, so I'd say he's doing just fine," said Tim, patting Alex on the back. "I'll head on down to the convoy to see what's in those armored trucks. If you can even fit anything in there. In my day—"

"We know. Marines walked everywhere, with twice the gear and no body armor," said Alex.

"You see that, Colonel? No respect for his elders," said Tim, shrugging his shoulders, and they all had a good laugh.

"We'll be right there, Dad," said Alex.

"Take your time," said Tim, heading down the road toward the armored vehicles.

"Grab a cup of coffee? Fresh brewed with a new batch of grinds," said Alex. "Looks nice enough to sit out on the deck.

"I'll take you up on that," said Grady. "But I need to push off in about fifteen minutes. I'm headed up over to Searsport next. I need to collect some personal gear."

"How many did Staff Sergeant Taylor lose?" asked Alex, aware that a fierce battle had been fought over the terminal the first night of the military coup.

"Five. The National Guard garrison took the brunt of the casualties. Eighteen out of the forty-two soldiers assigned to guard the terminal. They threw at least fifty Homeland mercs against the facility, supported by heavy weapons and several up-armored Humvees. Hit the place hard."

"Jesus. I'm sorry to hear that."

"They fought all night. We couldn't use the helicopters because the mercs breached the northern gate and took up positions near the fuel farm. We ferried half of the Sanford-based Ranger company up to Searsport to conduct a predawn attack. Finally cleared them out," Grady told him.

"What about the rest of the state? We heard some explosions. Sounded like they came from Waterville."

"A National Guard garrison was attacked on the outskirts of the city, but the same helicopters that brought you home managed to intercede. Homeland spread the battalion too thin. Searsport was the biggest attack, outside of the coordinated raid on the governor's mansion and state government in Augusta. Colonel Martin's Stryker battalion met them in force outside of the state capital. There wasn't much left of the Homeland force after that. We hit them all over the state with Medina's intelligence."

"And how is our former RRZ administrator?"

"Helping us keep the peace. Homeland doesn't want word spreading about this. As far as we know, it's been swept under the rug," said Grady. "They barely have the support of the military at this point. A few of the RRZs have been torn apart by these mercenary battalions, right under the noses of some very disgruntled and confused military commanders. The New England RRZ has a chance of surviving now, which is more important to D.C. right now than a petty control battle between two bureaucrats," said Grady.

"You're not a big fan of Dague or Medina?"

"What choice do we have?" said Grady. "The military can't be put in charge. The last vestige of trust in the government would be eradicated if the military took over. Those two will figure it out. They don't have a choice at this point."

Alex showed Grady to the kitchen, where Kate was pouring an extra mug of coffee.

"Kate, it's a pleasure to see you again," Grady said. "Feel free to slap me as many times as you'd like."

Kate eyed him warily, shaking her head. "A slap? I've been practicing a frontal kick, aimed low, for the past few days."

"Point taken," he said, looking to Alex.

"Don't look at me," said Alex.

She handed Grady the mug she just poured, the Marine hesitant to take her offer.

"I've decided it would be in nobody's best interest to assault you—today," she said. "Plus it sounds like my husband has found it in his heart to forgive you."

"I'm truly sorry," he said.

"I know," Kate said, her face softening. "I live with a man who still wakes up in a cold sweat, blaming himself for every Marine killed or injured under his command. I know it's not something you take lightly, and that it stays with you forever. But my son and husband are not part of your battalion. You had no right to send them up their without the full picture."

Grady swallowed hard.

"Never again," she said, pointing at him.

"Never again," Grady agreed.

"All right. I'll let the two of you catch up. I hear you brought four trucks with you?" she said, trying to smile.

"It's the least I could do to thank everyone," said Grady. "In addition to enough food to last your whole crew at least two years, we grabbed some gear from the Limerick compound. Solar panels, the whole system, along with the batteries, ham radio, personal effects. Nobody has gone near the place since we left."

Kate's eyes watered, her stern look melting.

"Thank you, Sean," she said, having trouble forming the words. "You don't know what this means to us."

"I should have brought this up to you a lot earlier," said Grady.

"It means a lot. We're truly grateful for everything you've done. We wouldn't be having this conversation if you hadn't helped Alex in Boston," she said.

"Friends help friends," said Sean.

"Then I should be glad some things haven't changed," she said, extending her hand. "Square?"

"Unless you need something," said Grady, shaking her hand. "I mean it. It'll be easier for us to get around the state now."

"I'd give you a hug, but I'm done hugging rifle magazines and body armor. I'll let the two of you catch up," she said.

"See you in a few minutes," said Alex, giving her a kiss.

Alex and Grady stepped onto the deck, basking in the warmth.

"Not a bad place up here," said Grady. "Now I can see why they call Maine vacationland. I never understood why people flocked to the southern coast. Same with

Cape Cod. The last thing I want to deal with on vacation are crowds of people. This is nice."

"I never understood why people wanted to vacation in the summer. I know the kids are out of school, but for shit's sake, why go from one warm place to another?"

"I never understood ski vacations either," said Grady.

"Don't even get me started. Going from cold to cold makes no sense either," Alex replied.

"I wonder how long it will be before any of us takes a *vacation* again," said Grady.

"I was on my way to warmer climates, maybe Europe, until my boat was taken by the state," said Alex.

"You don't want to go to Europe," Grady said gravely. "Things are falling apart quickly. The Russians have swept through half of their former satellite states, stopping at the Polish and Romanian borders. There's nothing in place to stop them if they want to drive further."

"I was thinking Argentina or Brazil," said Alex.

"Not a bad idea, though it's only a matter of time before the economic ripple effect starts to tear things apart down there. Mexico is essentially a no-man's-land, along with most of Central America. The Caribbean islands are folding one by one as the supplies from South America slow."

"Sounds like you're trying to sell me on staying in the U.S."

"Frankly, it's starting to look more and more like the best bet," said Grady.

"I was hoping to subsist on more than MREs and B-rations for the rest of my life," said Alex.

"I was going to surprise you on the walk back, but I might as well break the news over the best cup of coffee

I've had since last August. Harrison Campbell gave me a small cooler filled with heirloom seeds. Said he thought your garden might need a boost. Sounds like he was right," said Grady.

"He really did that?"

"He was adamant about it," said Grady. "Made me wait while he put it together."

"The RRZ relocation thing was bullshit, right? You still went out to visit him?"

"Medina did plan on moving the RRZ once the state government was neutralized. I knew that wasn't going to happen, but I promised you I'd talk to Harrison. He was touched by your generosity, and very happy to learn that the RRZ security zone wasn't moving north."

"I bet he was," said Alex.

"Well, I better get moving," said Grady. "I'll leave one MTVR, with a squad of volunteers to help you dig up the garden beds. Harrison led me to believe that you might need some help with that as well."

"Harrison must have been worried all winter about us," said Alex, leading him into the house.

"We were all worried about you. Like it or not, you're somewhat of a celebrity back at the MOB. Even more so now. I'd never say this around Kate, but if you're interested in a job with the RRZ, I'll make it happen. Just say the word," said Grady.

"I think I'm done with all of that, Sean," said Alex. "I just want to start over and enjoy what I still have."

"I don't blame you, Alex," said Grady, cracking a smile. "You have more than most up here. "If you change your mind, you know how to get in touch."

Alex swiped the ROTAC from the kitchen table on the way past, stopping to hand it to Grady.

"I'll drive down and let you know personally," said Alex. "Maybe after everything settles."

Grady accepted the ROTAC, nodding. "Hopefully, I'll be back with my family by then."

"I'll drink to that," said Alex, clinking Grady's coffee mug.

***

*

Acronyms and Terminology Used in
The Alex Fletcher Books

ACOG – Advanced Combat Optical Gunsight. A telescopic scope commonly issued to troops in the field.

ACU – Army Combat Uniform

AFES – Automated Fire Extinguishing System

AFV Stryker – Armored Fighting Vehicle used by U.S. Army

AN/VRC-110 – Vehicle based VHF/UHF capable radio system used by U.S. Marine Corps.

AR-10 – 7.62mm NATO/.308 caliber, military style rifle

AR-15 – 5.56mm/.223 caliber military style rifle

BCT – Brigade Combat Team, U.S. Army

Black Hawk – UH-60, Medium Lift, Utility Helicopter

CISA – Critical Infrastructure Skills Assembly

CQB – Close Quarters Battle, urban combat

CH-47 Chinook – Twin engine, tandem rotor, heavy lift helicopter

CIC – Combat Information Center

CONEX – Intermodal Shipping Container. Large metal crates typically seen stacked on merchant ships or in shipping yards.

C-130 – Propeller driven, heavy lift fixed wind aircraft capable of short landings and takeoffs.

C-17B Globemaster – Heavy Lift, fixed wing aircraft

C2BMC – Command, Control, Battle Management and Communications

DRASH – Deployable, Rapid Assembly Shelter

DTCS – Distributed Tactical Communication System (satellite based network)

EMP – Electromagnetic Pulse

ETA – Estimated Time of Arrival

FEMA – Federal Emergency Management Agency

FOB – Forward Operating Base

GPS – Global Positioning System, satellite based

GPNVG-18 – Panoramic night vision goggles, wide field of vision.

HAM radio – Term used to describe the Amateur Radio network

HBMD – Homeland Ballistic Missile Defense

HESCO – Rapidly deployable earth filled defensive barrier

HK416 – 5.56mm Assault rifle/carbine designed by Hechler & Koch.

Humvee – Nickname for High Mobility Multipurpose Wheeled Vehicle (HMMWV).

IED – Improvised Explosive Device

KIA – Killed in Action

L-ATV – Light Combat Tactical All Terrain Vehicle

LP/OP – Listening Post/Observation Post

MARPAT – Marine Pattern, digital camouflage used by U.S. Marine Corps

M-ATV – Medium Combat Tactical All Terrain Vehicle. MRAP

Medevac – Medical Evacuation

MOB – Main Operating Base

MP – Military Police

MP-7 – Personal Defense Weapon designed by Heckler and Koch, submachine gun firing armor penetrating ammunition

MRAP – Mine Resistant Ambush Protected vehicle

MRE – Meals Ready to Eat, self-contained field rations used by U.S. military

MR556SD – 5.56mm assault rifle/carbine with integrated suppressor.

MTV M1078 – Medium Tactical Vehicle used by U.S. Army, 5 ton capacity

MTVR Mk23 – Medium Tactical Vehicle Replacement used by U.S. Marine Corps, 7 ton capacity

M1919A6 – .30 caliber, belt fed medium machine gun fielded during WWII and the Korean War. Fully automatic.

M240G – Modern 7.62mm, belt fed medium machine gun used by U.S Army and U.S. Marine Corps

M27 IAR – Heavier barrel version of the HK416 used by U.S. Marine Corps. Replaced the M249 belt fed machine gun. Issued to one member of each fire team.

M320 – Rifle-mounted, detachable 40mm grenade launcher.

NCO – Non-Commissioned Officer (Corporal and Sergeant)

NEO – Near Earth Object (asteroid or meteorite)

NVD – Night Vision Device (used interchangeable with NVG)

NVG – Night Vision Goggles

PRC-153 ISR – Intra-squad radio. Motorola style radio (usually strapped to tactical vest) for squad communication.

ROTAC – Tactical Satellite Radio

RTB – Return to Base

Satphone – Satellite Phone

SNCO – Staff Non-Commissioned Officer (Staff Sergeant E-6 and above)

SUV – Sport Utility Vehicle

Two-Forty – M240 machine gun. See M240G

UH-60 Black Hawk – Medium Lift, Utility Helicopter

YCRB – York County Readiness Brigade. Harrison Campbell's group.

If you enjoyed The Alex Fletcher Books
you will love this conspiracy action-thriller series
FRACTURED STATE
Book 1 of this exciting new series

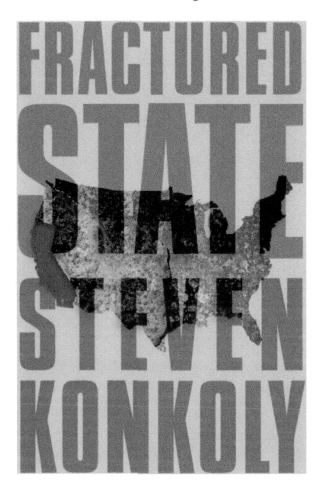

Available at Amazon Books
and other leading book vendors

Please consider leaving a review for Point of Crisis. Even a short, one-line review can make all of the difference.

Thank you!

For VIP access to exclusive sneak peeks at my upcoming work, new release updates and deeply discounted books, join my newsletter here:

eepurl.com/dFebyD

Visit Steven's blog to learn more about current and future projects:

StevenKonkoly.com

About the Author

Steven graduated from the United States Naval Academy in 1993, receiving a bachelor of science in English literature. He served the next eight years on active duty, traveling the world as a naval officer assigned to various Navy and Marine Corps units. His extensive journey spanned the globe, including a two-year tour of duty in Japan and travel to more than twenty countries throughout Asia and the Middle East.

From enforcing United Nations sanctions against Iraq as a maritime boarding officer in the Arabian Gulf, to directing aircraft bombing runs and naval gunfire strikes as a Forward Air Controller (FAC) assigned to a specialized Marine Corps unit, Steven's "in-house" experience with a wide range of regular and elite military units brings a unique authenticity to his thrillers.

He lives with his family in central Indiana, where he still wakes up at "zero dark thirty" to write for most of the day. When "off duty," he spends as much time as possible outdoors or travelling with his family—and dog.

Steven is the bestselling author of nearly twenty novels. His canon of work includes the popular Black Flagged Series, a gritty, no-holds barred covert operations and espionage saga; The Alex Fletcher Books, an action-adventure thriller epic chronicling the events surrounding an inconceivable attack on the United States; The Fractured State series, a near future, dystopian thriller trilogy set in the drought ravaged southwest; and THE RESCUE, a heart-pumping thriller of betrayal, revenge, and conspiracy.

He is an active member of the International Thriller Writers (ITW) and Science Fiction and Fantasy Writers of America (SFWA) organizations.

You can contact Steven directly by email
(stevekonkoly@striblingmedia.com)

or through his blog:
StevenKonkoly.com.